THE
FRAGRANCE OF
ROSES

REGALO ✹ GRANDE

THE
FRAGRANCE OF
ROSES

NIKKI ARANA

Revell
Grand Rapids, Michigan

IF
Arana

© 2006 by Nikki Arana

Published by Fleming H. Revell
a division of Baker Publishing Group
P.O. Box 6287, Grand Rapids, MI 49516-6287

Printed in the United States of America

Library of Congress Cataloging-in-Publication Data
Arana, Nikki, 1949–
    The fragrance of roses / Nikki Arana.
       p.   cm. — (Regalo grande ; bk. 3)
    ISBN 10: 0-8007-3050-X (pbk.)
    ISBN 978-0-8007-3050-5 (pbk.)
    1. Mothers and sons—Fiction. 2. Critically ill children—Fiction.
3. Cancer in children—Fiction. 4. Mexicans—Fiction. 5. California—
Fiction. I. Title.
PS3601.R35F73 2006
813′.6—dc22   2006006876

Unless otherwise indicated, Scripture is taken from the New King James Version. Copyright © 1982 by Thomas Nelson, Inc. Used by permission. All rights reserved.

Scripture marked KJV is taken from the King James Version of the Bible.

Internet quotes have been closely paraphrased for artistic purposes; however, every effort has been made to retain the original authors' intent. The extracts were drawn from the following sources between December 2004 to June 2005:

US GAO Report to Congressional Committees October 2002
www.cancer.org
www.marrow.org
www.ama-assn.org
www.aclj.org
www.atheists.org
www.themaxfoundation.org
www.bmtinfonet.org

To all parents who have stood on God's promises.
His Word is Truth.

For now we see through a glass, darkly; but then face to face:
now I know in part; but then shall I know
even as also I am known.

—*The First Epistle of Paul to the Corinthians*

PROLOGUE

1996—
Near Guadalajara, Mexico

The rocks cut his thin, bare legs as they hit their mark. But the taunting curses of the children that chased him left wounds that would never heal.

"Your mother is a *puta*."

The voice of Che Salinas, louder than all the rest.

Covering his head with his arms, he ran. Chin tucked, soundless tears streaming, he bit into his lower lip. He would not cry out. He was Cirocco, the son and namesake of an important man.

"Beggar." A young girl spat the word.

His mother had told him the story a thousand times. How his father had come to Mexico from Italy, looking for the woman of his dreams. And he had found her. He had fallen in love with Cirocco's mother the moment he had seen her. And though within days he had suddenly had to return to

Italy without her, he would be back for them soon and take them away from the poverty of the streets.

"Mongrel." Laughter.

But as the years had passed, Cirocco had heard rumors in his village that turned his mother's story of love into something ugly and shameful. The townspeople did not understand that the long nights she left him alone were spent looking for his father. Not hunting for "any *hombre* with a few pesos," as he heard whispered behind his back while he played alone on the streets of Santa Sophia. They knew nothing of his mother. She was good and kind. Someday he would be important like his father and then they would not dare talk about her.

The voices of his tormentors began to fade as he cut in and out of the roble trees. Winded, he fought for footing on the stony path that led to his hiding place at the rim of the steep, rocky canyon. His steps began to slow as he neared the top of the gorge. His knees buckled from exhaustion.

The earth beneath him gave way. He cried out, as brush and branches scraped his face. He began to tumble. Sky and earth spun wildly around him. Arms flailing, he slid. Head and back bouncing off the rocks that jutted out of the canyon wall, the craggy floor rushing toward him. A loud pop, searing pain, darkness.

When Cirocco opened his eyes, day had turned to night. A cool breeze had sprung up, moving across his face, awakening him. He tried lifting his arm to push himself up, but he had no strength. Every part of his body ached and racking pain sent waves of darkness over him, filling him with fear. He was going to die.

"Momma." The word echoed in the emptiness.

Surely she would come for him. Somehow she would know he needed her.

He gritted his teeth and tried to sit up. But he couldn't.

Stretching his right arm out to his side, he felt the ground around him, searching for a rock or branch to push against. His fingers touched something soft. He twisted his head back, squinting to make out the form . . . the lower half of his leg, partially severed. It was twisted grotesquely backward, toward his face.

Darkness hovered around him, pressed on him. He could feel himself slipping away.

"Momma." The breeze began to blow.

With all his remaining strength, he pushed his hand in his pocket. His fingers found the cross. Two horseshoe nails bound together with wire. It was his mother's. She had given it to him long ago, telling him to keep it in his pocket, to remember, no matter what happened, God was with him.

He closed his eyes. The suffocating darkness snatched his breath away. "*Dios*. Save me." He could feel his lips move, but he couldn't hear his own voice.

The gusting wind became a spiral, encircling him, drying the blood on his face and arms, sealing the cuts and gashes.

The ground beneath the boy began to tremble.

From somewhere above him he heard a rumbling sound as a boulder tore loose from the mountainside. He sensed more than heard it rushing toward him. Bouncing, rolling, gathering speed.

He pushed his head back, cutting his eyes to the right, watching the rock make its way toward him. As it neared, he began to weep. Still clutching the cross he threw his hands over his head and tried to roll out of the way. But his body wouldn't respond.

The last thing he saw was the rock ricocheting off an outcropping just above him. Passing within inches of his face, it fell with blunt force directly on the stump of his leg. Settling there.

The air became still.

As Cirocco slipped in and out of consciousness, he was aware of a presence. And though death encompassed him, a band of love arched over him like a wing, a fortress through which nothing could pass.

His life preserved . . . for a purpose.

A NGELICA REACHED INTO her pocket and pulled out her cell phone. Flipping it open, she checked to be sure the voice mail symbol hadn't appeared at the top of the screen.

Nothing.

They'd said they would call by five o'clock today. She glanced at her watch. It was only 3:40. She placed the phone on the kitchen windowsill, tilting the antenna toward the glass.

Glancing out the window, she could see her daughter, Anica, carefully cutting the zigzags of the crown she was making for her older brother, Manuel. The bright and talented eight-year-old held the yellow construction paper in one hand and cut free-form with her other. Angelica's lip began to tremble.

The oven beeped as it hit 325 degrees, bringing her attention back to the task at hand. She grabbed a wooden spoon and stirred the chocolate chips and pecans into the cookie dough.

After sliding the cookie sheet into the oven, she walked

over to the kitchen table and picked up the two pink party favor bags the children had dropped there on their way from the garage to the backyard.

When Manuel had been included in the birthday party invitation Anica received, Angelica had been thrilled for him. She hadn't realized he'd be the only boy. When they'd arrived, all the little girls had been making crowns. This was far beyond Manuel's ability and he soon busied himself with the chips on a nearby table. It wasn't long before the hostess asked Angelica if she could keep Manuel from "touching everything." And it wasn't long after that that Angelica was asked if she could keep Manuel in the other room.

Her answer had been to excuse herself and her two children from the party.

Angelica huffed a sigh. She wished she'd asked more questions before she'd taken Manuel to the party. She picked up the two pink bags and carried them to the counter next to the oven.

Turning back to the window, her gaze rested on her son. He sat across from his sister. He stared through thick glasses, his almond-shaped eyes mesmerized by the flashing scissors. Lips parted in a half smile. Unaware of the difference between this party and the one he'd left. Angelica blinked rapidly and took a steadying breath.

The sound of her cell phone interrupted her thoughts. Grabbing it, she flipped it open. *Let them say I got the job.*

"Hi, Angelica. It's Tex."

"Oh." Angelica tried to hide her disappointment. Tex Gaynor was Manuel's teacher and she often called on Friday afternoons to let her know how the week had gone for him. Angelica volunteered in his fourth-grade class. Still, she and Tex always tried to connect at the end of each week.

12

Angelica appreciated the extra effort and considered the woman her friend.

"Did I call at a bad time?"

Angelica could hear the concern in Tex's voice. "No. No. I'm waiting for the Sierra Center on Law and Poverty to call."

"I was going to ask if you'd heard, I've got that on my prayer list. Listen, I won't keep you. Manuel had a great week."

Angelica laughed. "Manuel always has a great week. The question is, how was it for you?"

"It's a pleasure having that little boy in my class. And before this year is over, I'm going to find out who he's talking to."

Angelica rolled her eyes. Everyone who knew Manuel knew about his invisible companion. The one-sided chattering had started shortly after he was stricken with acute myeloid leukemia, AML, at the age of five. After achieving remission, it seemed to subside. Yet even now, years later, Manuel would often glance up and begin laughing or suddenly stop midstride as if someone had called his name. "Well, if you find out, let me know."

"Blessings to you, dear."

Angelica flipped the phone shut and put it back on the windowsill.

For a moment she debated whether or not she should call the Center and ask if they'd made a selection. She hadn't come to the decision to go back to work easily, but once she started applying for jobs that advocated for the poor, she quickly became excited at the prospects of once again making a difference in the lives of people whom society seemed to care little about.

Manuel's birth had meant leaving her job as a public

13

defender. At the time, she hadn't realized it would mean giving up the law career she'd worked so hard for. But that soon became evident. It was only over the past year that her husband's landscape business had really taken off and the loving support she found at Manuel's school allowed her to consider returning to work.

The warm, chocolaty smell of the baking cookies told her they were ready and convinced her to wait on making the call. Right now, her son was the one who needed her.

Angelica fanned the cookies with her hand, looking over her shoulder. Out the window she could see that Manuel was wearing his crown and Anica had almost finished hers. Angelica gingerly picked up the hot cookies and dropped three into each one of the party bags.

"Mama. Mama." Manuel barreled through the sliding glass door, one hand on his headpiece, one hand splayed in the air. "My crown."

"Here my king . . . and queen." Angelica handed each of the children a party bag. "Let's go out and sit on the lawn, shall we?"

"Yes, my lady." Anica made a sweeping bow.

Suddenly, the music from the cell phone began to play. Angelica ran to the kitchen window. "Anica, take your brother out. I'll be there in a minute. This is that important call Mommy's been waiting for."

Oh, Lord, You know the plans You have for me. I pray this job is in Your will. She flipped the phone open. "This is Angelica."

"This is the nurse at Dr. Pearson's office. Dr. Pearson has received Manuel's blood work back from his physical. He'd like you and your husband to come in."

In past years the doctor's office had never called and asked them to come in . . . unless something was wrong.

14

The woman's words reminded her, with sickening clarity, of a similar call she'd received five years before. "Is something wrong?" Angelica's heart began to race.

"Dr. Pearson will discuss it with you when you come in. When can you meet with the doctor?"

"I . . . I don't know. My husband isn't here." Angelica tried to quell the panic she felt rising in her chest.

"Do you think you could come in this afternoon?"

"Uh. Yes, of course. We'll be there." Angelica pressed the End button, then pressed 1 to autodial her husband. "Please answer." She began pacing. The call went into voice mail. "Antonio, please call me, it's important."

Angelica knew Antonio always left his phone in the truck while he was working. She hesitated, then flipped the phone back open and pressed 2.

"Amante residence." It was Martha, Angelica's parents' housekeeper.

"Is my mom or dad there?"

"Just a moment."

How much should she say? She didn't want to alarm them. They adored their grandchildren and had been as devastated as Antonio and Angelica by Manuel's battle with leukemia.

"Hi, honey."

"Mom, could you come down and watch the kids for a couple of hours? I've got some things I need to do."

"Is something wrong?"

After years of discord, she and her mother had become close during Manuel's illness. She should have known her mother would sense something was up. "No, I just need to go find Antonio. He has an appointment he doesn't know about."

"Your father and I will come down. Maybe we'll bring the

15

kids home. Dad was going to barbeque. They could swim while we get dinner ready."

"That would be great, Mom. Thanks." Angelica disconnected and tried to reach Antonio again. No answer. She closed her eyes a moment and took a deep breath, then walked to the slider and opened it.

"Hey, kids, Grandma and Grandpa are coming and you're going to the ranch." She wished she were going to the ranch for the afternoon. The magical place of her childhood. The place she had met and fallen in love with Antonio. It was as much a part of her life as the earth and sky. Instead, she would be spending the afternoon in a doctor's office, praying that the doctor's news about Manuel would not be life threatening.

Both children jumped up and ran to the house, cookies and party bags forgotten. They were going to Regalo Grande.

Arms folded across his chest, Antonio narrowed his eyes slightly as he listened to the young man who worked for him.

The man continued in his native language, the dialect of the Mexican *campesinos*. "The baby keeps trying to come early. The doctor says my wife must stay in bed and take her medicine."

The boy, Carlos, had just turned eighteen when Antonio had hired him only a month before. Antonio never had more than a three-man crew. Santos and Pepito had been with him for years, but he always filled the third spot with "a neighbor." That was what he called the men who often crossed his path in need of help, and even more desperately, in need of hope. He'd begun the practice years ago when the owner of a rival lawn care company had needed a helping

16

hand. That was how he chose to honor the God who had blessed him so mightily with a wife he loved with every fiber of his being, two children who were the joy of his life, and a business that continued to grow each year. By keeping Christ's second great commandment to "love thy neighbor as thyself."

Antonio had read the situation when he'd interviewed the young man, though Carlos had given him only the barest personal information. Yet another boy becoming a father before he had become a man. Becoming responsible for a family before he'd become responsible for himself. A second-generation Mexican whose parents had probably come illegally and lived in poverty, as they had in Mexico. They believed their children, born in the United States, would seize the opportunities available here. But Carlos, like so many of the children of migrant laborers, had grown up in third world poverty, in a parentless home, without the culture or communal support of a Mexican village. And now, without a job, the opportunities of America would not be about what he could give to the country of his birth, but instead, what he could take from its treasuries.

And so Antonio had hired him, knowing he was taking a risk, knowing Santos and Pepito would raise their eyebrows and shake their heads, knowing that whatever the boy lacked in integrity and commitment to the clients of Affordable Lawn Care, Antonio must be prepared to make up.

Shoulders slumped, a trace of panic in his eyes, Carlos knotted his hands into fists. "She is out of her medicine, *Señor* Perez. That is why I need my check before Monday."

Antonio knew the story was true. He and Angelica had stopped at the couple's tiny apartment one Saturday to see if they'd like to join them in church on Sunday. Carlos's wife, hair tangled, face pale, and swollen legs extended, had sat,

17

unmoving, on the only piece of furniture in the room, a worn couch. Antonio and Angelica had stopped again the following Saturday with food, and Angelica helped the young woman bathe and fix her hair. Angelica's commitment was as deep as Antonio's, to reach out to the poor Mexicans, who were the brothers, sisters, and children of "his people." People he knew well. People he had grown up with in the fields near Guadalajara. People living the life he was born to and had only escaped by the grace of God.

Antonio's face softened and he dropped his arms. After a moment's thought, he smiled. "You're in luck. A man called me this morning. He had some trees that need pruning. He wants it done tomorrow, before his company arrives tomorrow night. Since it's short notice and the weekend, he offered to pay me extra."

"Really?" Hope crept into Carlos's eyes.

"Really. And I'll pay you tomorrow when you finish. You'll have the money you need, and more when you get your paycheck on Monday. I'll bill for the work and when he pays, we'll be even."

Carlos's face broke into a smile. "How can I thank you, *señor*?"

Antonio put his hand on the boy's shoulder. "When your child is born, take your family to church on Sundays."

Carlos avoided Antonio's eyes and color rose in the young man's cheeks. Stepping back, he put his hand out. "Deal."

Antonio grasped the boy's hand and gave it a shake. "Now go finish the weeding. Tell Pepito I'm going to the next house to get started."

Antonio watched Carlos as he strode across the lawn to finish his work. A man who needed pruning done had called that morning. But Antonio had declined the job. His schedule was full. He was working six days a week, from

18

early morning until late at night as it was and didn't need more work . . . but Carlos did. He sighed and glanced heavenward. Under the circumstances, it was the "neighborly" thing to do.

Antonio jumped in his truck and checked his watch. He'd been pushing himself all day, hoping to carve out thirty minutes to stop at the jewelry store and make the last payment on Angelica's ring. Now was as good a time as any.

As he drove to the mall, he went over in his mind every detail of the anniversary dinner he was planning. This would not only be a celebration of twelve years of marriage, but he would finally be able to give Angelica diamonds. It was something he had dreamed about since the day they were married. But every penny he'd made, he used to support his family or invested it back into the business. Angelica's parents were more than willing to help out financially, but Antonio had never permitted it. Personal gifts to his wife or the children were fine, but providing for his family was not.

He had admired the "eternity" ring in the jewelry store window for over a year. But it wasn't until ten months ago that he finally decided there was only one way to come up with a down payment. He sold his guitar. That had given him enough cash so that payments could be set up on the balance, which he faithfully paid at one hundred dollars a month. He was proud that he was making his last payment early.

Just as he pulled into the parking lot his cell phone rang. "*Sí?*"

"Antonio, where are you? Carlos said you went to the Allens'. So I drove over here to the Allens' house."

"I'm in my truck. I'm coming there." He knew his wife well. He could hear the controlled tempo of her voice. She was upset. "What's wrong?"

19

"Manuel's doctor called and said that the blood tests they took at his physical came back and they have to talk to us." Her voice trembled. "They want us to come in right away." He could hear her ragged breathing. "Antonio, I'm so scared. I can't go through this again."

"Don't be afraid. We don't know anything yet." A wave of nausea swept through him. He closed his eyes, willing it away. "His cancer has been in remission for almost five years. There's no reason for it to come back, Angel. I'll come home right now and we'll go talk to the doctor."

"Please hurry." The connection ended.

Antonio put the truck in reverse and stepped on the gas, narrowly missing a car parking next to him.

As he drove, his thoughts returned to the hell he and Angelica had lived through when Manuel had been diagnosed with cancer. Though it had been years ago, the fear embedded in that word was as powerful now as it had been then. How many nights had he awakened, slipped from his bed, and driven to the hills that surrounded Valle de Lagrimas, to pray for his son in solitude? Begging God to spare Manuel's life. How many times had he called God to account for His promises? Demanding the truth of His Word be made manifest in the situation.

A knot of uneasiness formed in his chest.

And how many times while holding his son, who was too weak from the chemo to open his eyes, face splotched with petechiae from constant vomiting, had Antonio, for just a moment, allowed himself to contemplate the enigmatic truth . . . there was only one truly perfect healing. And it was not found on this earth.

Antonio gripped the steering wheel and shifted in his seat. He immediately rejected the thought. As he had then.

Turning down Mountain View Drive, he could see Angelica sitting on the front porch of their house. Before he could put the truck into park, she was opening his door. As he pulled the key from the ignition, he felt her press into him. Turning toward her, still sitting, door flung open, he pulled her into his chest. He stroked her hair as she sobbed.

Pressing his cheek against the top of her head, he squeezed his eyes shut and clenched his jaw. He must be strong for her. There would be time for his tears later. He said nothing, letting her cry. Finally, her breathing began to steady.

He cupped her face in his hands and kissed her tears. "Are you ready to go?"

Angelica nodded silently.

Antonio pulled her into his arms one more time, holding her for a few seconds.

"Let's go."

"Let me go get my purse."

As Angelica walked to the front door, Antonio heard her cell phone ring. She stopped and turned toward him as she answered.

"Yes, this is Angelica." The color drained from her face. "Yes, we'll bring him right in." She flipped the phone shut. She tried to put it in her pocket, but it slipped from her fingers to the ground.

Antonio stepped out of the truck and picked it up.

"That was the oncologist's office. They want us to bring Manuel in so they can do a bone marrow biopsy."

Her gaze held his.

As the moments passed, she began to straighten.

Lifting her chin, she drew a deep breath. "We're going to fight. And we're going to win." She turned on her heel and went into the house.

Throwing her phone on the truck seat, Antonio slipped

behind the wheel and shut the door. As he started the truck, Angelica's cell phone started playing music.

He stared at it. The music continued to play.

"Hello."

"Is Angelica Perez there?"

"She's not available right now, could I take a message?"

"Tell her that the Sierra Center called . . . and congratulations."

It was him.

The woman whispered a prayer of thanks as she watched the boy through the traffic of Guadalajara's busiest street. Mama Rose had been right. He was becoming a handsome young man. Leaning as far as she dared from behind the parked car, she strained to catch a glimpse of his face. But he was hidden from her by the hordes of people on the crowded hospital sidewalk, their legs and hands veiling him from her view.

She could see his good leg was tucked under him, his other leg a straight stump. In a stilted, awkward motion, he used his hands to push himself along on the wheeled board toward the Cruz Roja.

She longed to run to him, to hold him, to beg him again to forgive her. No matter that he had said he hated her, no matter that he had cursed her and wished her dead.

She loved him.

He was her son.

2

Benito Amante summoned his sternest face. "Manuel, I told you not to wear your crown in the pool." The big, silver-haired man stood with his hands on his hips, towering over his grandson.

Manuel stuck his chin out, spread *his* feet, and put *his* hands on *his* hips. Benito took a step back, not wanting the rubber ducky around Manuel's waist to get him wet.

He glanced at his wife and stifled a chuckle. His grandson was as stubborn as Angelica had been when she was a little girl. And twice as tough.

Benito felt a closeness to Manuel that he felt with no other human being. It had begun when Manuel had faced the grueling physical therapy required of so many children with Down syndrome, and Benito had faced learning to walk again after a serious car accident he'd been in just before Manuel was born. Both endured months of hard work to overcome their physical disabilities. The little boy's steadfast determination was a constant reminder to Benito that giving up was not an option. But that had only been the beginning. As the years passed, the highly educated heart surgeon learned other lessons from his grandson: Sometimes slow is better. There is nothing wrong with cheering for the other team when your team is losing. And the capacity to love, and forgive, is not a measure of the mind but of the heart.

Manuel knit his brows together, thick fingers crumpling one of the crown's peaks. "No, Grrrampa. My crown."

Benito dropped his hands from his hips. Whenever Manuel called him Grrrampa, it melted Benito's heart. *R* sounds had not come easily to the little boy. The speech therapist had worked with Manuel for months. She instructed the family to make a growling sound to help him learn how to say "rrr" and even taught them the hand sign for "grrr," raising their hands to their cheeks, palms forward, and fingers curved into claws. Benito had worked tirelessly with Manuel all last year, making little clawing motions and softly growling "Grrr-ampa" to the child every chance he got.

"If you don't take off your crown, the water will ruin it."

Manuel stubbornly resisted. His face was not so much defiant as perplexed.

Benito tapped his lower lip with his forefinger, then knelt beside Manuel. "Could I wear your crown?"

Manuel's face broke into a broad smile and he took off the paper crown. With great ceremony, he put it on his grandfather's bowed head.

Benito rose, carefully balancing the headpiece. "Now, into the pool."

Manuel plopped down on the edge of the first step, pudgy hands grasping the rubber duck's neck.

Anica was perched atop one of the boulders built into the opposite side of the pool. "G-Mom. G-Dad. Look at me." Throwing her shoulders back, she took a deep breath, then dove into the deep end. A natural athlete, back slightly arched, toes pointed, Anica entered the water with barely a ripple. She swam the length of the pool underwater, coming up next to her brother, at her grandfather's feet.

"Now, Gen, there's a future Olympian if I ever saw one." Benito winked at his wife. Turning to Anica, he gestured to the lounge chairs on the pool deck. "Grandma and I are going to go sit in the bleachers and watch."

As Benito and Gen settled into the pillowed lounges, a groan escaped Benito's lips.

Gen turned to him. "Bad day?"

He removed the crown from his head and set it on the concrete next to his chair. "Not too bad." There was no point in dwelling on it. He'd suffered with chronic pain since the car accident. Over the years, his limp had grown worse, and lately he found his days were defined by what he could not do rather than what he could do. It was one of the reasons they had decided to sell Regalo Grande.

Benito released a deep sigh. "When the gardeners finish replanting the entry next week, I want to call the Realtor."

Gen raised her eyebrows. "We've got to tell Angelica *first*. You know she's going to feel we should have discussed it with her before we made our final decision."

He could hear the tension in his wife's voice. "I know. And that's why I didn't. There's nothing more to talk about."

It was his fault. He was the one who couldn't take the stairs anymore. And beyond that, though he would never admit it to Gen, or anyone, the financial burden of maintaining the large estate to his wife's standards was draining their assets. When he'd built the ranch, he dreamed it was something Angelica would always have, long after he was gone. But the car accident and subsequent business reversals left him no choice. Now he needed the income that the proceeds of the sale would provide.

If only Angelica had married a man who could support the

25

upscale lifestyle of Regalo Grande. Maybe something could have been worked out. But that wasn't going to happen. Antonio had made it clear throughout the marriage; he wasn't going to accept anything that remotely resembled charity. He would be the provider for his family. And much to Benito's surprise, Angelica apparently supported his position, even though it robbed her of the life she deserved.

Gen closed her eyes a moment, then laid her head back against the cushion.

Her hand slipped into his. "It's a beautiful afternoon. Let's enjoy it while we have it." He met her gaze and held it for a moment.

Benito let his eyes wander to the rolling hills of the Sonoma wine country that surrounded their property. He could see the cluster of ancient oaks where he and Gen had first stood surveying the property, choosing a home site. And below that, the slope that led to the barns and pastures where he had spent so many Sunday afternoons with his daughter, watching her ride her Arabian horse, Pasha.

His gaze returned to the grounds adjoining the pool. This was where he and Angelica had planned and held the fiftieth wedding anniversary party he surprised Gen with.

His attention turned to Manuel. Behind the boy, strung between two trees, was the hammock he'd rocked his grandchildren to sleep in, and next to it was the chair Manuel sat on last summer the first time he tied his own shoes.

Every treasured memory of the past thirty years had its roots in this ranch. Not just for him, but for Angelica too.

"You're right, Gen. It's time to tell her."

As Antonio drove through the wrought-iron gates that marked the formal entry to Regalo Grande, Angelica saw

Pasha trotting along the fence line of the lower pasture. The old stallion was well into his twenties. Still, he never failed to greet his mistress.

Angelica rolled down her window. The scent of the lupine and wild roses, and the jasmine that grew along the drive, filled her with memories of her childhood . . . and Poppy. He had worked for her parents from the day she was born until the day he died. He was a constant presence in her life, always available when her parents were not. His love for the Lord gave Angelica her spiritual foundation. Though he had been gone for over ten years, there was rarely a time she came to the ranch that she didn't think of him. Today, especially, she yearned for his quiet strength and unwavering faith.

Antonio pulled the truck in front of the arched, stucco entryway of Regalo Grande. The bougainvillea planted on each side were in full bloom, a wall of living lace.

Angelica unbuckled her seat belt and climbed down from the truck. She stopped a moment to take in the hills and valley. In a way she could not explain, she drew strength from this piece of land. It was more than her childhood home. It was a safe place. A place of remembrance and reflection, a place of innocence and dreams, a place her father had built with a promise that it would always be here for her. It was the home of her heart.

She glanced at her husband. He didn't fully understand her love of the ranch. But it was her hope and prayer that someday, somehow, they would live at Regalo Grande.

Antonio hurried around the truck and took her hand. "They're probably in the back with the kids."

As they approached the backyard, Angelica began to consider how much she should tell her parents about the situation. She didn't want to alarm them, but she needed their support.

"Daddy, look." Anica had spotted them the minute they were in sight of the pool.

Antonio stopped, giving his daughter his full attention as she jumped from the diving rock.

When she surfaced next to Manuel, she took her brother's hands in hers and kissed his cheek. "Hold on to me, Manuel, and I'll take you for a ride."

"Angelica, Antonio, we're over here." Her mother waved from a lounge chair. "Dad and I were just talking about you. We've been tossing around some ideas about the ranch and want to know what you think."

Angelica had noticed all the work being done at the entry when she and Antonio drove in. Undoubtedly, her mother had been reading *Architectural Digest* again. It seemed like every year or two her mother would decide the property needed a little sprucing up. Last time, it resulted in redecorating the guesthouse.

Antonio and Angelica crossed the pool decking. "Mom, not right now. We've got to take Manuel to the doctor." The words tumbled out, abrupt and rushed.

Both her parents turned to her. "What's wrong?" they said, speaking in unison.

Antonio quickly put his hand on Angelica's shoulder. "The doctor wants to be sure Manuel is cancer free."

Angelica could see her parents' relief. She gave her husband a sideways glance. He never ceased to amaze her.

Her father's gaze sharpened. "I thought he had his checkup last week."

"Oh, he did, Dad. This is just some additional testing. To be sure." Angelica turned toward the pool. "Mom, would you help me get him dressed?"

"Sure, honey." Her mother rose. "Why didn't you say something earlier?"

Angelica sensed that her mother wasn't satisfied with her story and quickened her steps. "I should have. I guess I just wasn't thinking."

Her mother touched her shoulder. "Why don't you let Anica spend the night? We'll bring her down in the morning."

Each of the children had their own room at the ranch, filled with as many clothes and toys as they had at home. Angelica slowed her steps. "Thanks, Mom. That would be wonderful." Turning to her mother with a smile of appreciation, she found the woman's eyes intent upon her face. Without a word being spoken, Angelica realized her mother suspected they weren't taking Manuel to a routine appointment.

As soon as Manuel was ready, Angelica and Antonio excused themselves.

Benito took Manuel's hand and walked with them to the truck. "Call us when you get back from the doctor's office."

"I will, Dad."

Angelica helped Manuel into the back of the king cab and fastened his seat belt. As soon as Antonio started the truck, Manuel began to wave gleefully. "Bye, Grrrampa. Bye, Grrrampa."

Angelica quickly got into the front seat and shut the door. "Hurry, let's go before Dad asks if he can come."

As they started down the drive, Angelica could feel the fear she had lived with during Manuel's illness five years earlier returning. She closed her eyes. Her thoughts filtered back over the previous months. Had there been anything, a sign, an indication, something she should have noticed? Her heart raced. The fevers. She had taken him to the doctor. A virus, they said, give fluids and rest. She hadn't questioned it because the fluids and rest seemed to help. Other than Manuel being a little tired, which was understandable since he'd been fighting a virus, there was nothing.

29

She drew a deep breath. She would remain positive. It *was* a virus. Nothing was seriously wrong. *God, I trust You. I believe You healed Manuel. A blood test means nothing to You. Your will is sovereign and Your will will be done.* Manuel's giggling broke into her thoughts.

Turning in her seat she could see her son, eyes squeezed shut, shoulders up under his ears, turning his head side to side as if someone were tickling him under his chin. "What's up, sweetie?"

"Crown."

"Crown?" Angelica tilted her head, watching him. "Is your crown at Grandma's?"

Manuel opened his eyes, then waved his hand at the empty seat next to him. "Crown."

She reached across the back of the seat and patted his leg. "Silly boy. We'll get your crown when we pick up Anica tomorrow."

Antonio turned his eyes toward her, tapped his finger on the steering wheel, and raised his eyebrows. She knew immediately what he was thinking. They were nearing the Children's Hospital at the Sierra Medical Center.

After Manuel's treatment for AML had been completed, he had follow-up visits with the oncologist every month for eighteen months. Then every three months for a year, and finally every six months. But even with the longer periods between visits, the sight of the hospital always meant a battle. As Antonio turned into the parking lot, she braced herself.

"No. No doctor." She could hear Manuel pulling his legs up to his chest. His voice rose and his words became abrupt and belligerent. "No. No doctor."

Angelica got out of the truck and opened Manuel's door. He was in *the* position. Knees under his chin, arms locked

30

around his legs, lying on his side so his body covered the seat belt buckle.

Angelica felt Antonio's hand on her shoulder, gently moving her to the side. He stepped in front of her and leaned into the truck. Then he bent over Manuel and worked his arms around Manuel's body until he was lying face-to-face with him.

"No. No. No."

Angelica could hear Manuel struggling in Antonio's arms.

Antonio began to speak in Spanish. His voice soft, low, lilting. "Daddy is here, little one. I am with you, don't be afraid." Over and over, he repeated the words.

Every time Angelica witnessed this ritual, she was fascinated. Taking Manuel in his arms when Manuel was frightened or upset, and whispering to him in Spanish was something Antonio had done since their son was an infant. She didn't believe that Manuel understood a word of Spanish. But if the words were spoken in English, it didn't help at all. As the minutes passed, Manuel began to grow quiet.

Angelica heard the click of the seat belt being released.

Antonio stood, Manuel in his arms, the child's head resting on Antonio's shoulder.

She shut the truck door. Starting toward the offices, she glanced at Antonio. His jaw was set, his eyes narrowed, his lips in a rigid line; the suffering Manuel had endured through the months of his treatments was reflected in Antonio's face. Manuel's eyes were closed, a slight smile on his lips, at peace in the arms of his father. It was as if Antonio had taken Manuel's place for the moment. And Angelica knew if it were possible for Antonio to do so, he would have.

When they entered the hospital, they went immediately to the oncology section and checked in at the front desk. The entire pediatric section of the hospital had a nautical theme.

The windows looked like portholes. Big, brightly colored fish swam along the walls just above ocean blue carpets.

Antonio set Manuel down in the waiting area in front of a shadow box displaying sea treasures.

"No. No doctor. No shot." Manuel's voice rose. "No go. Go home, now." He sat where he had been standing and folded his arms across his chest.

The oncologist's nurse peered through the doorway that led to the exam rooms.

Angelica gave the woman a weak smile. "Sorry."

For a moment, she and the nurse looked at each other. They both knew reasoning never worked with Manuel, though negotiating had been tried with some success. But there was one thing that worked like a charm.

Angelica tilted her head. "Is Dr. Dorak with patients?"

The nurse winked at her. "He's expecting you. Just a sec. Let me see if I can find a wheelchair. We haven't kept one here since Manuel stopped coming regularly." She disappeared behind the door.

Angelica could feel the heat rising in her cheeks as the other people in the waiting area stared at them.

One child whispered, "What's wrong with him, Mommy?"

"He's retarded. Like the girl at school nobody likes."

The woman's stage whisper might as well have been a shout. Angelica spun on her heel and glared at her. The woman looked away.

Angelica strode across the room, sat down in the empty chair across from her, and stared at her.

The woman studied the carpet.

Antonio knelt down beside Manuel and stroked his hair, then kissed the top of his head. "I love you, precious little one."

The swish of the door to the exam rooms opening broke the sudden silence in the waiting room.

The woman across from Angelica raised her head, then caught her breath. "Dr. Dorak!"

"What's happened to *him*, Mommy?" The little girl next to the woman leaned forward in her chair.

Dr. Dorak smiled at Angelica from the wheelchair he was sitting in.

Angelica rose. "Well, Doctor, you can see Manuel has come to visit you."

"So I heard." The doctor looked toward Manuel. "Good afternoon, Dr. Perez. I'm ready for my exam, young man."

Manuel jumped up and raced to the doctor. He took the stethoscope from the doctor's hand, hung it around his own neck, then stepped back, planting his hands on his hips. "It time for *you* now." Manuel stepped to the back of the wheelchair and pushed it in a circle. When it faced the door to the exam rooms, he wheeled it through the door and down the hall. The nurse, Antonio, and Angelica followed.

In the exam room, after Manuel had "examined" Dr. Dorak, Manuel pointed to a chair for Dr. Dorak to sit in and Manuel climbed into the wheelchair. The nurse stepped up to Manuel and put a blood pressure cuff on his arm.

Dr. Dorak stood. "Let's step into my office while Beth updates his chart."

As Angelica made the short walk to the doctor's office down the hall, her chest tightened. Memories flooded through her the minute she stepped through the office door.

"Please, have a seat." Dr. Dorak gestured to the two chairs across from his desk.

The chairs, the office, the doctor, words from the past echoed through her mind . . . *"We'll do everything humanly possible for him."* A death knell. That's what the words had

33

sounded like that day five years ago. She and Antonio had reached for each other, then wept as they endured the news of Manuel's diagnosis. Acute myeloid leukemia. *Please, God, not again.*

Dr. Dorak opened a file on his desk. "Dr. Pearson sent me Manuel's CBC results. The white blood cell count was high and his hemoglobin was low. Have you noticed any changes in his behavior recently?"

Angelica glanced at Antonio. "Nothing, really. He's had a few bouts with the flu since school started." She searched Dr. Dorak's face. "Anica was sick one of those times too, as I remember. There was nothing unusual about it."

"What we want to do this afternoon is take another blood sample and do a bone marrow biopsy."

Angelica slowly nodded her head. Her shoulders slumped. Antonio reached across the space between them and put his hand on her arm.

"After the aspiration I'll order flow cytometry, chromosome analysis, and some molecular genetic tests to be used as a baseline during his follow-up. First though, I'll have the lab take a preliminary look to see if there are any abnormal cells. If we see any blasts, we'll start chemo right away . . . tonight."

"Tonight?" Angelica's stomach turned over, tears pricked her eyes. "What does all this mean?"

"We'll know more after the biopsy." He fingered the corner of the file.

"Here we are."

Angelica turned toward the opening door as Beth led Manuel into the office. Her gaze shifted back to Dr. Dorak.

His eyes met hers. He rose. "Ready?"

"Is anyone ever ready for this?" She held the doctor's gaze a moment, then stood. "Let's get started."

Angelica and Antonio returned to the exam room and helped Manuel get into a hospital gown.

Angelica took a seat on a nearby stool. Antonio sat on the exam table and held Manuel in his lap. Within moments, the nurse joined them.

Amidst Manuel's loud and adamant protests, Beth administered a shot of Versed. Slowly, he began to settle down, his body relaxing, his eyes drooping. As the child's chin dropped to his chest, Antonio slipped from beneath him and laid him gently on the table, then stood next to his head and stroked his cheek.

Dr. Dorak stepped into the room. He selected a syringe from a tray of instruments that Beth had assembled for him. The syringe was as large as the ones Angelica had seen the vet use on Pasha. She clenched her hands into fists. Hadn't Manuel been through enough during his short life?

Antonio turned Manuel onto his stomach, then bent over him and put his arm around the child's upper body, speaking to him in low tones.

As the needle plunged into Manuel's hip, he cried out and began to struggle. Antonio's arms tightened around him.

Manuel screamed.

The draw was difficult. The thick, bloody substance barely moving up the vial.

Angelica bit her lip, fighting nausea. She wiped her sweating hands on her thighs, then dropped her head and took a deep breath.

Finally, Dr. Dorak removed the syringe. Manuel's moans became whimpers as Antonio lifted his son into his arms.

Dr. Dorak turned to his nurse. "Beth, get this to the lab for flow and chromosome analysis. Tell them I want a preliminary reading stat." He walked to the sink and began washing his hands. "Why don't the three of you go to my

35

office and make yourselves comfortable. I'll be paged as soon as the lab makes a sample slide and looks at it."

"Thank you, Doctor, for everything you're doing." Angelica stretched her arms toward Antonio. "Let me have him."

"I'll see you two soon." Dr. Dorak closed the door as he left.

After Angelica helped Manuel get dressed, they returned to Dr. Dorak's office. Angelica sat down and Antonio put Manuel in her arms, then he pulled his chair tight to hers. Sitting down next to her, he took her hand.

As the time dragged by, they spoke of how long Manuel's remission had been and how that worked in his favor. They went over, again, every detail of the recent fevers, concluding it was only a virus. And they prayed for their son. Asking God to pour out His mercy on their family. Asking God to continue the remission He had granted Manuel for the past five years. And asking God to heal Manuel as only the Creator of the universe could, completely and unconditionally.

But would He?

Dr. Mark Dorak stood outside his office door holding the sheet of paper Beth had given him. He could hear Antonio and Angelica talking. The couple had been down this road before. He remembered Angelica well, though it had been at least five years ago.

He first learned of her in the newspaper several years before he became Manuel's doctor. She went by Amante then. A young attorney assisting the chief public defender in a high-profile legal case . . . and strikingly beautiful.

The picture that accompanied the article was taken just as Angelica was leaving the courthouse. She had looked directly at the photographer. Her dark hair framing her face, her eyes intent, her expression determined. He remembered thinking she was a rising star.

When he met her during Manuel's first illness, it was clear she'd made a choice between a career and motherhood. He was impressed by her dedication to her children and especially with the patience and compassion she showed Manuel. He was also taken by her unfailing faith in God. He shook his head. That faith was about to be challenged in ways she never dreamed possible.

And he admired and respected her husband. During Manuel's first illness Antonio had been an unshakable source of strength to his wife. The fruit of the Spirit evident in all his ways.

Mark drew a deep breath. His desire to care for children with cancer was something God had called him to do. It had come from a tragic situation his senior year in high school. His girlfriend, Maggie, lost her little brother to the disease. After a wrenching, desperate battle with leukemia, Jeremiah died at the age of eight. Watching that child and the family suffer had set Mark on a course that resulted in him becoming a pediatric oncologist. And he excelled in every aspect of his profession, Jeremiah and Maggie never far from his mind. His thoughts returned to that time, over thirty years ago.

He'd been planning to volunteer for a yearlong mission in South America with his church after graduation. But when he learned of Jeremiah's unexpected diagnosis of cancer, he decided not to go. The ensuing months were a living hell. It called into question everything Mark thought he knew about God.

But then, in the final minutes of Jeremiah's life, in the profound culmination of what he now understood was a divine plan, in one life-changing moment, God revealed His truth . . . a crown upon a crystal sea. That moment became a wellspring from which Mark had drawn throughout his career.

His thoughts returned to the present. Someday he hoped he would be able to do more for the children he cared for and their families.

He opened the office door, walked behind his desk, and took a seat. He laid the piece of paper he had been holding on the desktop in front of him.

Angelica had her arms wrapped around her son, her cheek resting on the top of his head. She looked directly at Mark.

The eyes of Maggie were suddenly before him, asking . . . why.

He dropped his eyes to the paper in front of him. He understood all too well, it was the question every loved one asked, yet it was something only God could answer. And sometimes it was not in this life but in the next one . . . beyond the crystal sea.

He raised his head.

"I have the preliminary results."

It had become his ritual each day at noon to position himself against the wall that surrounded the public toilets. Calle Dolores was a busy street halfway between the Cruz Roja and San Juan de Dios. Lunchtime crowds of American tourists and working Mexicans could mean enough money for food for a few days. Cirocco considered this his lucky spot, not just because it provided good business for him, but it seemed that at least once a week a passerby would stop and hand him fifty pesos, sometimes more. Not that he wanted charity. This was his job and he earned his money. Still, it helped. Many times, it meant the difference between going to bed hungry and sleeping well.

Someone was approaching. He took from his lap all but one of the plastic sacks he'd scavenged out of alleys and trash piles, and tucked them under the wheeled board he sat on. Lifting his arms over his head, he offered the remaining sack to the *Americana* who'd stopped in front of him. She put a coin in his palm and took the plastic bag. The edge of her pointed shoe scuffed his leg as she stepped past him and entered the bathrooms.

He looked in his hand. Five pesos. He smiled. It was going to be a good day. He had that feeling earlier. It was his birthday after all. Today he was eighteen.

A plastic sack dropped in his lap, the pointed shoe missing him this time.

He raised his eyebrows. Often the Americans didn't return the sacks, leaving the paper in the toilets.

He loosely tied off the top to stop the stench, then crushed the soiled paper inside the bag down until the bag was flat. He tucked it behind his back, then pulled a fresh sack from beneath the board. Lifting his arms in the air, he offered it to the *señor* who had stopped in front of him.

He felt two coins drop into his palm. *"Gracias."*

Maybe he would be able to leave early and get over to Diego's. The man owned a food stand near San Juan de Dios. He let Cirocco sleep under the stand on cold or rainy nights, and he often gave Cirocco food that was left over from the lunch rush.

Diego had recently returned from a long trip to visit his aunt, Lucita, who had raised him. She'd been very sick. She had worked with Diego at the food stand before she moved away from Guadalajara to live with one of her sons in America, and Cirocco considered her a friend. He was anxious to hear how the woman was doing.

Cirocco's stomach growled.

Yes, this would be a good day to go and visit Diego and ask about his aunt.

3

ANGELICA GLANCED AT Manuel. He'd fallen asleep in her arms. She could hear Antonio's steady breathing next to her. She closed her eyes a moment, bracing herself. Finally, lifting her head, she turned her eyes to Dr. Dorak. "What do the preliminary results show?"

"Acute myeloid leukemia."

"What?" She could hear him speaking, but the words didn't register.

"The cancer is back."

The room seemed to darken and she suddenly felt alone. Her arms tightened round her son and she put her cheek against his face, cupping him in her shoulder. This was impossible. They had prayed. They had believed.

"What will we do now?" Antonio's voice seemed far away.

"We'll admit him. I'll schedule surgery to put a port in his chest tonight and we'll start chemo right away."

Angelica reached for Antonio and he wrapped his fingers around hers. She sought Dr. Dorak's eyes. "What are Manuel's chances for remission?"

"Our objective isn't just achieving remission; it's achieving remission so that a hematopoietic stem cell transplant can be done. That's his best chance at beating this. I'll have the full results of the biopsy back tomorrow and I'll set up his protocol. We'll know more then." Dr. Dorak held her gaze. "We're going to do everything humanly possible."

Those words. The death knell. She hated them. The implication that "everything humanly possible" might not be enough. And after five years of remission, apparently last time it hadn't been. The cancer was back.

Memories of the wretchedness of the disease gripped her like spidery fingers. The malignant tumors showing their hideous blue-green faces around his eyes, the joint pain, the vomiting, vomiting, vomiting of chemo. And the fear. The constant, paralyzing fear that Manuel would die, that they would lose the fight, that God would not hear their prayers. Hell on earth. For Manuel, for her, for Antonio.

Her husband's voice brought her back to the present. "How does the stem cell transplant work?"

"First, we need to find a match. You and Angelica will likely be a half match. But there is a 25 percent chance that Anica will be a full genetic match, the same tissue type, meaning her HLA—human leukocyte antigens—will match Manuel's perfectly. If they do, we'll be able to do the transplantation using her stem cells as soon as Manuel achieves remission."

A 25 percent chance.

Angelica cleared her throat. "What if Anica isn't a match?"

"We'll also request a donor search through the National Marrow Donor Program. That's a database of over five million people. The search will include some Canadian and European registries."

42

"Manuel's half Mexican. You said he needs a genetic match. What about Mexico?"

"Mexico doesn't have a registry. But there are people of Mexican descent registered in the donor program."

Antonio leaned forward in his chair. "I want to be tested when Anica is tested. I am Mexican. I will match. I'm sure of it."

If Anica wasn't a full match, *someone* in the family would be. A trill of hope flashed through Angelica's chest. The doctor had just said that she was, at the minimum, a half match. "I want to be tested too. And I know my parents will want to be tested."

Dr. Dorak nodded. "Of course." The doctor's voice softened. "But, if Anica doesn't match, the registry is the most likely source of a donor. Manuel's HLA was inherited from both of you. It's part of his genetic makeup given to him through generations on both sides of your families."

Antonio sat back in his chair. "I will be a match." His voice was firm.

Angelica looked at him. Couldn't he hear what the doctor was saying? This was the problem with him. He had no education; he wasn't well read; he was self-made and didn't understand anything except landscaping. He wasn't going to be a match. And she probably wasn't either. She could feel tears slipping down her face. *The registry. Please, God. Let there be someone in the registry.*

Antonio's gaze met hers. First recognition, then hurt flashed across his face. Biting her lower lip, she closed her eyes. He knew her so well.

She dropped her head. He was good and kind. His love for her and Manuel believed all things, hoped all things . . . endured all things.

Forgive me.

43

"Mama?" Manuel's chubby hand was on her cheek. "You sad. No cry, Mama. Manuel hug." He tried to lift his arms to her.

Angelica caught her breath. When had he awakened? Quickly, she pushed her hair back from her face, letting her fingers drop below her palm, trying to brush her tears aside.

She pulled Manuel up on her lap. "You rest. Mommy's not sad." She slipped off his glasses and kissed his eyelids closed. "Think of fairies dancing under the moon." She smoothed his hair from his forehead.

A sweet smile settled on his lips and he drifted back into a sedated sleep.

Looking at Manuel, innocent and helpless, unaware of his desperate situation, made her heart ache. They *would* find a match for him. If it wasn't Anica, then it would be someone else. There was somebody, somewhere, who could save her son's life. And they would find him.

Angelica lowered her voice. "Thank you, Doctor, for everything you're doing. We'll go take care of the admission."

Cell phone music rang through the office.

"I bet it's Mother." She turned to Antonio. "We didn't call and now she's checking on us." She retrieved the phone from her purse. "What time is it?"

"Six forty."

"No wonder she's calling, but this isn't something I want to explain over the phone. It's going to upset them terribly." She flipped the phone open.

"Hi, Mom." She bit her lower lip as she listened. "We're still here at the hospital talking to the doctor. We learned some things and we'll tell you about them when we see you." She silently shook her head as her mother continued. "The

44

full results aren't back yet. I promise I'll call you later." After saying good-bye, she closed the phone.

She slipped her free hand under Manuel's knees, signaling Antonio to take him.

Antonio stood and lifted the child into his arms.

As Antonio and Angelica walked through the hospital corridors to the inpatient wing, the sounds and smells of the hospital brought the reality of their circumstances into focus. Until Dr. Dorak had given them the preliminary results, she had clung to the hope that this was a false alarm, that God would spare them, that they would leave the hospital and drive up to the ranch to tell her parents how it had turned out to be nothing. But the doctor's pronouncement had changed everything.

She looked at Manuel, face turned into his father's shoulder, arms relaxed as they swayed with his father's strides. Blinking rapidly, she clenched her hands into fists. Cancer, the demon from the pit of hell, was not going to take Manuel from her.

Benito balanced the cordless phone on his shoulder. "Sandi, I want to tell our daughter before we list." His eyes drifted across the family room to Gen, who was working a puzzle with Anica on the big coffee table. "We're going to be seeing her in the morning. I'll call you the first part of the week." He cleared his throat. "Thank you." He shut off the phone.

Gen snapped Idaho in between Washington and Montana. "When the phone rang, I thought maybe it was Angelica." She glanced at her watch. "We should have heard from them by now. She said she'd call as soon as they got the test results. She definitely gave me the impression it wouldn't be long."

Benito shrugged his shoulders. "Maybe they decided to go out to dinner."

He didn't believe that and he knew Gen wouldn't either. Ever since Gen had talked to Angelica earlier in the evening, they had both avoided the topic. He'd been retired for years; still, he knew the medical profession. When Gen had repeated her conversation with Angelica it hadn't rung true. But, with Anica constantly within earshot, he had to let it drop.

Gen looked at her watch again. "Hand me the phone. It won't take a minute to call and make sure everything's all right."

Benito could feel himself tensing as he watched his wife dial.

Gen smiled at Anica as she pressed the Off button on the phone. "She's not answering. I bet they're out to dinner." She rose, walked to Benito, and handed him the phone. With her back to their grandchild, her face filled with concern.

Benito took the phone from her and placed it in the cradle. "Anica, it's almost nine. Time for bed. Martha will help you get ready, then G-Mom and G-Dad will come up and tuck you in."

As soon as Anica left the room, Benito voiced what both were thinking. "Something's going on."

"Ben, this whole thing is starting to bother me. Her exact words were, 'We learned some things and we'll tell you about them when we see you.' That was over two hours ago." Gen sat on the edge of the couch. "I know the pediatrician's office isn't open this late."

Benito felt a chill as he realized the truth in what his wife was saying. "You're right. In fact, I doubt it was open when you called her earlier."

The distress that tinged his wife's voice increased. "At the pool, when I was helping her with Manuel . . . I don't know . . . there was an awkward moment . . . she seemed like she was hiding something. I felt like I shouldn't pry. I don't know . . ." Her voice trailed off. "I guess I should have asked more questions." She looked at him.

Benito grabbed the phone and dialed Angelica's home number. No answer. He tried her cell phone again. The voice mail picked up. He waited for the beep.

"This is your father. Call me immediately." He jabbed the Off button and dropped the phone in its cradle.

He couldn't quell the uneasiness rising in his stomach. "I'm not about to sit around here and wait until tomorrow morning to find out what's going on. If something is up with Manuel, I want to know about it. Now." He started down the hall. "Kiss my granddaughter good night for me. Tell her I had to run out for a minute."

Gen was right at his heels. "You wait, I'm going too. Bring the car around. I'll run upstairs and tuck Anica in, then meet you out front."

Moments later Gen slid into the car next to him. They drove to their daughter's home and found the house dark. At Dr. Pearson's office the parking lot was empty.

Benito pulled the car to the side of the road. Gripping the steering wheel, he stared straight ahead.

Gen reached across the seat and rubbed his arm. "What should we do?"

Benito pursed his lips. Pulling from the curb, he gunned the accelerator. "There's only one other place they could be." He and Gen exchanged glances. Neither spoke.

As Benito pulled into the parking area of Sierra Medical Center, he began scanning the parked cars. As he continued through the medical center to the children's hospital, he spotted Antonio's truck. He pulled into a parking space.

They hurried into the building.

As they approached the counter, Benito stepped in front of his wife. "I'm Dr. Amante. Our daughter, Angelica Perez, and her husband are here with our grandson. The patient name is Manuel Perez. We'd like to visit."

"Just a moment." The woman behind the counter entered some information into her computer. "Yes, he's on level three. You can take the—"

Benito spun on his heel, grabbed his wife's hand, and headed toward the elevator. He didn't need directions. He'd spent plenty of time on level three of the hospital five years before. By the time he reached the nurses station, his pulse was pounding.

"I'm Dr. Amante. I'm here to check on my grandson, Manuel Perez. Where's his room?"

"He's not back from surgery."

"Surgery!" The word exploded from his lips. Heads turned.

"Ben, keep your voice down." Gen addressed the nurse. "I'm sorry. We've been trying to reach our daughter and we're concerned."

Benito interrupted her. "Which operating room was he taken to?"

The nurse took a step back. "Why don't you take a seat? I'm sure they'll be back soon."

Benito leaned across the counter and lowered his voice. "Young lady, I'm not taking a seat anywhere except next to my daughter. I know where the operating rooms are. You can tell me which one, or I can go find out myself."

The nurse stared at him silently.

"Fine." He brushed past his wife. "Let's go."

He could hear Gen behind him, running to keep up. He made his way through the maze of halls and doors, scanning the waiting areas as he neared the operating rooms. Finally, he slowed his steps as he looked through a doorway, recognizing the gray chairs clustered in groups, the low tables with magazines . . . his eyes stopped on the large window in the back of the room.

Long ago he'd stood in front of that window. He dropped his eyes, remembering an afternoon years before. He'd pleaded with God to give mercy to his grandson. His gaze returned to the window. He'd been a fool.

"Mom! Dad!"

Benito turned at the voice behind him. "What's going on? Where's Manuel?" His voice was louder than he'd intended. Angelica burst into tears.

"Oh, honey." Gen pulled their daughter into her arms. "Daddy's not angry. We're just concerned." She guided Angelica to one of the chairs. "Sit down and tell us about it."

Benito cursed himself under his breath and took a seat opposite his daughter. "I'm sorry, Angel."

Taking a shaky breath, Angelica raised her chin. "Manuel's in surgery. They're putting a port in his chest."

Gen's hand flew to her lips.

Benito closed his eyes and turned his face away.

When Manuel had first been diagnosed with acute myeloid leukemia, Benito had made it his business to find out everything he could about the disease. Having been a heart surgeon, he had access to many resources and the knowledge to assimilate what he read. As Manuel had improved, he'd researched cure rates and relapses. He recalled that the survival rate for relapse was about twenty-four percent, using any treatment protocol other than a bone marrow

49

transplant. And even with a bone marrow transplant, the chance of success was only about fifty-fifty.

He turned toward his daughter. Did she have any idea what they were facing? "What did the doctor say?"

"They plan to start chemo as soon as the port is in."

"Chemo's not going to be enough." Benito stood. "Manuel is going to need a bone marrow transplant as soon as the cancer's under control. Where's the doctor?"

"Dad, sit down, please." Angelica proceeded to relate to him all the doctor had told them. "Tomorrow Anica, Antonio, and I will be tested to see if we match."

"I want to be tested too." Gen glanced around the room. "Where is Antonio?"

"He's in the chapel room downstairs."

Benito rolled his eyes. Frankly, it didn't surprise him. With no education, no connections, no way to take charge, it was the only option someone like his son-in-law had. Looking outside himself, hoping that the powers that be would somehow intervene.

"I'm glad. God hears our prayers." Gen reached for Angelica's hand. "Jesus is the great physician."

Benito slumped back in his chair. What nonsense. Where were God and Jesus when Manuel was born with Down syndrome, or when Manuel was first diagnosed with AML? Where were they now? Benito's eyes drifted to the window at the back of the room. He scowled. He'd given God and Jesus a shot. It was time to take control. It was time to gather every resource available and fight for Manuel's life.

Antonio stepped inside the chapel room door. The room was empty.

Bowing his head, he walked toward the altar. He stopped

in front of the simple table and lit a candle. The flame shot up, straight and strong.

He knelt in front of the candle. "*Dios*, my heart breaks."

He folded his hands beneath his chin, sorting through his thoughts, trying to grasp all that was happening. He didn't understand why God had allowed this. "You have given me a son and I love him with all that I am. He is life to me. But now, he is sick. So sick." He raised his eyes heavenward. "You are my only hope. Only You can help us. Show me what to do."

He waited. Wanting a sign. Something. Anything to tell him God heard his prayer and would answer it.

As the moments passed, silence pressed on him.

"You command the morning and set the days in their place. You speak life into being and death fears You. You are God. Please hear me." His voice became desperate. "Please help me."

The candle flame began to flicker, drawing Antonio's eyes to it.

Suddenly, the flame filled his scope of vision and there was nothing in the room but the golden light. Transfixed, he stared at it. Seeing within its midst a door. And through the door, a glassy sea sparkling like crystal. Upon the sea was a throne and before the throne . . . a crown.

The presence of overwhelming love filled him and a peace settled over him. The flame and the love seemed to become one, now a fire that did not burn.

The light became so intense Antonio dropped his face to his knees.

For a moment, shadows flickered around him, then suddenly disappeared.

He raised his head.

The vision was gone.

Moments passed. Unsure what might happen next, he didn't move. Never in his life had he experienced anything like this. He had had many experiences with God through the years, but it was his grandmother, Maclovia, who first spoke to him of God's love. Later he learned of God's love become man, and that His name was Jesus. Still, none of that had prepared him for this.

As he sat, trying to make sense of all that had happened, words from the Bible that he had been reading just that morning came to him: "'Eye has not seen, nor ear heard, nor have entered into the heart of man the things which God has prepared for those who love Him.' But God has revealed them to us through His Spirit."

Revealed by His Spirit. He was filled with conviction. God's will would be done in the life of his son. God's great love for Manuel would bring healing. Antonio felt a weight lift from his shoulders.

He stood and picked up the flickering candle. Turning it to the right and to the left, he examined it, but there was no evidence that anything out of the ordinary had transpired. There was nothing remaining from the moments before except the deep and profound sense of love and peace that filled him.

He blew out the flame and set the candle on the table.

As he opened the door to leave the room, he realized a woman was on the other side, her hand on the knob.

"You're not supposed to lock the door. The chapel is for everyone."

"I didn't lock the door." He looked at the knob. "See, there is no lock on it."

The woman frowned and pushed past him.

He quickly stepped out of her way. "I'm sorry that happened, *señora*." She was probably struggling with her own grief and meant nothing by her rudeness.

As he hurried back to the waiting area near the operating room, the scene in the chapel replayed in his mind. He did not understand the mysterious power of God. But he did know the transforming power of God's love. Surely, that had been God's answer to his prayer. God was with him. God would never leave him or forsake him. God would heal Manuel.

"Antonio."

Angelica was running toward him.

"Hurry. It's Manuel. Something terrible has happened."

4

INCOMPETENCE, I TELL you. I'm still thinking of taking it up with the chief of staff." Benito shoved his chair back, narrowly missing Martha as she cleared the breakfast dishes.

"Keep your voice down or Anica will hear you." Gen's voice broke. Waiting a moment, she composed herself. "The surgeon said that Manuel's lung collapsing during surgery was an extremely rare complication. Going over it and over it doesn't help. It just keeps me upset. How many times did something unexpected happen to you during surgery?"

For a split second, Benito saw himself standing in an operating room, bright lights glaring. All faces turned toward him, the young heart surgeon, as the patient was pronounced dead. If only he'd known more. If only he'd done more. He glanced at his wife, she knew nothing about it. He had shared the incident with no one, and even now, thirty years later, the memory stirred feelings he preferred to keep buried. "There's no excuse for incompetence."

Gen rose. "When Angelica called this morning, she said that Manuel's been moved from Pediatric Intensive Care into a private room. That must mean he's improving."

Benito looked at her. They'd been married over fifty years, and for as long as she'd been his wife he'd protected her from the trials and tribulations of life. She'd had dreams of being an interior designer when he met her. She loved to entertain and was a wonderful hostess. The lifestyle he'd been able to give her at Regalo Grande had allowed her to indulge her interests with the flair and passion that were so much a part of her personality. It had only been over the past few years, since his accident and Manuel's diagnosis of AML, that she had become emotionally fragile. Despite his concerns, he must continue to protect her by keeping his feelings in check. It was his duty. "Yes, it probably does mean he's improving. As soon as you're dressed, we'll get down to the lab and have our blood drawn."

Benito went to his office to wait for his wife. He shut the door and swiveled his chair to the computer. The screen still showed the site he'd been studying when Gen called him to breakfast. He began reading where he left off.

The outlook for a child whose AML relapses is very poor. Different drug treatments in varying combinations have been tried, but they have not been successful. Sometimes the child can be put into a clinical trial that is testing a new chemotherapy regimen. The hope being that remission can be attained and a stem cell transplant performed.

The outcome of a transplant depends on the match between donor and patient with respect to particular blood cell proteins called human leukocyte antigens (HLA). Each individual carries six proteins that are the result of genetic mixing of their ancestors over the millennia; therefore treatment of AML with stem cell transplantation from a sibling with a compatible tissue type increases the chances of success.

Benito sat back in his chair, trying to process the information. He had basic knowledge about matching in the context

55

of his work as a surgeon. But this kind of detail was far beyond his area of expertise.

HLA. Genetic makeup. Tissue type. He began to realize the truth of what he was reading. The HLA antigens that must be matched were genetic markers on the surface of Manuel's white blood cells, inherited from his parents. A fingerprint of sorts. Manuel would most likely need a donor with some Hispanic blood. It was imperative Anica be a match. His eyes returned to the screen.

"If a related match cannot be found, an unrelated match may be located through the use of the National Marrow Donor Program (NMDP)."

Benito filtered through his memory. He'd been familiar with the program in years past. He let his breath out and a smile tugged at his lips. As he recalled, the donor base was huge. He typed "NMDP Hispanic Minorities" into the Search field at the top of his screen.

Scanning the results, the smile left his face. "Special Need for Minorities," "Minorities Underrepresented in Donor Program," "Lack of Minorities in the Registry." He clicked.

Because of genetic differences among racial and ethnic groups, particularly African Americans and Hispanics, patients from minority groups may never have the same probability of finding matches, and therefore access to transplants, as Caucasian patients. Patient matching rates depend, to some extent, on the number of people in the patient's group on the Registry. All minorities are at a disadvantage for this reason.

Manuel was only *half* Mexican. Surely, that would open up more possible matches. He continued to follow one link to another, finally, ending up on family sites—web pages desperate parents had designed, pleading with minority members of the public to register with a donor program. Family after family logging their futile search for a stem cell match for their child. Hispanic. African American. Pakistani.

Not wanting to accept what he was reading, he broadened his search. Spotting a link titled, "To improve the lives and survival rates of patients suffering with blood-related cancers *worldwide. . . ."*

He clicked on the words.

The picture of a handsome man, black hair and moustache, arms wrapped around a smiling boy standing on a beach, filled his screen. The boy's hair was tousled by a sea breeze and the man's face was filled with joy. Father and son on an outing.

Benito leaned forward in his chair to read the text next to the picture.

"Maximiliano M. Rivarola died of leukemia at the age of 17. Max was born in Argentina. At the age of 14, he was diagnosed with chronic myelogenous leukemia. Despite a vast worldwide search, a bone marrow donor was never found."

For a moment, Benito sat staring at the screen, slowly shaking his head. "No."

His eyes drifted to the face of the young boy. Innocent, hopeful eyes engaging him.

"No. No. No. No."

He lowered his head and wept.

"Good morning." Dr. Dorak stepped to the foot of Manuel's bed. "Looks like our boy is doing better this morning."

"He sure gave us a scare last night." Angelica glanced at her husband, sitting next to her.

Antonio smiled. "My boy is strong and a fighter. He's going to be okay."

Angelica looked at the doctor. He only nodded, then turned his attention to the chart he was holding. "I've got the results from the blood test."

When they had worked with Dr. Dorak during Manuel's first illness, Angelica had learned he'd lost someone close to him to cancer when he was in high school. The experience deeply affected him, and ultimately influenced his decision to become an oncologist. He had shared with her and Antonio his dream to develop a camp for kids with cancer and their families, someday. The only thing stopping him was that property in the wine country was too expensive. He thought perhaps when he retired, he could relocate to a less expensive area and see his dream become a reality.

She admired him greatly, not only for his dedication and commitment, but also for his constant positive attitude and endless patience with Manuel. There was something about his manner that always made her feel hopeful. Whatever he was going to tell them would be told with compassion and understanding. He was not only an impressive doctor but also an extraordinary human being.

"The results show Manuel's white blood count at one hundred ten thousand. The previous count was seventy thousand."

"Isn't normal between five and ten thousand?"

The doctor nodded. "His hemoglobin is six, and his platelet count is thirty thousand."

Angelica felt Antonio's arm slip around her shoulder. They both knew these counts were very serious.

"We'll continue the chemotherapy for five days, then take another biopsy." He raised his head. "I've sent down the request to the lab so yours and Anica's blood can be typed."

"My parents will be here soon with our daughter. They're going to be typed too."

Dr. Dorak closed the chart. "How are your parents? I haven't seen them in such a long time."

"They're both doing great. Very healthy. And so glad that they may be able to help."

"I remember what a tremendous support they were for you." He looked from her to Antonio. "Extended family is very important and they'll play a critical role over these next few months." He winked at Angelica. "Your dad really kept me on my toes."

Angelica winced at the memory of her father's questioning every detail of Manuel's treatment, as if the doctor had been practicing thirty days instead of nearly thirty years.

As though reading her thoughts, he added, "He really loves that boy. He's a good grandfather."

"I know he's hoping he'll be the match."

Dr. Dorak hesitated. "I've spoken to the hematologist about your situation. He isn't aware of any rule about age, but the registry, for example, prefers donors under the age of sixty. We agreed that in the absence of a younger donor candidate, perhaps testing could be moved up a little." He shifted the chart from one hand to the other. "Manuel received one hundred percent of his genetic makeup from you and Antonio. His grandfather would, on average, only be a quarter match. I can explain it to him if you want me to."

Antonio stroked the back of her hair. "Don't worry, Angel. Anica or I will match. I am sure."

Angelica closed her eyes a moment. "I understand. But why wouldn't you want to test every possible person?"

Dr. Dorak pulled a chair around to face them and sat down. "It isn't just that a viable match is unlikely, the hematopoietic stem cells of a seventy-year-old man will also be seventy years old. After a traumatic experience of being seeded in a new and very hostile environment, they wouldn't work anymore. Even if they did, they wouldn't last long." He waited patiently for her to respond. "Does that make sense?"

"Yes, thank you."

The doctor stood. "I'll have some of the biopsy results later today." He shook Antonio's hand and left the room.

Within minutes Anica charged through the door, rushing up to Manuel's bedside. "Oh, he's sleeping." Her face filled with concern. "What's that thing?"

Angelica gathered her daughter in her arms. "That's a tube that gives him his medicine. That helps him get well."

Anica's face relaxed. "G-Mom and I prayed for him this morning." Anica flashed her grandmother a smile as her grandparents entered the room. "Tomorrow morning I'm going to ask the whole church to pray for him, Mom." Her young face became serious. "Jesus can do anything."

Angelica kissed her daughter's cheek and tightened her arms around the little girl. They'd chosen Anica's name because it combined parts of their names. And the child had proven to be a true combination of her parents' strongest qualities, having her mother's bright mind and her father's gentle compassion. Little escaped her notice and it was both a joy and a challenge raising her.

Benito walked around the hospital bed, then squatted down beside his grandson, awkwardly rubbing Manuel's cheek with his finger.

Manuel's eyes opened slightly. "Grrr . . ." The tiny sound disappeared in the air and his eyelids drifted shut.

Benito rose, blinking rapidly. "Let's go get our blood drawn. The sooner the better."

"Dad." Angelica brushed her hair back from her face.

"Dr. Dorak said that the donor should be under sixty." Her father's face darkened. "And besides, it's highly unlikely that a grandparent would be more than a quarter match."

Her mother stepped next to her father. "That means Manuel will only have three people in the family that could match, instead of five."

"Mother, it really isn't that simple. Genetic matching is complicated. We're hoping and praying one of us matches. If not, then we'll have to find an unrelated donor and—"

"Look, Angelica. I spent hours last night and this morning researching HLA matching. I am fully aware that probability is not in my favor. But I'm a doctor and during my forty-year career I've seen all sorts of unexpected and unexplainable anomalies that have resulted in a positive outcome for the patient. I don't care if it's one chance in a million. I'm going to pursue it for Manuel's sake."

Angelica felt overwhelmed. She'd counted on him all her life for advice and guidance. He'd been one of the most respected heart surgeons in the country but this wasn't his field of expertise. She didn't want to embarrass him by telling him he was wrong, and more than that, he was too old to be of help. "I know exactly how you feel, Dad. I'm certainly not going to fight with you about it. If the lab will do the test then do it."

She turned to Anica. She'd asked her parents to tell her daughter no more than that Manuel was very sick. "Manuel's blood is not healthy. He needs healthy blood. Would you like to give some of your healthy blood to him?"

Anica's eyes widened. "How?"

"Well, right now we'll all go down to the lab. They'll take a little blood from each of us and then they'll test it. The person whose blood matches Manuel's will have a chance to help him more."

Angelica held her breath. The child had been with Angelica numerous times when Manuel had gone to the doctor. She knew exactly how blood was drawn.

Anica wiggled out of her mother's arms. "That means there's going to be a needle." She put her hands on her hips, waiting for an answer.

Angelica nodded.

Anica looked toward her brother. Slowly, her hands dropped to her sides. "Can I sit in Daddy's lap?"

Antonio stood and swooped her into his arms. "Yes, precious, and will you sit with me when it's my turn?"

Anica giggled. "Daddy, you're brave. You're not afraid of anything."

Antonio looked over her head at Manuel.

"Then we will be brave together."

Angelica rose and took his hand. "Yes, we will be brave together."

As they left the room, Angelica turned for one last look at Manuel, with the tube dripping poison into him that was so toxic if it touched his skin it would burn it. Yet it was the only chance of saving his life. She swallowed the nausea that rose in her throat.

Please, God. Your Word says You have known us from the beginning. You knew this would happen. I trust that Your divine plan has already provided what Manuel needs. That You have hidden the cure in one of us.

Angelica sat down at the kitchen table and kicked off her shoes. God bless Faith Community Church. Going there for the morning service had lifted her spirits and renewed her hope. It had been years since she'd gone to church alone, but she and Antonio had agreed that as long as Manuel was in the hospital, one of the family would be with him. She and Antonio would alternate shifts on weekends; she and her parents would alternate on weekdays, so Antonio could keep his business going.

Before the service was over, a prayer chain had been set up and numerous families had volunteered to help with child care, meals, and errands. Thankfully, the parents of Anica's best friend, Katie, offered to care for Anica for the next few days. The O'Connells came home with them after church and helped pack Anica's bag. They left with her just moments ago.

Angelica looked at her watch. It was already after one o'clock. Dr. Dorak thought he would have preliminary test results back from the HLA typing tests by later in the afternoon . . . for all five of the samples. Her father had not been deterred by any of Dr. Dorak's facts, and had decided they didn't apply to her mother either.

She was glad her father had insisted. At church, many people had shared stories of similar situations where there had been spontaneous remissions, or long shots had paid off. Even healings.

She jumped up from the table energized. They were going to beat this thing.

Angelica picked up the phone. There was one thing she wanted to do before she went back to the hospital. She pressed the familiar numbers on the keypad.

Manuel's teacher answered on the second ring.

"Hi, Tex. It's Angelica."

"How are you, dear?"

Angelica gave her a summary of what had happened. "I really don't know when he'll be back in school. We'll know a lot more when we find out how he's responding to the chemo."

For a moment the line was silent. "I'm so sorry, Angelica. I know all the children in class will miss him. When he's feeling better, even if he can't attend, I hope he'll come by for a visit."

Angelica smiled into the phone. Since the beginning of school, this woman had gone well beyond what was required of a teacher accommodating a special needs child in a mainstream class. She had taken a sincere interest in Manuel and he had responded to her. She'd told Angelica when they first met how she'd been teaching over thirty years and always considered it a blessing to have a differently abled child in her class. Angelica had immediately felt a bond with her.

"Tell everyone he misses them too. Anica will be in school tomorrow and she'll help keep everyone informed."

"She's something else, that girl. I'm sure she will." There was a pause. "Did you ever hear from the Sierra Center about the job?"

Angelica caught her breath. It seemed like a lifetime ago that Antonio had told her they called. "Yes, I did. I'm so glad you asked, I completely forgot about it." She hesitated. "Tex, could you please do me a favor? I'm feeling so overwhelmed right now, could you call them for me and tell them what's happened? That I appreciate their offer, but I won't be able to accept the position."

"Of course, dear. I'd be glad to."

After giving Tex the phone number of the law center and saying good-bye, Angelica hung up the phone and changed her clothes.

Driving to the hospital, she reflected on the pastor's closing prayer that morning. Appealing to God, in His mercy, to provide the genetic match that was so critical to Manuel's recovery. Her eyes drifted to the clock on the car's dash. In a few hours, she would have the answer to that prayer.

64

When Angelica got to Manuel's room, her parents were already there with Antonio. He had deep circles under his eyes.

Angelica stepped next to her son and was glad to see he was sleeping. She bent down and kissed him.

There were small red dots under the surface of his skin around his eyes. Petechiae. Caused by blood leaking from his capillaries. He must have been vomiting. She looked at Antonio.

Her father answered. "Manuel didn't tolerate the chemo very well during the night. They've added anti-nausea drugs to his drip."

"Bless his heart," her mother whispered.

Angelica sat down next to her husband.

He took her face in his hands and turned her toward him. "Don't be afraid. He is resting now."

Angelica looked into Antonio's eyes, and as she had since the day she met him, she found peace there. Every wrenching circumstance that had happened in the past, every horror that threatened their future, kept at bay. She was not alone. They would fight for their son. She must stay positive.

She sat back in her chair. "You look exhausted. Have you had anything to eat today?"

He smiled at her. "Not yet." He rubbed her hand.

"Mom and Dad, why don't you and Antonio go to the cafeteria so he can get a bite to eat, then I'll meet you at Dr. Dorak's office."

"Good idea." Her father's voice was unnaturally loud as he shot from his chair.

Angelica caught her mother's eye. Both stifled a smile. Her father had always been deeply uncomfortable with any displays of emotion. She knew part of the reason was the required discipline of his profession, but she also knew part of it was because of his childhood. The unwanted child of an alcoholic mother and a workaholic father. Emotions always kept in check behind a wall of self-control.

Antonio stood, extending his hand to Angelica. "You're coming with us. Manuel is asleep and he will be fine."

"What if he wakes up and is frightened? I need to stay here."

Her father's brows drew together in a frown. "Angelica, you've got a long night ahead of you. Manuel isn't going to wake up if you leave for a little while. Trust your family doctor." He winked at her.

Antonio took her hand. "Come on. Walk with me."

The cafeteria wasn't crowded and they finished eating well before the time of their appointment.

Angelica took Antonio's hand. "Let's take the long way around to the oncology wing and walk through the park."

As they followed the winding sidewalk through the hospital grounds, Angelica turned her face toward the cloudless sky, letting the California sun warm her. It was a beautiful fall day. For just the briefest moment, in the scent of the air, and from the angle of the sun, she was able to capture the ambiance of hundreds of other fall days. Before. Before the blood test, before the diagnosis, before this meeting. That unburdened, familiar place of memory. Would things ever be the same again?

The oncology wing was unnaturally quiet without the comings and goings of weekday workers. There was only one other couple in the waiting room when they took their seats.

A nurse appeared at the door. "Are you Mr. and Mrs. Perez?"

Antonio stood and nodded.

"Come this way."

All four followed the nurse to Dr. Dorak's office.

"Good afternoon. Please, have a seat." The doctor gestured to the chairs.

Angelica looked at the doctor's face. He had a pleasant expression. Did that mean good news?

He was shaking her father's hand and exchanging pleasantries. Was he delaying the inevitable?

Finally, he moved behind his desk and sat down. "Let's go over the tissue typing test results and our options."

"Options?" Benito's voice filled the room.

Angelica felt her stomach knot. Her eyes flew to Dr. Dorak's face.

"I'm sorry. There was no full match within the family. We will have to search for an unrelated donor."

"Hola, amigo." Diego laid down his big greasy knife and extended his arm to Cirocco.

Gripping the man's arm, Cirocco pulled himself up. Then he hopped behind the counter, facing the street. He sat on Diego's empty stool.

Diego grabbed his knife, scooped up a handful of chopped meat, and threw it into a hot frying pan. Cirocco leaned over the pan, inhaling the savory steam.

Smile wide and silver tooth gleaming, Diego handed him a long-handled spoon. "Stir that and help yourself." He dipped the point of his knife at a stack of tortillas. "They're still warm."

Cirocco carefully extracted a sliver of meat from the pan with his fingers and popped it into his mouth. "How is Lucita?"

Diego set his knife down and crossed himself. "Aye, yi, yi. Praise God she's alive. That woman is like a mother to me."

He took a rag from his back pocket and swept the bits of meat that hadn't made it to the pan into his hand. He turned to Cirocco. "It's her diabetes. She lost her leg."

After laying a tortilla in his palm, Cirocco ladled some meat onto it. He'd known about the woman's health problems but he had no idea they were that serious. "I'm so sorry for her."

Diego expertly threw the scraps in his hand across the counter into Cirocco's skillet. "Oh, no need for that. They made her a new leg." He shoved the rag back into his pocket. "They gave it to her."

"*Gave* it to her." Cirocco stopped, the rolled tortilla midway to his mouth. "What do you mean?"

"It's through her church. They help people who need legs and arms."

Cirocco rested his hand on the counter, the tortilla warm in his fingers.

Only in America could this be true. "Free?"

"*Sí, amigo.*" Diego nodded his head. "Maybe it's good for you?"

Cirocco sat staring at Diego.

"Maybe you could go there?"

They gave her a leg.

Moments passed.

Finally, Cirocco shook his head. "There is no way for me to go there." He stuffed the tortilla in his mouth and chewed thoughtfully. "There is no way I could buy a plane ticket or get a visa."

Diego reached into an ice chest and pulled out a bottle of Coke. "Lucita and her son and his family live very near the border. They cross back and forth with no problem. Maybe they could meet you in Tijuana and help you." He put the Coke in front of Cirocco. "Me and Lucita talked about it."

Cirocco tapped his foot on the rung of the stool. "There is no way I could get enough money to go to America."

Diego wiped his hands on his apron, reached for his tip jar, and dumped the contents on the counter.

Cirocco's eyes widened.

Diego picked through the coins and placed a handful in an empty tin cup. "I'm going to put this under the counter for you." He gave a decisive nod of his head. "It's a start."

"No, no. That is *your* money."

"You think about it. I can't help you much. But, if you change your mind, I'll give you what I can."

Cirocco knew he would not change his mind. Diego was not a rich man. He had a wife and eight children. If Diego were going to buy a ticket to go to America, it should be for one of his own sons. The man had no obligation to him. No one did.

Cirocco looked into Diego's eyes. "You are very kind and I thank you. But I cannot take your money." It was better that way. He would take care of himself.

Diego turned his palms up and shrugged his shoulders. "I understand." He bent over and placed the cup on the back corner of the shelf. "Still, *amigo*, it is something to think about."

Diego's generosity touched Cirocco deeply, but it was foolishness to think such a thing was possible. He straightened on the stool. Even if he got to the border, there was no guarantee he could cross. He'd heard hundreds of stories about how hard it was to enter America. Why would he attempt such a thing? Here he had a job and a few people he could count on.

A breeze blew across the counter of the food stand, scattering a stack of paper plates into the street.

Cirocco reached across the counter and put his hand on the remaining stack while Diego rushed out to the front of the stand.

"Let me help you." A pretty, young woman knelt beside Diego and gathered the plates.

Cirocco froze.

It was her.

He'd seen her many times on the streets near San Juan de Dios, though she hadn't seen him. She first caught his attention because of her smile. Pretty, pink lips, straight white teeth. She had walked past him, talking and laughing with a young boy, her long black hair keeping time with her steps.

He'd dropped back and followed her for a distance, watching until she and the little boy had gone into a store. And then he waited, not taking his eyes from the store's door as one minute turned into twenty. First, praying she would return so he could catch another glimpse of her, then fearing she would return . . . and see a beggar on a wheeled board leaning against the wall of a building. Finally, he left, tucking the chance meeting away, safe from the reality of his world. Visiting her only at night, behind closed eyes.

He felt heat crawling up his neck.

She rose and stepped toward the stand, holding the plates out toward Cirocco. "Where did that wind come from?" It gusted again, blowing her hair close to her face and under her chin, as if framing it for Cirocco's consideration.

His heart was pounding.

Diego's hand passed in front of Cirocco, taking the plates from the girl. "*Gracias, señorita.*"

70

She looked toward Diego and nodded her head. "You are most welcome, *señor.*"

Turning to go, her eyes briefly rested on Cirocco. Pretty, pink lips parting in a smile.

5

N o, it is a mistake." Antonio clenched his fist. "The test is wrong."

Angelica looked at her husband, then at her father. "Dad?"

Fear flashed across her father's face.

His expression shook her to her core. The man to whom she had turned her entire life for support and strength seemed stunned, helpless. The doctor's words became real. They would have to search for an unrelated donor.

The full impact of what that meant surged through Angelica. She tried to get her breath, but fear, hopelessness, and grief gripped her like a vice. Manuel would die if a donor could not be found. She heard her father's voice in the distance. "You have someone here who handles donor searches, I assume."

"Yes." Dr. Dorak's voice cut through her thoughts. "I'll be in touch with the Unrelated Donor Search Coordinator tomorrow morning. She will initiate contact with the National Marrow Donor Program."

Angelica felt a wave of panic. She suddenly realized that

deep down she had believed one of them would match. "There're millions of people registered in that program, aren't there?"

Dr. Dorak paused, considering her question. "Yes, there are millions of people registered. But I think you're asking if there is a good probability that a match will be found for Manuel."

Antonio took Angelica's hand in his. "Is there?"

Dr. Dorak hesitated for a moment. "Manuel is the child of a mixed marriage. The half of the HLA type Manuel inherited from Angelica is a relatively common one and that will help."

Angelica heard her father exhale.

"However, the other half from Antonio is a rare HLA type . . . even in Mexico."

Antonio dropped Angelica's hand.

"In a situation like this, if there is no match in the registry, the best chance lies with Antonio's extended family. Some of Antonio's immediate family or relatives will carry his uncommon haplotype. Then it will be a matter of Angelica's more common European haplotype also being present."

"Is that even possible?"

The doctor turned to Angelica's father. "I understand your question."

Angelica looked from the doctor to her father. It was as if the doctor were acknowledging something that had not actually been said. She swallowed the lump in her throat. What did her father know about finding a match for Manuel that he hadn't shared with her?

Dr. Dorak continued. "First, let me explain that when I say common or rare, it's all relative in that any haplotype is a rare one. Millions of them are possible in any given population.

"Now, having said that, each haplotype may exist in any population with a certain degree of overlap as there is no definite separation between the populations. Angelica's haplotype will certainly exist in some Mexicans." His face grew serious. "Yes, a match is possible. There are some non-Hispanic white haplotypes that are fairly common in Mexico. Still, we are not talking about an absolute certainty by any stretch of the imagination. Only a small possibility."

Antonio ran his fingers through his hair. "I will leave for Mexico tomorrow."

Dr. Dorak's face filled with compassion. "I understand why you would feel that way. But I think it would be premature at this time. The NMDP should be tried first."

Antonio slowly shook his head, his eyes drifting to the floor.

No one spoke.

Silence fanned the fear that gripped Angelica. "It's going to take a miracle to find a match, isn't it, Doctor?"

He'd been thinking about it all night. Cirocco rolled onto his back. Morning was just beginning to light the skies over Guadalajara. His eyes traveled to the shelf above his head. He could see a sliver of the gray metal cup through a split in the wood.

Using his hands, he scooted out from under Diego's food stand, then pushed himself up on his good leg. Standing behind the wooden counter, he surveyed the street for a few moments.

Cirocco hesitated, then leaned on the counter, as he had the afternoon before. He drew a deep breath, raising his chest, squaring his shoulders.

She had smiled at him.

Diego had noticed it too, though he said he'd never seen the girl before. Was he blind? Cirocco had observed her on the streets surrounding San Juan de Dios many times.

What had she thought when she saw him standing there? Did she think Diego worked for him? She hadn't tried to hand the plates to Diego, even though they were side by side in the street. She'd risen and turned to him.

Everything in his line of vision disappeared as he revisited that moment in the benevolent and timeless place of his memory.

The darting movement of a bone-thin dog sniffing the sidewalk across the street caught his attention.

Cirocco recognized the animal. The dog often trotted alongside Cirocco as he scavenged in the alleys, he and the dog sometimes nosing through the same trash cans.

Cirocco's shoulders slumped. That's where he lived his life. Two feet off the ground, in the black gaps that separated buildings, where dogs sniffed and tires sprayed filthy water from rain-soaked streets.

The reality of his past and the certainty of his future became palpable. He knotted his hand into a fist and slammed it on the counter. He wasn't going to live like a dog anymore. The ideas and schemes he'd played out in his mind during the night coalesced into conviction. Whether it was fear or faith, he couldn't say. But what had seemed impossible, now seemed imperative. He was going to America. And he was going to get a leg.

"I will do it," he whispered. "I will . . . I will." The words became a chant as the whisper became a shout.

The dog across the street gazed at him with dull eyes. Cirocco shook his fist at the animal. "I will."

Waves of excitement washed through him. He had to tell somebody.

Mama Rose.

He squatted down and grabbed the wheeled board from under the stand. Rolling the board behind his back, he slid onto it.

He took a cursory look at his hands and shirt. He would clean up first. This was a very important occasion. He wheeled to the sidewalk and took off for the park.

When he arrived, the sprinkler was shooting water in wide circles. Some of the water washed over one side of the statue in the middle of the grounds, and then pooled at its base.

Cirocco hurriedly rolled down the walkway to the base of the statue. He slid off the board and sat on the marble landing. Taking off his shirt, he quickly rinsed it in the pooled water, then ran his shirt over his face, hair, and upper body.

Shivering, he dropped the shirt in his lap and pushed himself back up the walkway. He circled around to the sunny benches on the south side of the park. There he wrung the shirt out and spread it on the seat of a bench.

A smile tugged at his lips. Mama Rose would be surprised to see him. Years past, he had visited the American missionary weekly at the room she lived in next to the church, Iglesia Biblica Centro, or at the Cruz Roja where she volunteered. But over time, his visits had come further apart. Mostly because he didn't want to hear about how Jesus loved him . . . though there'd been a time he believed that.

He rubbed the stump of his leg.

The first thing she would say was that she would pray for him. He chewed his lower lip. He knew there was a God; it was just that God had never seemed to care much for him. Still, it wouldn't hurt to have someone put in a good word for him. Especially for something as important as this. He picked his shirt up off the bench and squeezed out the water that had collected in the edges of the fabric. Then he snapped it in the air, encouraging it to dry.

His first memory of the woman was the fragrance of roses. A man had driven him and his mother to the hospital from Santa Sophia after his leg had been crushed by a boulder. The weeks that followed were a maze of confusion in his mind. Part of the time spent in this world, part of the time in some other. But through the pain and fear that marked that dark time, there had been the scent of roses.

At first he'd thought it was his mother sitting at his bedside praying for him. And he called out to her. But as the drugged fog cleared, he realized that the woman stroking his forehead was not his mother. In fact, it seemed his mother was unable to visit more than once every few days. And eventually, not at all.

So he began to call the woman who cared for him in the hospital Mama Rose. And by the time the doctors said he could go home, he understood he would go home with her.

Sometimes his mother picked him up from the church where Mama Rose lived, and took him to different houses or hotels. Those were the days he lived for. But whether he stayed with his mother an hour or an afternoon, he saw little of her. She had to work, she explained. She needed money to give to Mama Rose to take care of him and she needed money to take care of herself.

By the time he was thirteen, he knew what that work was. And one day, with devastating clarity, he realized why she did it. It was because of him. Because he was a cripple and he would never be able to take care of himself or her.

He felt his shirt. It was damp, but he didn't care. He jammed his arms through the sleeves and pulled himself onto his board. He began pumping his hands on the pavement, picking up speed as he rolled down the walkway.

That terrible day, that terrible day was upon him. He pumped harder, as though he could leave his memories in the park. But they clung to him, flashing in vivid detail . . . him crouching beside the hotel room door, hoping to hear his mother's footsteps, instead, hearing snatches of a conversation.

First his mother's voice, "He's my son and I love him."

Then a man's voice, "Ines, I told you, I don't want to be strapped with a kid, especially not a crippled one. Drop it. By this time tomorrow, you'll be in Mexico City. We'll be looking at apartments."

And the next day, she left. Telling him her work was taking her away, but that she would send money to Mama Rose and would soon return for him.

But a year had passed before she returned. And she returned with that man. He stood at the door while Cirocco's mother explained to Cirocco that he had to stay with Mama Rose awhile longer. He could see the man's face behind his mother's shoulder. The cool eyes telling him he was a cripple and no one wanted him.

Cirocco's palms stung as they slapped the pavement. At first he'd begged her to stay with him. But when the man took her hand to lead her away, Cirocco felt an acidic anger and seething hatred rise from his belly to his mouth. Unable to control the feelings, they became words, spewing into the air. He hated her.

It was not until months later, when he began to revisit memories of his mother, that he realized the truth. It wasn't her fault. She was good and kind and loved him. It was his fault and he hated himself for it. He was no good for her. He was no good for anybody.

By the time Cirocco reached the church, he had managed to get control of his thoughts. He had a plan. That was what mattered now.

He rolled around to the back of the building, through a door he knew was always open, and then down a long hall. As he approached the kitchen, he could hear Mama Rose humming.

When he got to the kitchen, her back was to him. Gray hair pulled up into a casual bun, a simple sundress hanging from her ample shoulders, and an apron tied askew across her broad hips. She began to sing, her rich voice filling the room with praises to the Lord as she kneaded dough on the counter.

Seeing her, he suddenly felt vulnerable. What if she didn't think he should go? What if she wouldn't give him her blessing?

He put his foot on the floor and pushed himself up until he was standing. He balanced against the doorjamb. "Mama Rose?"

Her floury hands flew up in the air. "Is that my boy?" She wheeled around, recognition instantly on her face.

Wiping her hands on her apron, she rushed toward him. "Cirocco, honey. How good it is to see you. I was just thinking about you." She pressed her plump cheek against his and wrapped her arms around him. "Bless you, child. You've been on my mind." Cirocco closed his eyes, melting into her soft bosom.

Stepping back, she looked him over, her dimpled smile transporting him to his childhood. "Looks like you've come just in time." She hugged him again. "Hon, if you were any skinnier, you'd be dead." She clucked her tongue. "Now, you come sit at the table and talk to me while I make you breakfast."

She rubbed some butter on her dough, then put it in a bowl and covered it. Then she began to chop tomatoes, onions, and cheese.

Cirocco hopped to the sink and washed his hands, then took a seat at the table. Maybe it would be better to ease into telling her about his decision. He thought for a moment. "Diego went to visit his aunt in the hospital. He thought she was going to die. But they saved her. He told me about it and everything he saw there."

Mama Rose stirred the chopped food into a skillet of tortilla strips. "How is she doing?"

As the food cooked, Cirocco related all that Diego had told him about Lucita's experience, casually mentioning Diego's suggestion that Cirocco might be able to visit Lucita.

Mama Rose put a full plate of *chilaquiles* in front of him. "Dear Lord, bless this food and this child." She took a seat across from him. "Now eat."

Cirocco took a deep breath.

"I'm going to get a leg, just like Lucita did."

Mama Rose's mouth dropped open.

"I've thought about it a lot." He waited, hoping she'd say something.

"It's free." His words came rushing out. "They do it for free. I just have to get there."

"What are you talking about, child?"

"I'm going to America."

"How on earth *will* you get there?"

Cirocco leaned forward. His heart began to pound as he laid out his plan for her. "I thought about it all night. Diego is giving me some money. Enough for a bus ticket to Puerto Vallarta. I know I can find work there and I will make enough money to travel farther north on the bus. I will work my way to the border."

As he spoke, Mama Rose's face became a mixture of bewilderment and concern. "I don't know, son. This sounds very risky, very dangerous." She fingered the cross at her neck. "What if you don't make enough money to continue north?"

"Then I will stay in Puerto Vallarta until I do."

"Where will you stay? You don't know anyone."

Cirocco had already thought of that. It was why he'd chosen Puerto Vallarta as his first stop. He learned all about it from Jose, who sometimes worked the toilets with him. "My friend, Jose, has been there many times. He told me there are magnificent hotels on the oceanfront, with big *palapas* scattered across the beaches and showers for the American tourists to use. He said at night there are few people on the beach and the police are busy in town. Life there is good." He searched her face. "I will be okay, Mama. Please, give me your blessing."

Mama Rose reached across the table and took his hands in hers. "It isn't my blessing that you need, son. Let me pray for you."

Cirocco released a deep sigh and bowed his head.

He felt Mama Rose's hands tighten on his.

"Dear Lord, please give Your angels charge over this boy. You know the plans You have for him, plans to give him hope and a future. I ask You to give him the desires of his heart, going before him and opening doors for him so he can receive the leg that You have for him. I pray Your Holy Spirit will speak to him and guide him from this moment forward. I ask this in the precious name of Your Son, Jesus Christ."

As the prayer ended, Cirocco felt a deep sense of foreboding pass through him. He lifted his head and looked at Mama Rose.

But her head was still bowed, her lips moving in silent prayer, as tears silently slipped down her cheeks.

Cirocco slowly turned his head to the right, then to the left.

Somewhere behind him was the unmistakable scent of roses.

It was *his* fault. There was something in his blood he had passed on to Manuel.

Dios, forgive me.

Antonio pulled out of the hospital parking lot, his knuckles white as he gripped the steering wheel. Angelica had insisted that he go home because he'd been at the hospital since Friday afternoon.

What if this thing, this haplotype that had come from his blood, had caused the cancer to begin with?

He shuddered, remembering the way Benito had looked at him when the doctor said the Mexican part of Manuel's blood was rare, and could interfere with getting a match. He would never forget that look as long as he lived. Benito was a doctor; maybe there was more to it, and he knew that.

What did Angelica think? Did she blame him too? A cold chill slithered up his spine. Her parents had never wanted her to marry him. Now did she think they were right?

Despair settled on him, the weight of it making it hard for him to breathe. He pulled the truck over to the side of the road and shifted it into park. He leaned forward, pressing his forehead against the steering wheel.

Acute myeloid leukemia. Words hissed from hell, coming into his life, trying to steal everything he loved.

He began to replay what the doctor had said, thinking

about each point he had made. *Rare . . . uncommon . . . no match*. The words pricked his ears like the point of a tine.

He squeezed his eyes shut. *Jesus.*

Minutes passed.

Help me.

Slowly Antonio's head cleared and he began to think about all he had overcome in his life. Extreme poverty, the desert of California, lack of education, a language, a new culture, and even a family that would not accept him.

He rolled down the truck's window to get some air. A gentle evening breeze drifted in.

But he had not been alone. Through it all, he'd had a champion fighting his battles when he could not, holding him up when he was too weary to go on, walking before him when he could not see.

Jesús. Jesucristo.

Antonio sat up. He was not going to accept a death sentence for his son, or a grandfather's condemnation, or his wife's fear. He had a defender. A champion. A dread champion.

Something deep within him stirred . . . a feeling, giving rise to a thought . . . the thought crystallizing into certainty.

He knew what he was going to do.

Antonio put the truck in gear, made a U-turn, and headed back to the hospital.

When he arrived at Manuel's room, Angelica was sitting next to his son, holding his hand and softly singing to him, her back to the door.

Antonio watched her.

His beautiful Angelica. His first love. The mother of his children. She had given him heaven on earth by agreeing to be his wife, and he thanked God every day for allowing him the privilege of being her husband. He wanted her to

83

know she could count on him, that he would shoulder this burden.

He whispered her name.

Angelica turned toward him, her lips forming a silent O.

She rose, facing him. As she held his gaze, her lips began to tremble. "What are we going to do? I'm so scared."

He stepped toward her, pulling her into his arms, holding her as she wept. "Don't cry." He pressed her head into his shoulder, blinking back his own tears. "Please, don't cry."

Gradually, her sobs subsided. "Oh, Antonio, I don't know what we're going to do."

He brushed her hair away from her face. "I do."

Angelica tilted her head back, looking into his eyes.

He pulled her into his arms. "I'm not going to wait for the doctor's permission or the donor program. I'm going to Mexico to find a match for Manuel."

Benito sat behind his desk fingering the Realtor's card.

The meeting in Dr. Dorak's office had disturbed him deeply. Nothing that had been said sounded encouraging. He stirred the martini he'd made.

It was clear from Angelica's questions that she recognized the seriousness of Manuel's situation. It was also clear that she was the one who was going to have to deal with it. Antonio didn't have a clue what was going on.

His eyes drifted to the picture on his desk. Angelica as a teenager, sitting on Pasha bareback, hand knotted in his mane. The horse's neck in a pronounced arch, anticipating her signal to take off into the hills surrounding the ranch.

Benito huffed a sigh. Angelica never should have married Antonio. He was a nice young man and had done all right

. . . considering. But Angelica deserved a better life than the one she had settled for.

He picked up the picture and ran his forefinger over her hair. She was still his little girl. And she still needed him.

The one thing that had not come up in Dr. Dorak's office was the matter of insurance. Antonio was self-employed and they couldn't afford good insurance. When Manuel had first been diagnosed with AML, battling the insurance company had seemed almost as difficult as battling the cancer.

He tapped the card on the desk.

If a match was not found for Manuel through conventional channels, who would pay for searches in other registries, in other countries? The issue had occurred to him in the doctor's office and he'd thought about little else since then. He didn't have the reserves and assets he once had. He'd suffered a severe financial setback just before his accident when he'd formed a company and tried to bring a new drug to market. Then, just as he was getting back on his feet, the accident had ended his career as a surgeon.

Angelica knew nothing about his finances. No one did. From all outward appearances, everyone assumed that he and his wife lived a secure life of leisure on their California estate.

Benito leaned back in his swivel chair and folded his arms across his chest. He had to get the ranch sold. There had been no real hurry before; now it was imperative. If it became necessary, he would spare no expense to save his grandson's life.

He looked at Angelica's picture again. She loved the ranch. He dreaded telling her he was selling it, especially now. And considering all she had to deal with, he would never want her to know that Manuel's illness was the impetus for his decision.

He drained his martini glass, then picked up the phone and dialed the number on the Realtor's card.

6

ANGELICA SLIPPED HER front door key into the lock. She eased the door open, stepped into the living room, and stood a moment, listening.

Hoping Antonio was still asleep, she set her purse and coat in a chair, kicked off her shoes, then tiptoed down the hall to their bedroom. Peeking through the door, she saw him sprawled on his back across the bedspread, still dressed. Jacket askew, booted feet hanging off the end of the mattress.

She walked to the edge of the bed and sat down next to him.

He didn't move.

Even though they'd been married almost twelve years, she still thought him one of the most handsome men she'd ever met: tall, tanned, muscled. Possessing a natural magnetism. Although he seemed oblivious to his appeal.

A smile tugged at her lips. There'd been numerous occasions over the years when predatory women had tried to enlighten him, only to receive a firm, but gentlemanly, rebuff.

Her thoughts returned to the night before, in the hospital room when he'd taken her in his arms, telling her of his plan to go to Mexico. She'd felt loved and protected . . . she yearned to feel that way again.

She lay down next to him and kissed his lips.

Slowly, his eyes opened.

Turning toward her, their faces just inches apart, looking into her eyes, he smiled at her. And before she could speak a word, before she could tell him how much she needed him, he reached out and pulled her to him.

For the next few minutes, in that sheltered, safe place, Angelica drew from her husband's quiet strength and thanked God for bringing him into her life.

"Do you have to go to work?" She felt his arms relax.

"What time is it?"

"It's a little after seven. You took the truck, so I had Mom bring me home. Dad's with Manuel."

Antonio rolled onto his back. "After I left the hospital last night, I drove over to Pepito's and told him what was going on. He's going to take care of things while I'm gone. He knows the routine and the people as well as I do."

"I've been thinking a lot about that . . . your plan to go to Mexico."

Antonio rolled over, facing her, angling his arm out and resting the side of his head in his hand.

Angelica grabbed a pillow and dragged it under her head. "How will this work? Who'll do the testing down there?"

"I'll have to wait until I get there to find out. I thought I'd go to the hospitals. There are big hospitals in Guadalajara. I'm sure they have doctors who treat cancer and can tell me where to get testing done."

"I don't know, Antonio. Anybody can draw the blood, but the tissue typing is only done in specialized labs, according to what I understand. And what are the rules in Mexico about something like this?"

Other questions had come to her during the night. Would doctors here blindly accept testing done in Mexico? What did it cost? If a match were found, how would the person get here? It had taken months to get Antonio's papers. Manuel might not have months. She looked at her husband. He had no idea what he was taking on.

Angelica sat up. "I don't see how this can work. There are so many things we don't know. I feel like we're David, fighting Goliath."

Antonio turned over, threw his legs off the bed, and stood. "You've got to have faith, Angel." He walked around the bed and sat next to her. "You and I have been through a lot of things together, but we've always found a way. This *will* work out."

He took her by the shoulders and turned her toward him, his voice intense. "You've got to believe."

Angelica shrugged his hands away. "I want to believe. I do. But it just isn't that simple."

Antonio drew away from her, his lips in a thin, firm line. "I didn't say it was simple, I'm saying it's possible."

Angelica stared at him. He was right. They had always faced life together, and together they had overcome whatever life had handed them. "I'm sorry." She drew a deep breath. "It's just that it seems like everything has gone wrong. Of course, we have to try."

She chewed her lower lip. "I can start by making a list of all the things we need to know. I'll set it up on the computer."

Antonio's face softened. "As soon as I get cleaned up, I'll come and help you."

Angelica nodded, then quirked the corner of her mouth.

"But I still feel like all we've got is a slingshot and a pebble."

Antonio smiled at her. "According to what I understand"—he tilted his head as if mocking her with her own words—"that's enough."

Angelica put her arms around her husband's neck and looked into his eyes. What a blessing he was. "You're right."

As she walked to the family room, her thoughts filtered back over the years, searching for memories to draw on. Anything to strengthen the tenuous hold she had on hope.

She remembered how she'd taken on the cause of the poor as a public defender, how she battled Immigration for Antonio's papers, and how she fought for Manuel during his first bout with AML. Through it all, she never wavered, never doubted. What had changed since then?

She stopped midstride, a realization pushing to the forefront of her mind. Manuel's cancer. It had spread into her life, proliferating fear, killing hope. She set her jaw. That was going to stop right now.

For the rest of the morning, she and Antonio sat at her laptop researching everything from plane fares to laboratories in Mexico. In some ways she felt encouraged; in other ways she felt more overwhelmed than she had before they started. They prepared a list of questions for Dr. Dorak, and Angelica printed out two copies.

"Now that Pepito's covering for you, would you mind staying with Manuel tonight?" Angelica took the list of questions from the printer. "The O'Connells are bringing Anica here at six o'clock and I feel like I need to spend some extra time with her." She folded the papers and stood. "I'll go to the hospital now and stay with Manuel. Why don't you take a nap? If you come in about five, I'll take Dad home and then get back here to meet Anica."

"Yes, *señora*." Antonio jumped up, delivered a crisp salute, and snapped his heels together.

She started laughing.

He swooped her up in his arms and carried her to the kitchen table. "You sit here, *General* Perez, while I fix us something to eat."

Angelica ignored his sarcasm. "I can eat at the hospital. I feel like I've already been away from Manuel too long."

Antonio got bread from the cabinet. "If you don't take care of yourself, you're not going to be able to take care of him."

Angelica gulped down the sandwich Antonio made for her, took a quick shower, and changed her clothes.

"See you later," she shouted down the hall as she rushed out the door.

During the drive to the hospital, her mind was spinning with all the information she'd found on the Internet, her questions for Dr. Dorak, and, most of all, concern about Manuel.

Angelica stopped at Dr. Dorak's office on the way to the pediatric inpatient wing and left him a copy of her questions and a message to call her. When she arrived at Manuel's room, her father was crouching behind a chair peeking at Manuel.

She could have sworn she heard him say, "Woo hoo, I see you."

"Dad?"

"Ahem." He grabbed the back of the chair and awkwardly pushed himself up. "I was just moving this chair over by Manuel." He pushed the chair to the bedside and motioned for her to sit. "For you."

"Thanks, Dad. I guess you heard me coming down the hall." She took the seat.

His face relaxed. "Yes. Yes, I did."

She glanced at Manuel. "Looks like he's drifting in and out." She rested her hand on his arm.

"You know, sometimes he opens his eyes and for just a second or two he seems to be looking at something. I mean clear-eyed and focused. Then he giggles and closes his eyes." Her father pulled a chair next to hers. "It's the strangest thing." He looked at her a moment and shrugged.

Then he proceeded to give her a complete rundown of everything that happened in the room since he'd relieved her earlier that morning: how many times the nurses had been in, what they had done, whether they had done it right, and how Manuel had responded.

Angelica also learned that the physician on rounds, Dr. Justin, had come by instead of Dr. Dorak. Dr. Justin was apparently too young and inexperienced to be covering for Dr. Dorak. He was only in the top third of his class in medical school and had to think too long about the questions her father had asked him, like the statistical probability of the National Marrow Donor Program having a match for Manuel.

"Dad, what do *you* think the chances are that a match will be found in one of the registries?"

A look of uncertainty flashed across her father's face. "I have no idea, but there must be someone somewhere who matches."

"That's exactly what Antonio and I were talking about this morning. He's decided to go to Mexico right away and have all his family tested."

"He decided that? I didn't think he'd pursue that after the doctor told him to wait."

91

It was all Angelica could do not to snap at her father. This was so typical of him. He never gave Antonio credit for anything. "Not only did he decide he should go, he's already made arrangements with Pepito to take care of the business while he's gone."

"Oh."

Surprise was evident in his voice.

A picture of her father crouching behind the chair when she'd walked into the room flashed through her mind. He was a good man and he meant well. She decided to drop the subject.

For the next few hours they spoke of how they would share time taking care of Manuel when he went home and the things they would do as a family when he was fully recovered.

"Hola."

Angelica turned at the voice behind her. "Antonio! Is it five already?"

"No, I'm early. But your mom called the house. So, I told her I was coming in and you would take your dad home."

Angelica looked at her watch. "It's early enough that I'll have time to stop at the school and visit with the kids' teachers after I run Dad up the hill."

Angelica gave Antonio a quick update on Manuel, then she and her father left.

As Angelica neared Regalo Grande, she found herself looking for the red tile roof along the ridge of the Sonoma Mountains. There was something about seeing it that always made her feel secure. Perhaps it was the innocent years of her childhood that she spent there, or the memories of her beloved Poppy, the grandfatherly man who helped raise her, or just the massive solidity of the stucco and tile structure. Whatever it was, it called to her, it was part of her.

She smiled inwardly. She'd met Antonio there.

"Dad, this probably sounds silly to you. But do you think Antonio and I and the kids could stay in the guesthouse one weekend after Manuel is better?"

When he didn't answer, she glanced at him. "Dad?"

"Of course. Anytime. But why would you want to do that?"

She turned the minivan up the long driveway that led to the house. "Oh, I don't know. The kids could ride Pasha and go swimming. Antonio and I could take a walk under the oaks, by the stream. I'd have him bring his guitar. He hasn't played it in a long time." She breathed a contented sigh. "There's just something about the ranch that feeds my soul."

Her father didn't respond.

"Don't you feel the same way?" She pulled in front of the arched entry and stopped the van.

"I do, Angelica." His voice was low and tentative. "But unto everything there is a season."

She looked at him. "What does that mean?"

He stiffened. "I'm selling the ranch."

"Selling the ranch!" Angelica's voice rose. "Why?"

"There're a lot of reasons." He paused a moment. "It's just too big for us."

She could hardly comprehend what he was saying. "You've never said anything about selling the ranch."

"I can't take the stairs, and they're hard on your mother too."

Angelica dropped her hands from the steering wheel. "What are you talking about? You've never complained about the stairs. You walk with Manuel all over the ranch."

"There are things you know nothing about."

Her father's words were clipped. Her heart began to

93

pound. "Is there something wrong with you, or Mom? Are you sick?"

"No, it's nothing like that." He paused. "It's just that we're in our seventies now and Regalo Grande is our biggest asset. It has a huge equity, and that money tied up in a property like this just doesn't make sense at our age."

Angelica stared at him, stunned. "This is an investment decision? Now? This is something you feel you *must* do now?"

Her father's face was a mixture of anger and sadness. He unbuckled his seat belt.

"Angelica, I don't feel like I have to justify my decisions to you. I know you're upset, I know you love the ranch. But frankly, I'm surprised at your lack of understanding. It seems just a little selfish to me."

He opened the door and got out. Bending down, he leveled his eyes with hers. "Sometimes life doesn't work out exactly as we expect."

He slammed the van door and went into the house.

Shaken, Angelica sat for a moment. One part of her wanted to run after her father and apologize. She should have been more understanding, she should have chosen her words more carefully.

The other part of her felt betrayed.

She backed the van around and headed down the drive.

Why did it have to be now, when Manuel was so sick, when her world was falling apart, when she needed her family most?

Nearing the gates at the entry, she slowed down, looking toward Pasha's pasture. The horse was trotting along the fence, as if following the van. Angelica's eyes teared up. What would happen to him? Would he be put in a stall somewhere at a boarding facility?

Angelica stopped the van, shoved the gearshift into park, and jumped out.

As she ran across the field to the pasture, she felt the breeze blowing up from the valley.

Pasha stopped, then turned and with a labored stride, loped toward the gate.

By the time Angelica got to the gated section of the fence, he stood waiting for her, nodding his head up and down as she pulled back the metal latch.

She wrapped her arms around his neck and the old horse bent his head over her shoulder. She buried her face in his mane.

The horsey smell, his coarse mane in her hands, and his warm breath triggered a flood of memories. She could hear the sound of the stream flowing under the oaks. Tears slipped down her cheeks. The rushing water became the sound of music, beautifully haunting notes from the strings of a guitar. She began to weep. The music became words. Poppy's voice, *"Oh, Miss Angel. You look beautiful. Praise Jesus, He bring my girl home safe."* It echoed in the wind.

Home. This was home. No other place would ever be. She pressed her face into Pasha's neck. "Poppy, Poppy. I miss you so."

Sobbing, bereft of words, she prayed.

Don't take everything from me.

Why did she feel like she was being forced to choose?

If You must take something, take Regalo Grande, but not my son.

She stepped away from Pasha and wiped her face with the back of her hands. She scanned the valleys and mountains that surrounded her.

But then, I beg You, heal my heart.

By the time Angelica pulled into the parking lot of Foothills Elementary, she had gone over her father's words a dozen times.

She was sure selling the ranch wasn't an arbitrary decision that he had come to easily. His expression had told her that much. But his inference that there was some financial reason didn't ring true. She was part of the Amante Family Trust, and in the past he'd consulted her numerous times for legal advice in business matters. Though she didn't actually transact business in the trust, he'd never given her any indication that there was a problem.

She parked the van and sat for a moment reflecting on the conversation again.

It made no sense, and that made her angry. He should have leveled with her.

Her cell phone rang.

It was Dr. Dorak.

"Well, Angelica, you're way ahead of the game. I went over your list of questions."

"We just want to be proactive with Manuel's treatment." She dug in her purse for her copy.

"Of course. I'll help you all I can. I've submitted a request for the preliminary search for a donor at NMDP and have been in touch with the transplant physician."

Angelica glanced at the list of questions, refreshing her memory. "Do you know if there are labs in Mexico that do this kind of testing?"

"I'm sure there are, but your best bet would be to talk to the HLA lab up here. I do know they'll want to retest even if another lab has reported a match."

Angelica continued down the list. At the end of the conversation, she felt like more questions had been raised than had been answered.

There were two things Dr. Dorak had repeatedly stressed. There were no guarantees that a match would be found among Antonio's extended family, and if testing were to be done in Mexico, the broader the search, the better the chance of success.

The obvious sequitur to that point sent a wave of apprehension through her. Who was going to pay? She felt overwhelmed.

"Doctor, I don't know if you're a praying man. But sometimes I feel like prayer is the only thing that is going to get us through this."

He seemed to hesitate in answering her. "Yes, prayer can be powerful."

She said good-bye, then grabbing her purse, she got out of the van. She would have to deal with the insurance company tomorrow. Right now she needed to visit with Anica's and Manuel's teachers.

As she walked toward the school office, she looked around the parking lot and noticed Tex's Prelude. The handicapped tag was hanging from the rearview mirror, though it wasn't parked in a handicapped spot. Manuel's teacher had a pronounced limp, but moved about with ease. And though she had special parking privileges, Angelica had never known her to use them.

Angelica smiled, recalling the first time she'd paired with Tex for playground duty. Angelica had hardly been able to keep up with her.

Angelica checked in at the school office and learned Anica's teacher, Mrs. Neumann, had already left for the day.

She hurried down the hall to Manuel's classroom. "Oh, glad I caught you."

Tex looked up from behind a stack of papers. "Angelica, dear." She stood.

Angelica quickly stepped toward her. The women hugged.

"I was just correcting a math quiz." Tex sat back down and pushed the pile of papers to the side of the desk. "How is Manuel doing?"

Angelica drew a deep breath and tried to smile. "It's been a rough few days."

Suddenly she felt exhausted. She reached for the desk to steady herself.

Tex rose. "Are you all right?" She rushed to Angelica's side and put a hand on her shoulder. "Sit down, dear." She guided Angelica to a chair.

"I'm sorry." Angelica wiped her forehead. "I'll be fine."

Tex brushed the hair away from Angelica's face. "You rest here. I'll go to the teacher's lounge and get you a cup of tea."

Tex returned with two cups of tea. She handed one to Angelica, then quietly shut the classroom door.

As Angelica sipped the steaming liquid, she poured out her heart to the older woman—her fears for Manuel, Antonio's plan to go to Mexico, even her father's decision to sell Regalo Grande.

When Angelica finished, Tex looked at her for a moment, then set her cup on the desk. She scooted her chair toward Angelica and stopped, their knees just touching. She reached out and held Angelica's hands in hers.

"When I was about your age, I was in a serious car accident."

Angelica held the woman's gaze.

"My pelvis was crushed and my back injured. My husband was killed."

Angelica gasped. "I'm so sorry."

"Those were the darkest days of my life."

Tex's grip tightened on her hands and Angelica watched as the woman's face transformed before her, softening, filling with love.

"But into that darkness came a light. And that light lifted me and carried me and healed me."

Angelica felt a peace settle over her as Tex continued. "We've never talked much about it. But I gathered from Manuel that you're a believer."

"From Manuel?"

Tex smiled. "He told me he loves Jesus the first day of class. We were talking about making friends in school and Manuel said, 'Jesus Manuel friend.'"

Angelica raised her eyebrows. "I can't say I've ever heard him say that, but yes, we are believers."

"Then you know that God allows storms in our lives to refine us, while He works all things for His purposes. He knows about Manuel's cancer and He is working in Manuel's life right now. And He's working in the lives of every single person who is being touched by this situation. There are no coincidences when it comes to the will of God."

Angelica nodded. Suddenly, she felt a draft on her feet, as if someone had opened the classroom door and come in. She glanced toward the back of the room. The door was still closed. She turned back to Tex.

"After my accident, God called me to teach, and in time He showed me why."

Angelica felt a slight tremor in the woman's hands. "What did He show you?"

"That there is a battle going on for the hearts and minds of our children. I pray protection over them every day."

"Excuse me." A voice boomed across the room.

"Jack, you startled us." Tex squeezed Angelica's hands and rolled her chair back to the desk.

"I didn't think it was necessary to knock."

"Hello, Mr. O'Hare." Angelica smiled, acknowledging the principal.

"Good afternoon, Mrs. Perez. The office said you had stopped by, and I was hoping you'd still be here." The principal walked across the room to where Angelica was sitting. "How's Manuel?"

"He's on chemo and that's never easy. But he's a fighter."

"I hate to bring this up, but I received a call from Hugh Bris's mother this afternoon. It seems Anica instigated something today that offended her son."

Angelica's eyes widened and her heart skipped a beat. "What?"

"Apparently on the playground after lunch, she and her friend Katie were asking some of the children if they wanted to pray for Manuel."

Angelica held her breath. "And?"

"And that offended Hugh Bris, according to his mother." He turned to Tex. "And you were on duty during that recess?"

Tex nodded.

"Hugh told his mother that you joined in the circle."

Tex nodded.

"Did you pray in front of the children?"

"Jack, I assure you, I didn't utter a word." She held his gaze.

"Frankly, Tex, I'm surprised we're having this conversation again. You're fully aware that it is the school's position that we should not be a forum for religious rituals. And certainly, under no circumstance, should you be participating in anything of the kind."

Angelica's mouth dropped open. "What are you talking about?"

"It's the law, Mrs. Perez. It's a clear violation of our First Amendment." He softened his tone. "I understand how Anica and Katie might not know they shouldn't be praying in school, and I'm not going to suspend them. But please have a word with your daughter so it doesn't happen again."

Angelica locked eyes with the principal and slowly rose from her chair. "My son is fighting for his life in a cancer ward. And if I understand you correctly, you are saying that his sister and her friends are not allowed to pray for him during school."

He took a step back. "Yes, that's the school's policy. The ACLU has represented our district in the past on matters like this. It's not news."

"Well, it's news to me, Mr. O'Hare." She kept her voice controlled. "I pray, in the name of Jesus, that what you're saying isn't true."

Angelica turned on her heel and walked out of the room.

She was so angry she was shaking. She'd heard bits and pieces from time to time about this kind of censorship in public schools. But nothing as blatant as this. Surely the principal was wrong. The position he was taking was ridiculous. People were free to pray anywhere they wanted.

This was America.

ANGELICA HAD TRIED all morning not to think about how much was riding on this meeting. But as she and Antonio followed the director of the HLA lab to his office, she couldn't ignore the butterflies in her stomach. Somehow, they had to link Antonio's family in Mexico to tissue typing in California.

"I appreciate your taking the time to see us, Dr. Cohen." Angelica took a seat across from the director, and Antonio took a chair beside her.

The lab director sat behind his desk. "Dr. Dorak said a search is being done to find a stem cell match for your son. Have you heard from the donor program yet?"

Angelica shook her head. "Not yet, but Dr. Dorak thinks he'll get the preliminary report by this afternoon. It's been four days."

Dr. Harold Cohen smiled. "Even after the preliminary report, the search continues. There are new donors every day." He adjusted his glasses and folded his arms on the desk. "Now, tell me how I can help."

"Our son has an uncommon haplotype, and it seems the

best chance of finding a match will be in Mexico. We're hoping you'll be able to help us with the logistics. My husband has arranged to leave for Guadalajara in a few days, but we're not sure what he should do when he gets there. Have you ever dealt with a hospital or a lab in Mexico?"

He gave a slight shake of his head. "No, I haven't. But I have had situations very similar to yours. Minorities are dramatically underrepresented among registered donors, so it isn't uncommon for families to go to Mexico to look for a match, particularly among family members."

Angelica leaned forward in her chair. "How do they get the blood tested down there?"

"We usually mail a kit to the family. It has complete instructions. The blood is drawn there and mailed back to us. We do the testing here. It's not even necessary to fly down."

Angelica couldn't believe what she was hearing. "Really?" She looked at Antonio. "This is wonderful. God is so good."

She faced the doctor. "I can't believe it's so simple. I should have realized this has happened to other people, there are so many Hispanics in California. What a relief. I wish we'd talked to you sooner." Clasping her hands together, she looked toward her husband. "This is answered prayer. We're going to be able to get your family typed."

Antonio sat quietly, his face sober.

"Antonio?"

Finally, he drew a deep breath and turned to the doctor. "My family has no address."

Dr. Cohen pursed his lips. "No address?" He looked at Angelica, waiting for her to continue.

She felt a spark of anger. Why was everything always so difficult when it came to dealing with Antonio's family?

They couldn't visit because they couldn't get passports, they couldn't correspond because they couldn't read and write, and now they couldn't help Manuel because they couldn't get mail.

How many times had she asked Antonio over the years to speak to his parents about moving to a nearby town? Where their lives would be easier, where they could enjoy modern-day conveniences. Like toilets, electricity, phones . . . and mail. Every time they visited his family, she asked him to bring it up with them. But he never had.

The silence was awkward. The doctor had obviously assumed that her husband's family lived in Guadalajara and maintained a certain lifestyle.

"Over the years, we've mailed things down there." She leaned back in her chair. "To a church in a nearby village, Santa Cruz del Astillero. His mother goes there from time to time and they give the mail to her."

Angelica saw a flicker of understanding pass across the doctor's face. She felt heat rise in her cheeks.

The doctor's expression grew serious. "The kits will only last a week, maybe two."

"I will take the kits to Mexico." Antonio lifted his chin, looking the doctor in the eye.

Dr. Cohen nodded. "That sounds like the best idea. How many kits will you need?"

"I have many in my family." Antonio paused. "Many aunts and uncles and cousins. Maybe fifty."

"Dr. Dorak said the broader the search the better," Angelica added. "Maybe we should take a hundred."

Dr. Cohen's eyes widened. "Usually this is done when there are immediate family members who would be a likely match. The complete typing costs between fifteen hundred and two thousand dollars."

Angelica stared at the doctor, stunned.

Finally, she spoke. "This isn't going to work, is it?"

The doctor steepled his fingers under his chin. "What kind of health insurance do you have?"

"Western States."

He shook his head. "We've dealt with them before. They pay for a very limited number of tissue typings." He paused. "But I think there's a bigger issue here you might not be fully understanding." He folded his arms and leaned on his desk. "Finding a match to the uncommon haplotype Manuel received from Antonio is most possible within Antonio's family, but unless there is also a match for the other three antigens Manuel has, you haven't really improved your situation. Antonio can provide the uncommon half match. It's the second half that makes the perfect combination and gives your son the best chance of a full recovery."

The image of her father and Dr. Dorak talking when they'd all been in Dr. Dorak's office flashed across Angelica's mind. The sound of her father's voice . . . *"Is that even possible?"* . . . and Dr. Dorak's response . . . *"I understand your question."*

Angelica dropped her head. That's what her father had meant. And it was why Dr. Dorak had said there was only a small possibility of finding a match.

Angelica lifted her eyes to the director. "Is this hopeless? Are we just grasping at straws?"

"Well, you've got some challenges here. But I've been the director of this lab too long to say anything is hopeless."

Dr. Cohen turned to Antonio. "How far out of Guadalajara do your parents live?"

"About thirty minutes to the north, by car."

The director picked up a pen and began to tap it on his desk. "HLA class one serology can be used as a screening test.

It's a low-resolution test that indicates whether the donor is a good candidate for a match. The cost here is about three hundred and fifty dollars. In Mexico it's probably less."

He looked at Antonio. "If you could make arrangements with a hospital or private laboratory down there to do the low-resolution screening, you would be able to eliminate everyone who has no chance of matching Manuel. If one of the people tested presented as a matched donor, then the second phase of testing could be done."

"One of the people?" Angelica interrupted. "You're saying there would only be one *possible* match out of fifty or a hundred people?"

The doctor nodded. "And that would be very, very lucky." He turned to Antonio. "Has your family lived in the same area for a long time?"

"My family and their families before them. Over the years, some have left, but most return. Sometimes with wives and children."

"I don't know what the state of your finances is, but I would encourage you to test as many people in that area as possible . . . maybe a thousand." He hesitated. "Again, you might want to wait until the search being conducted through the NMDP is completed in a few months."

Angelica struggled to find her voice. "A thousand?"

She stared at him, blinking rapidly. "What do you think our chances are then . . . I mean statistically?"

The director's face filled with compassion as his eyes held hers. "Zero, if you don't try."

Antonio pulled out of the bank parking lot onto the street. As he wove through town toward Sonoma Mountain, he reflected on the meeting he and Angelica had had with Dr. Cohen that morning.

They had both felt overwhelmed by the doctor's advice. At one point, Angelica said if no one in the Perez family was a match then Antonio should come back home because they were up against impossible odds.

He'd heard the frustration in her voice when she talked to the doctor about where his parents lived. Several times during their marriage, Angelica had pressured him to insist that his mother move, saying it would be a better situation for his whole family, particularly as his parents got older. What she didn't understand was that the fields and mountains were his mother's home, the place of her childhood, where she'd met his father, the birthplace of her children.

Angelica had hardly spoken during the drive from the laboratory back to the hospital. The silence said everything she would not say. The uncommon haplotype had come from him. His family's situation complicated things. They did not have the money to do all the testing necessary in Mexico.

When they'd arrived at Sierra Medical Center, she'd turned to him and said, "I guess we'll pay for the testing by draining what savings we have and putting the rest on credit cards."

He heaved a deep sigh.

The fact that she and the doctors didn't seem to think a match would be found for Manuel in Mexico was something he could not understand. He'd heard Angelica ask Dr. Cohen about "statistical."

Other than attending an English as a Second Language class at the community center when he first came to America, Antonio had taught himself to read and write. He was not completely sure what the word meant, but he knew it had to do with mathematics.

He'd also heard Benito talking to Dr. Dorak. They discussed letters. Like A positive and O negative and other letters and signs he didn't understand. Everyone seemed to think Manuel's life depended on numbers and formulas and facts. Taking blood and examining it, then saying it was good for him or was not good for him. Antonio's grip tightened on the wheel. No one seemed to understand that Manuel's life depended on God and His provision. God would decide if his son would live or die. God would open doors . . . and shut them.

He thought about the meeting he'd just had with the bank manager.

After he'd left Angelica at the hospital with her mother, he'd driven to the bank that had given them the loan on their house. He and Angelica had borrowed money from the bank when they started his business, and the last time Manuel was sick they had borrowed to pay the medical bills. He felt sure he could borrow money from them again to pay for the testing in Mexico.

But the banker said the most he could borrow was a few thousand dollars, unless Angelica's parents signed the loan papers with him. He didn't want to ask the Amantes to sign on his loan. This was his family and his responsibility.

He turned up the hill toward Regalo Grande.

He reached over to the small velvet box on the seat next to him, fingering it. Before he'd gone to the bank, he'd gone to the jewelry store in the mall to see if he could get the money back that he paid on Angelica's anniversary ring. But the jeweler said no. He could pick out a different ring, but he could not get his money back. So he gave the jeweler the final payment and took the ring with him.

He leaned across the seat and opened the glove compartment with two fingers, dropped the black velvet box into it, then let the door snap shut. Returning his attention to the road in front of him, he saw the For Sale sign at the foot of the driveway that led to Regalo Grande.

Benito's decision to sell the property had upset Angelica terribly. With the split shifts she and Antonio had been spending at the hospital, they had not talked about it very much. But he could see that it had caused a rift between father and daughter. Awkward, stilted words shared in the hospital room, narrow conversations about Manuel, and never a mention of Regalo Grande. It had been only a few days, but he could see it was wearing on them both.

Antonio slowly shook his head. He resolved to do what he could to repair their relationship.

He had his own ideas about why Benito was selling the ranch. At first, he'd noticed little things. The gardener didn't come every day, as he once had. The wine racks were not full. One evening when they were there for dinner, he heard Martha complaining to someone over the phone about having to press Benito's shirts, instead of taking them to the cleaners. Still, at the time, none of it struck him as particularly unusual.

But when Benito told Angelica he was selling the ranch within days of Manuel's going into the hospital, Antonio felt a check in his spirit. Angelica was the man's only child and he adored her. To sell the ranch at such a traumatic time in her life made no sense, unless Benito already knew what they had found out that morning. The search for a blood match for Manuel would be very expensive if one was not found through the donor program.

Antonio parked the truck in front of the arched entryway next to Benito's car and climbed out. He was glad to see Angelica's mother had apparently not yet returned from the hospital.

He knew nothing about the letters or the "statisticals" he'd heard talked about. Would Benito think him stupid for coming here? His stomach clenched. He had no choice.

He turned and faced the valley, closing his eyes for a moment, gathering his thoughts. A breeze swept over him. He breathed deeply. In some ways, the breeze seemed unique to Regalo Grande. Angelica had told him she'd ridden in the hills and valleys of Sonoma Mountain all her life but nowhere else was the gentle wind as consistent as it was right here. Today it carried the scent of roses. Probably from the landscaping along the drive.

He walked to the front door and knocked.

Angelica hurried into the hospital room. Even though she'd only been at the meeting with Dr. Cohen a few hours, it always made her uneasy when she was away from Manuel.

She put her purse down in a chair. "How's he doing, Mom?" Leaning over the hospital bed, she tucked the sheet around Manuel's waist.

"He's been asleep most of the time you've been gone. But Dr. Dorak came by."

Angelica turned toward her mother. "And?"

"He said he'd like to see you and Antonio when you have a minute."

Angelica frowned. "I wonder why?"

"He didn't say. He was here about an hour ago."

"Can you stay a little longer? I'll walk over to his office and see if I can catch him."

"Sure, honey. I'll stay with Manuel, you go on."

"Thanks, Mom." Angelica grabbed her purse and hurried out the door. As she walked, she took her cell phone from her purse and pressed the autodial for Antonio.

He didn't answer.

She slapped the cell phone shut and heaved a deep sigh. She loved her husband, but right now she was frustrated. The meeting with Dr. Cohen had made it clear that the odds were not in their favor for finding a match for Manuel in Mexico. And it was going to cost a lot of money to try. But Antonio seemed intent on ignoring the facts. As if he just assumed she would figure out how to pay for everything. Maybe he thought going down there was doing his part.

Angelica quirked her mouth. The truth was, Antonio didn't understand a lot of things. A situation like this really brought attention to his lack of education.

If only the National Marrow Donor Program had a match. Then all of these problems would be solved. They should be hearing back any day from the NMDP.

She stopped. Maybe that was why Dr. Dorak wanted to see them. He'd probably heard something. Maybe Antonio wouldn't even have to go to Mexico. She broke into a jog.

When she got to Dr. Dorak's office, Beth ushered her right in.

Dr. Dorak rose. "Please, have a seat."

She slipped into one of the chairs.

The doctor settled himself behind his desk and leaned forward. "I heard from the NMDP today."

Angelica held her breath, clenching her purse in her lap.

"They haven't found a match yet."

"What do you mean, yet? Have they checked the entire registry?"

"They've made a preliminary search."

"How many donors is that?"

"Several million."

She stared at him as his words wiped out the glimmer of

hope she'd felt moments before. Her hands fell to her sides. "Oh. I see." She stood. "Thank you."

Turning, she walked briskly from his office.

Fighting tears, she ran down the hall and out the doors to the hospital grounds. His words edged into her mind. *"They haven't found . . ."* No, she didn't want to hear it.

She dropped her head and put her hands over her ears. A myriad of voices assailed her. *"Western States doesn't pay for many typings . . . My family has no address . . . it will be about three hundred fifty dollars for each test . . . they haven't found a match."*

When her steps finally slowed, she found herself in the little park next to the hospital. Feeling alone and abandoned, she sat on an empty bench and took her phone out of her purse. She pressed the number for Antonio.

No answer.

She squeezed her eyes shut as she tried to choke back a sob.

This was too hard. Too hopeless. Where was her husband when she needed him?

Benito looked up from the stack of mail on his desk. "Martha, see who's at the door?" His eyes drifted to the picture of his daughter. He picked it up.

Angelica had kept her distance from him ever since he'd told her he was going to put the ranch on the market. She hadn't been up to visit since the For Sale sign had been put on the drive.

His stomach knotted. It was tearing him up.

"Antonio!" He laid the picture facedown.

Antonio tipped his head. "Good afternoon, *señor.*"

Benito stiffened. "Has something happened to Manuel?"

112

"No." Antonio shifted from one foot to the other. "He is resting."

Benito gestured to the chair beside his desk. "Then what brings you here?"

Antonio took the seat. "I'm going to Mexico next week."

"I see." The fact that his son-in-law seemed to think a match would be found for Manuel in Mexico was something he couldn't understand. "Don't you think you should wait until the search is finished with the donor program? The chance of finding a full match for Manuel in Guadalajara is a statistical long shot."

Antonio drummed his fingers on his knee, then cleared his throat. "What is 'statistical'?"

"Statistical?"

Antonio nodded.

"Um. It's numerical datum." Benito paused, frowning. "In this case it means that if you consider all the combinations of HLA that are possible, finding the exact combination Manuel needs by testing a few people in Mexico would be extraordinary, almost miraculous."

"Miraculous?" Antonio sat back in his chair. "That I understand."

Finally. Maybe now he'd be able to get a handle on what they were facing and wait for the sophisticated computerized search through NMDP.

Antonio seemed to relax. "I believe that too." He folded his hands in his lap. "Manuel's life has been a miracle, no?"

What a thing to say. Life had been nothing but a struggle for the little boy. "How's that?" Benito tried to keep the frustration out of his voice. He leaned back in his chair and folded his arms across his chest.

"He almost died when he was born, but God breathed life into him." A look of awe passed across Antonio's face, and he slowly shook his head. "I have wondered if that is why he seems filled with love instead of words." He smiled. "When he hugs me, I feel what a lucky man I am.

"And when he was sick last time, God protected his life, then returned it to him." Benito saw something flicker in Antonio's eyes. "And I believe He will again. That is why I am here."

Benito sat for a moment observing his son-in-law, moved by the raw emotion on Antonio's face . . . the love of a father for his child. He dropped his arms from his chest.

"So this is the reason you're so committed to going to Mexico?"

Antonio's gaze didn't waver. "Yes. I love my son and I cannot let him die for lack of a miracle I did not look for."

Antonio had been in the family for twelve years, but as Benito listened to him speak he realized he didn't really know Angelica's husband, Manuel's father. He knew only the Mexican who had cleaned the stalls at Regalo Grande.

"This morning, Angelica and I went to see the director of the laboratory that tested Manuel's blood. He said if I was going to Mexico, then it would be good if many of my people were tested. And to do that I need your help."

He hesitated. "I have been to the bank and they will not lend me the money I need to pay for the testing in Mexico."

All the years Antonio had been married to Angelica, he had refused to let Benito help them. To come here now had to be hard. "How much do you need?"

Antonio continued. "I won't know until I get there. I'm thinking seventeen thousand five hundred dollars to test all of my family and aunts and uncles and cousins."

Benito shifted in his chair. "How'd you come up with a number like that?"

"I estimated how many relatives I have. The most the test would cost is three hundred and fifty dollars each because that is what is charged here. If the cost of the test is less, I will use the money to test other people that live there."

Benito pursed his lips. "What does Angelica think about this?"

"I haven't told her yet because I don't have the money together. I was hoping . . . ," he rubbed his hands on his jeans, ". . . that you would lend me the money. I can pay you monthly when I go back to work."

"I see." Benito tilted his head to the side and nodded. "I think we might be able to work something out." The boy had clearly given this a lot of thought. He pulled his chair up to the desk. "But what are you going to tell Angelica?"

Antonio's gaze moved to the picture lying facedown on Benito's desk, then returned to Benito's face. "Why don't you call her and tell her you have an idea of how you can help Manuel?"

Benito smiled and for a moment studied the young man sitting across from him.

Angelica had done all right for herself.

"But, *señor*, I insist you let me pay you back."

"I respect that. We can work out those details later."

Antonio stood and extended his hand to Benito. "I'm planning to leave Monday night."

"We'll work out payments when you get back."

They shook hands and Antonio turned and left the office.

Benito sat back down at his desk. He opened his file drawer and took out the binder with his stock accounts. Paging through it, he considered each of his investments. It wasn't a good time to sell any of them. He sighed and put the book back in the drawer. He'd talk to his stockbroker tomorrow.

"Ben, where are you?" Gen's voice broke into his thoughts.

"In my office."

His wife appeared at the doorway. Face pale, lined with worry. "Was that Antonio I passed on the road?"

"Yes, he just left. What's the matter?"

"I wish I could have caught him." She dropped her purse and coat in the chair. "Dr. Dorak got the preliminary report from the donor program."

Benito felt his stomach knot.

"There was no match for Manuel. Angelica is devastated." Gen shook her head. "But, God bless that doctor. He sat her down and told her they would keep looking and this was not the time to lose hope."

Benito picked up the phone and dialed Angelica's cell number. As he waited for it to ring, Antonio's words played back to him. *"I cannot let him die for lack of a miracle I did not look for."* Suddenly, the words seemed prophetic. Benito hung the phone up.

Stunned, he sat for a moment. *A miracle I did not look for.*

Benito picked up the phone and dialed the number for Dr. Dorak's office.

"Hello. This is Dr. Amante. Would you give me the name and number of the director of the laboratory that's doing the tissue typing for Manuel Perez?"

He would dance. That's what he would do when he got his leg.

Cirocco backed his board up against the wall surrounding

the public toilets. He would return to Mexico and he would find her. She would see him walking toward her and wonder who the tall, important man with the pretty woman holding his hand was. He smiled.

He would take off his sunglasses and then she would shout, "Cirocco!" He blinked rapidly. She would be so proud of him.

"Hey, kid."

Cirocco snapped his head back.

A peso dropped on Cirocco's head as a fleshy hand snatched a bag from his lap. The peso twirled down his chest, bounced off his board, and rolled into the street.

Keeping his eye on the coin, he wheeled after it. Finally retrieving it from the dirty pavement.

He stopped. Looking in the direction of the fat man, he tossed his head and spit. When he had a leg, things would be different. He pushed the peso into his pocket, then gathered the scattered sacks as he returned to his spot on the wall.

They would go to Santa Sophia. And they would dance in the plaza on a Sunday afternoon, when the mariachis played. Hearing the music, he bobbed his head.

Maybe his uncle would be there and play the guitar. When he was younger, his mother had often spoken of his uncle and the magical guitar. She'd said her brother had been born with the gift of music and when he played, you could hear angels sing.

Cirocco had never met his uncle, though his mother had said he visited them when they'd lived in Santa Sophia. Cirocco had clung to that for years. Praying, with the trusting innocence of the very young, that his uncle would return for them.

What a fool he had been. By the time he started living with Mama Rose, he figured out God wasn't going to bring back his uncle. And soon afterward, he accepted that God would not be bringing back his mother either.

Cirocco snapped a bag open, getting it ready for his next customer.

He didn't need God now. He was going to get a leg. He would leave on the bus Tuesday right after he went to see Mama Rose. He'd promised her he would come and say good-bye.

Leaning back against the wall, he surveyed the streets, the park in the distance, the skyline behind it. This was his world.

And he hated it.

Tuesday . . . Tuesday his life would change forever.

8

When will Manuel be coming home?"

Angelica pulled the van into their driveway and turned to her daughter. The visit at the hospital had been difficult for Anica. The toxicity of the chemotherapy had been so severe that Manuel had developed sores in his mouth, down the back of his throat, and in his esophagus. He was still vomiting and had diarrhea. His pain had been apparent to his sister.

"His doctor said we have to wait until Manuel is eating and feels better." She took Anica's hand. "It's going to be okay, sweetie."

Anica unfastened her seat belt and faced Angelica. "Is it really, Mother?"

Anica's brows were knit, her hazel eyes searching Angelica's face.

Angelica leaned across the seat and gathered Anica into her arms. She wasn't surprised at her daughter's direct and penetrating question. Anica had always been precocious and faced the world with her hands on her hips.

Angelica rested her cheek on the top of her daughter's head

and bit her lower lip. Anica was too young to be worrying about life and death. She should be riding bikes and playing with her friends. "Yes, honey. Everyone is doing everything they can. It's going to be okay."

Anica wiggled out of Angelica's arms. "Then why are you crying?" She hesitated, then blurted out, "And why are G-Dad and G-Mom selling their house? Is it because Manuel won't be coming there anymore?"

Everyone in the family had gone out of their way to protect Anica from the uncertain and unsettling events of the past two weeks. Angelica quietly took a steadying breath and tried to gather her thoughts.

"I'm crying because I'm sad that Manuel is sick and that you have to go through this with him."

Anica's eyes filled with tears. "I want Manuel to come home, and for us to play at the ranch like we used to." She reached for Angelica.

Angelica wrapped her arms around her, comforting her daughter as she cried. Gradually, Anica's breathing became steady and she straightened, moving back into her seat.

"But why are G-Dad and G-Mom selling their house?" She sniffled.

Angelica thought for a moment. "I'm not really sure. I guess they're getting older and feel like they need to make a change. Sometimes we have to make changes, even when we don't want to."

Her own words condemned her, bringing back memories of the conversation she had with her father when he told her he was selling Regalo Grande. She had hardly spoken to him after that, until he called and told her he would pay for the blood testing in Mexico.

Angelica looked at her daughter. Selling Regalo Grande was going to be hard on everyone. Not the least of which would be her father, who had built the estate for her and her mother. She felt ashamed of herself. She owed him an apology.

"Go tell Daddy we're here and to hurry. We have to meet with G-Dad at the ranch before we go to the airport."

Anica jumped out of the car and ran into the house.

When her father had learned that no match for Manuel had been found in the preliminary search of the NMDP, he'd called her and told her he wanted to help pay for the testing in Mexico. They estimated that testing all of Antonio's relatives and the cost of the trip would amount to about twenty thousand dollars. And even though she and Antonio knew they would pay it back, it was still a huge relief to know the payments could be made after this crisis was over.

Angelica folded her arms across the top of the steering wheel and rested her forehead on them. "God, forgive me for the way I treated my father and please give me wisdom for my daughter and her questions." She released a deep sigh. "I'm trusting You, God. This is almost more than I can bear."

She heard the garage door opening in front of the van.

Anica skipped out and Antonio followed her, wearing work clothes and his old straw hat. He looked like a migrant laborer.

Angelica shook her head slowly as a broad grin inched its way across her face. Every time they traveled to visit his family, they had words about the clothes he would wear. He usually indulged her as far as agreeing to wear slacks and a sports shirt until they were actually ready to make the forty-five-minute drive north from Guadalajara to the area where his family lived. Then he would change into old work clothes that were typical of the Mexican farmers who lived in the fields and hills surrounding Guadalajara. He never spoke

121

with his family about the success he'd found in America. Visits home were a time he used to reconnect to his roots. To honor the people and land of his heritage.

Anica climbed into the backseat. Antonio threw his suitcase and valise on the empty seat next to her, then jumped in the van beside Angelica.

She frowned at him. "I guess you know you look like a bum. You should wear nice clothes and look like the successful businessman you are."

Antonio gave her an innocent grin. "If I was going to visit successful businessmen, then I would dress like one."

She clicked the garage door opener and backed out of the driveway. "Does that mean you've packed some decent clothes to wear when you meet with the lab director?"

He mocked her stern look. "You'll be happy to know I not only brought a sports coat, but also my gold cross and my belt with the silver buckle."

She gave him a playful slap.

"And my visa is in my shoe."

Angelica rolled her eyes. He always carried his visa in his shoe whenever they traveled. He had had to stay in Mexico for months after they were married to get his permanent visa. Without it, he couldn't reenter the United States. And since 9/11 they had become impossible to get. He said that when he'd crossed into the United States he kept his papers in his shoe and there was no reason to change now.

The days had been a blur since Manuel had been admitted to the hospital, not giving her a moment to think about what lay ahead. But now, as they drove to the ranch, the reality that her husband was leaving and she would be alone for the next few weeks, if not longer, settled on her. She glanced at him. There was no point in thinking about it. They were doing what was best for Manuel.

"Do you have everything Dr. Cohen gave you to take with you?"

Antonio nodded.

"I hope Dad got the banking mess straightened out. If we can't transfer money down there, we're nowhere." She tightened her grip on the steering wheel. "What if you can't find a lab that will work with Dr. Cohen and Dr. Dorak?" She looked at Antonio. "What if you don't find a match and all of this was for nothing?"

Antonio patted her hand. "Angel, you've got to believe. There's so much we don't know about this whole thing. But God knows. If He is with us, who can be against us?"

She huffed a sigh.

"Mom, I thought you said everything was going to be okay."

Angelica cut her eyes to the rearview mirror. Anica's questioning gaze met her. "Of course it is, honey. I'm just thinking out loud. I've got a lot on my mind."

"Daddy says you've got to believe. I believe." Anica paused. "I prayed in school today too."

Angelica's eyes shot to the rearview mirror. "Did you pray quietly to yourself, like we talked about?"

That conversation with Anica, after the principal's directive that she couldn't pray in school, had been like walking through a minefield. Angelica had felt unprepared for it. Not knowing what the law allowed, and not having the time to find out, she had to take Principal O'Hare at his word while deep down she believed it was wrong to tell her daughter not to turn to Jesus and pray for her brother whenever she felt drawn to do so.

She could see Anica's face brighten. "Yes, Mom, I did."

Angelica felt herself relax.

"And so did Jimmy and Pete and Katie."

Angelica's eyes widened. "And how did that come about?"

"Jimmy and Pete used to eat lunch with Manuel. They always ask me about him."

Angelica had volunteered at the school numerous times and knew both boys. Jimmy Shultz's parents had been missionaries in Africa until Jimmy's sister was born. Since then, they'd settled in Valle de Lagrimas and his father was in charge of the outreach program at Faith Community Church. "And?"

"And we decided to start a club. Jimmy's the president . . . 'cause he's in sixth grade. We're going to meet every day at lunch break and pray for Manuel."

Angelica felt like saying, "Don't do that." She didn't want another confrontation with Jack O'Hare. She had enough to deal with.

"Why don't you guys meet at our house after school? Maybe I could work out a carpool with Jimmy's mom."

"Oh, no. We want the club to get real big. We're going to ask lots of kids to join." Anica was adamant.

Angelica knew that tone of voice all too well. Her strong-willed, stubborn daughter had been Manuel's advocate since she was old enough to talk. And her bright mind and natural determination had equipped her well for the job. She wouldn't be detoured easily.

"Anica, your club is a good idea, but I'll need to talk to Mr. O'Hare, honey, before you start inviting other children to join. Remember, I told you praying at school would have to be between you and Jesus."

"Oh, don't worry, Mom." Anica's tone was dismissive. "Jimmy said it's our right."

Angelica glanced at Antonio.

124

He shrugged his shoulders, then whispered, "You're the lawyer."

"Jimmy said his father's starting a Good News Club when Jimmy goes to junior high next year, and they're going to pray and read the Bible and everything."

God bless Ed Shultz. That man was on fire for the Lord. She remembered the morning he'd given his testimony at church about his family's experience in Africa. They had lived under the threat of death the entire time they were there. Literally rising every morning and asking God to preserve their lives for one more day, so they could spread the gospel of Jesus Christ to the unsaved.

"Besides, Mom, Jimmy said there's nothing to worry about. The Holy Spirit will be in our club and He will defend us."

Angelica looked at Anica in the mirror. "How will He do that?"

"Oh, you just ask Him to."

Anica's casual confidence convicted Angelica. She felt like she was being mentored by eleven-year-old Jimmy and her eight-year-old daughter. "Anica, I'll call Jimmy's dad and talk to him, and then I'll talk to Principal O'Hare about it. We need to follow the rules."

"What if the rules are wrong, Mom?"

For a moment, Angelica didn't know what to say. Antonio turned toward her, one eyebrow raised. He was clearly amused. Probably thinking she should march into Jack O'Hare's office and say she had her rights. There was going to be a prayer group for Manuel, and if the principal didn't like it, he could take it up with the Holy Spirit.

She shot him a withering glance. "Then you try to get the rules changed."

The rest of the way to the ranch, Angelica steered clear of

the subject by reminding Anica of the last time she'd visited Grandma Perez in Mexico and how much fun it would be for Daddy to visit his family again.

When they got to Regalo Grande, Martha took Anica to feed Pasha carrots and apples while Angelica and Antonio met with Benito in his office to go over all the details of Antonio's trip that involved paying for the lab work in Mexico.

Sitting with Antonio across from her father gave Angelica a sense of déjà vu. She'd been in so many doctors' offices it suddenly felt as though she were at another appointment. She looked at her father, wearing a shirt and tie, gray hair neatly combed, stacks of files on his desk, running a tab on the adding machine. He could have been a bank manager. And there was an edge in the air. Almost as if the angry words she'd exchanged with him days before had somehow followed them into the office.

Suddenly, a wave of sadness washed over her. She had allowed the relationship with her father to change. And even though their deep love and sense of obligation to Manuel had trumped their petty differences, things were not the same.

She glanced around the room. Two shelves of the cherrywood bookcase were filled with Angelica's awards for scholastic achievement. On one wall was a collage of framed newspaper articles that had been printed about her when she'd been not only the valedictorian but also the youngest student ever to graduate from her law school.

Her gaze drifted to her father's desk. A picture of her as a teenager sitting on Pasha was near the phone, at an odd angle. Behind it, an empty martini glass.

Her eyes shot to her father's face.

He turned toward her, the adding machine tape in hand. "I've been working on this all day. And—"

126

"Dad, before we get started I want to say something."

He dropped his hand to the desk.

Angelica got up and walked to his chair. Bending down, she wrapped her arms around his neck. "Dad, I'm so sorry I was cross with you the other day. Can you forgive me?"

He didn't speak.

She pressed into his neck and closed her eyes, catching the scent of his aftershave, following it through a lifetime of memories, compressed into seconds. "I love you so much. Thank you for everything you do."

Her father patted her arm. "Me too." His voice was husky and he cleared his throat. "Now, we've got a lot to do."

For the next hour Benito recapped the maze of national and international banking rules and regulations he'd navigated through. He explained the effects of exchange rates, banking fees, and daily transfer limits. As her father spoke, Angelica realized how naïve she and Antonio had been. In the past, they had simply taken the money they would need on their trips with them.

She glanced at her husband. Was he going to be able to follow all of this? He never had a bank account when he lived in Mexico, and she handled all the finances since they'd been married.

"Dad, we're talking about needing up to twenty thousand dollars. Wouldn't it be easier to just set up an account here and give Antonio access in Mexico with an ATM card?"

Her father leaned back in his chair. "Yes, that would be easier. But we're not talking about twenty thousand dollars."

"What do you mean, Dad?"

Her father's face became somber. "I've consulted with Dr. Dorak and Dr. Cohen, and it's my judgment that we'll give Manuel the absolute best chance of survival by maximizing the search in Mexico. That people group has the highest potential of yielding a full match."

"How many people do you mean?"

"I've arranged financing to test a thousand people. Three hundred fifty thousand dollars."

Angelica's eyes widened. "A thousand people! We can't pay back that kind of money."

Her father nodded. "I'm fully aware of that. Frankly, it wasn't easy for me to come up with the money. But it's like a very astute young man once explained to me, we can't let Manuel die for lack of a miracle we didn't look for."

His eyes met hers.

"I put a second mortgage on the ranch."

Antonio knelt beside his daughter and gently brushed the hair back from her face. "I love you and I'll be home soon."

Anica's hazel eyes filled with tears. "I'll miss you, Daddy."

He pulled her to him for one last hug, then rose. He could see the departure monitor from where he stood. His flight was boarding.

Antonio turned toward Angelica, taking her face in his hands, searching her eyes, refusing to hurry his good-bye. She met his intimate gaze, her eyes slowly closing as he kissed her parted lips. A vow of love exchanged, without a single word being spoken.

Antonio stepped back. "I'll call you tomorrow." He patted his pocket. "I'll reprogram my cell phone for international calls as soon as I get there."

He picked up his carry-on bag and made his way through security. Turning, he waved at his wife and daughter across the crowded concourse, then headed up the ramp to the departure gates. Hearing the second call for his flight, he broke into a jog.

After having his ticket checked, he boarded the plane and took his seat by the window. Within minutes he felt the big jet moving, preparing for takeoff.

As the plane headed down the runway, gathering speed, Antonio's eyes drifted to the window. He felt a vague sense of restlessness as he watched the ground fall away beneath him. A feeling of leaving home, not going home. He would always consider himself Mexican, but during the twelve years he'd lived in America he'd come to love her. She had been good to him, giving freely of her opportunities.

He rested his head against the seatback and closed his eyes.

No one knew he was coming. Communication with his family was difficult since they had no phones or regular mail. But from the point of view of his mother or sisters, a son or husband suddenly appearing after a year or two of absence was as it should be, an affirmation of God's provision, and if a loved one never returned . . . an affirmation of God's sovereignty.

The last time he and Angelica had visited he'd been surprised and pleased to see how his mother's house had expanded. With his father, himself, and his five brothers all working and sending her money, she was able to build a large solid structure next to the jacaranda tree that had provided shelter for them from the day he was born until the day he left for America. Now the old tree defined her front yard.

Antonio hoped all his brothers were working in the area. They went wherever work could be found. But a private sports complex and soccer facility where many of Mexico's soccer teams trained, Club Guadalajara, had been developed near Santa Cruz del Astillero a few years before. Its restaurant and hotel allowed many of the people who lived in the fields to find work close to home.

He wanted to be sure every member of his family was tested, even Ines . . . and her son.

He let out a long, deep sigh. He'd been thinking about his older sister ever since he made the decision to come to Mexico. Angelica knew very little about her and he hadn't brought it up. Not because he wanted to keep secrets from his wife, but in deference to his mother, who had not spoken the girl's name in over fifteen years. Angelica knew only that the young woman had disappeared long ago.

If she had been found dead, it would have been easier. But Ines had run away with a man, an older man. She, leaving her family great shame; he, leaving his wife and children without a provider. Antonio's parents suffered the humiliation with forgiving hearts, both toward their daughter and toward their neighbors, who found the topic a compelling subject for every occasion. But as the years passed, Ines didn't return and rumors began to make their way from the distant town of Santa Sophia, all the way beneath the spreading boughs of the jacaranda tree where Antonio and his family lived. Ines Perez was a prostitute. His parents' absolution turned into anger and her name had not been spoken from that day forward.

Antonio was nearly fifteen when he told his mother he was going to look for work in nearby villages and would be gone for a while. He traveled by foot to Santa Sophia to look for the sister who helped care for him as a child. Who often went without food so he could eat, and slept on the bare ground next to him, using her blanket to cover him on cold nights. He'd never forgotten her and still loved her deeply.

Antonio had found her in Santa Sophia living in a hovel with her little boy. He held her as she poured out the story of

130

her broken dreams. How she ran away from the hopelessness of the fields, into the arms of the handsome and mysterious *majordomo* who hired her to work the blue agave crops near their home. How she became pregnant soon after arriving in Santa Sophia, then lost the baby during one of her lover's drunken rages. How he left her shortly after that.

She told him going home was not an option, her shame was too deep. Starving and desperate, she began to work the streets, eventually traveling into Guadalajara. She found the hotels that serviced the steady stream of tourists and visitors to the city were quite happy to help her build her business. A careless night with a young Italian businessman resulted in a second pregnancy and the birth of her son.

Antonio's heart had gone out to her. He begged her to let him try to make amends with their parents. But Ines couldn't bear the thought of facing the people she had devastated. She made Antonio promise to keep their meeting a secret.

He traveled to see her several times after that. The last time, just before he left for America. He found only her son, being cared for by a neighbor.

This time he would find her.

Suddenly, he felt drained, burdened. The full weight of opening old family wounds, the search for a blood match for Manuel, the incredible financial burden that surely lay before him, rested on his shoulders.

And there was still the other problem. The one Angelica had only mentioned once when they'd first talked about his coming to Mexico, though he'd thought of it a hundred times since then. If he found a donor, how would the person get a visa to come to the United States for the rest of the testing? *Dios, I can do nothing without You. Please go before me and make these crooked paths straight.*

He turned his head and rested it on the hard edge of the

window. Letting his gaze drift to the night sky, he found the moon and a thousand stars displayed before him.

Who am I, Dios, that You would take notice of me?

Tears pricked his eyes. Not only had God noticed him, God had sent His Son to die for him . . . and Jesus Christ had risen from the dead.

Nothing was impossible for God.

Never before had the importance of that truth been as real to him as it was at this moment. A thousand stars or a thousand faceless donors, God knew them all intimately. He scanned the sky; he must trust God to make a way for him.

Antonio dropped his seatback a few inches, stretched out his legs beneath the seat in front of him, and put his hat over his face. Tomorrow he would begin his search for a donor, for his sister, and for her son, Cirocco.

Cirocco pushed himself along the busy sidewalk away from Iglesia Biblica Centro, toward the bus station. The bus would be leaving at noon. Noon straight up, they had said. And he would be on it. This day was the beginning of the rest of his life.

Saying good-bye to Mama Rose had been much harder than he'd thought it would be. And she'd done exactly what she always did. She prayed for him. A smile tugged at his lips. He was glad.

She'd knelt beside him just before he left the church and taken his hands in hers. She asked Jesus to give him favor on his journey and fill his life with blessings. Then she said something that moved him deeply. She asked Jesus to give him his dreams.

She said, "Jesus, this is Your child and I ask You to give

him the desires of his heart." And right when she said that, he felt a warmth from her hands that traveled up his arms and filled his chest. Somehow—he blinked rapidly—it seemed like Jesus was telling him He'd heard her. For the first time since the accident, Cirocco believed. Jesus cared about him and was going to help him. And then she asked him if he'd like to see his mother again.

It had been strange. They had not been talking about his mother. And Mama Rose didn't ask as if she were waiting for his answer, but instead, as if she were asking for permission. As if his mother might walk into the room at any moment. He tilted his head, remembering. He smiled. She hadn't fooled him. He said, "You'll always be my Mama Rose."

She handed him a small sack with tortillas and fruit that she and a visiting friend had packed for him that morning. He had that tucked in his lap. Wedged tight next to it was the tin cup holding Diego's tip money, the money Cirocco had managed to save over the past week, and the extra money Mama Rose had just given him. As he rolled along, he repeatedly glanced into the cup at the bills and coins, hardly able to believe he not only had enough money for his ticket to Puerto Vallarta, but he would also have some left over to help him get by until he could begin earning money there.

He felt a push from behind, propelling his board forward.

"Hey, move it, stump boy."

As Cirocco's board picked up speed, his heart began to pound. He recognized the voice. It was one of the boys who lived on the streets. He'd tormented Cirocco in the past, once at the public toilets and several times around San Juan de Dios. He felt the boy's hands on his back again, pushing him faster.

The board began to rock on its wheels.

"Hey, what's the matter?" The boy had broken into a run behind him. "Can't stop, huh?"

He felt his tormentor push him again.

"Look out, man," the boy said, laughing. "You're gonna crash."

People in front of Cirocco jumped out of the way as he careened down the sidewalk.

He grabbed the tin cup with one hand and put his other hand over the top of it. Hitting the curb at the intersection, he became airborne, the board dropping from beneath him and the cup flying from his hands as he crashed onto the street.

Cirocco struggled to sit up. Dazed, he watched the coins roll in every direction, most disappearing through the heavy steel grates that covered the storm drains.

As his vision cleared, he noticed several of the bills scattered nearby. Ignoring the blood he tasted on his lips, he crawled in frantic, jerking movements across the grates toward them.

A wind gusted, carrying the bills away.

His tormentor rushed in front of him, chasing the money down the street, scooping it up as he ran.

Cirocco looked toward the sidewalk, calling out to passersby, "Stop him. Stop him." But no one responded.

Within moments the boy was out of sight.

Cirocco pushed himself up on his knee and the stump of his leg. He could feel the grate biting into his flesh.

Then it started. Somewhere deep down inside his belly. Hands still on the pavement, he arched his neck back. A guttural, keening wail tore from his lips. Again and again. He couldn't stop it.

Finally, he dropped onto the pavement.

Between sobs he heard church bells, somewhere in the distance, striking noon.

9

"How's it been going, Dad? Has Manuel eaten anything since Anica and I left last night?" Angelica set her computer case and purse in a chair.

Benito was sitting next to Manuel's bed. "No, and he won't talk either. It's the ulcers in his mouth, Angelica. He's going to need something for the pain."

"Has Dr. Dorak been in yet?"

Her father shook his head. "What's in that black bag?"

"Oh, I brought my laptop so I can get some things done while I'm here. I want to do some research."

"There are some excellent cancer sites—"

Angelica heard the musical tones of her cell phone. She opened her purse and grabbed the instrument. "Hello."

At the sound of Antonio's voice, relief washed over her.

"I'm glad you got there safe and sound. I'm here at the hospital with Dad. They moved Manuel to a new room last night. It has a couch that folds out to a bed and small bath. I guess he's going to be here for a while longer."

She acknowledged her father's waving hand. "Dad wants to know if you've been to the bank."

"No . . . I'm j—t getting a car." His voice cut in and out.

She shook her head in her father's direction.

"Who stayed wi—Manuel las—night?"

"Dad did. Anica and I stopped here after we took you to the airport and Dad and I worked out a shift schedule. I'll be here eight until four, then Anica and I will come back in the evenings so she can visit Manuel. Mom will cover four until nine and Dad will take the night shift. The O'Connells are taking Anica to school for me and watching her until I get home."

"Thank them for me. Let me t—k to Manuel."

"He hasn't talked since yesterday. We think it's because of his mouth sores." As Angelica stepped toward Manuel she noticed he was drooling. Not only wouldn't he swallow food, now he wouldn't swallow his own saliva. Her stomach churned. "I don't think he can talk, Antonio. His mouth and throat are very sore." She put the phone to Manuel's ear. "This is Daddy."

Manuel's face registered recognition of his father's voice. Angelica put her ear next to Manuel's, listening as Antonio told him how much he missed and loved him.

Manuel tried to speak, but it came out as a whimper.

"That's okay, sweetie, you don't have to talk." Angelica put the phone to her own ear and rose.

Manuel's whimper became a ragged whisper. "Love . . . Daddy." He began to cry.

"He said he loves you." She waited a moment, not trusting her voice. "I love you too." She turned her back to Manuel. "We've got to find a match, Antonio. Somehow, somewhere. We've got to help him."

"Keep—faith. I'll c—l again soon. Bye for n—w."

"Bye." She closed her phone and looked at her father.

"Angelica, I'm going to stay here until Dr. Dorak comes in. I want to be sure he prescribes something to alleviate Manuel's pain."

She faced her father. "Dad, you're exhausted. I can talk to the doctor."

"Not like I can." Benito stifled a yawn and settled back in his chair.

Angelica gave him a weak smile. "That's true, Dad. It's just that you need to get your rest. You've got dark circles under your eyes." Angelica didn't want her father to know that when it came to Manuel's treatment, she appreciated his input and opinions, but she felt he was out of his area of expertise. She hated seeing the doctor constantly put in the position of having to justify his decisions about Manuel's treatment.

"I'm not that tired." Benito folded his arms across his chest.

"Good morning."

Angelica and her father looked toward the voice.

"Dr. Dorak. We were just talking about you." Angelica returned her phone to her purse.

Benito stood. "I'm glad you're here early so you can prescribe something for Manuel. He's not eating and he won't talk. The inside of his mouth is inflamed and irritated."

Dr. Dorak put his hand on Benito's shoulder. "I understand your concern. I've been watching that." He stepped toward Manuel. "I've ordered morphine to be started." He opened Manuel's chart.

Angelica listened as Dr. Dorak and her father discussed Manuel's condition. As they spoke, she couldn't help but notice the doctor's skill in handling her father. By the time the discussion was over, her father's arms rested casually at his sides and a quick nod of his head punctuated each of Dr. Dorak's assessments and recommendations.

Her father turned to her. "Well, now that I've taken care of that, I'm going home." He picked up his jacket from the couch and took a deep breath. "I'm exhausted."

After saying good-bye to Manuel, he left the room.

Angelica looked at Dr. Dorak. "I'm sorry he always grills you like that." She felt heat rising in her cheeks.

The doctor met her gaze, his face amused. "If that's the most difficult problem I have to deal with today, I'll consider myself lucky."

His words immediately put her at ease. "I guess you learn to deal with difficult people when you're taking care of sick children."

He grinned. "Actually, dealing with the families of my patients is one of the things I enjoy most."

Angelica tried to hide her surprise, the doctor's genuineness touching her. She hadn't had many personal conversations with the doctor, but during Manuel's first battle with cancer she learned that Dr. Dorak had never been married. She'd wondered why. It seemed like he would have been a wonderful husband and father.

"Well, I can't tell you how much we appreciate you."

He smiled at her, as if wanting to say more. But instead, he looked down at the chart.

"Antonio called from Guadalajara this morning."

The doctor moved toward the foot of Manuel's bed. "I wish we'd been able to locate a lab to work with down there before he left."

Angelica straightened. "Me too. But my husband is very resourceful and I have complete confidence that he'll find a lab." Antonio's gentle, constant admonition, *you've got to have faith, Angel,* echoed in her mind. "And a match."

"Keep that positive attitude. Dr. Cohen and I are in constant communication and ready to work with any lab that can do the testing. Being proactive like you are makes a big difference."

Dr. Dorak closed the chart. "I'll be back later this afternoon to see how our patient's doing." He turned and left.

Manuel's whimpering drew Angelica's attention and she hurried to him. His eyes were closed and he seemed to be in a restless half sleep. She sat with him, stroking his hand until the nurse arrived and started the morphine. When his body had yielded to the numbing drug, she rose, took her laptop from its case, and settled into the small couch near Manuel's bed.

After turning the computer on, she located the Word files where she'd saved Internet information that morning.

She rubbed her forehead. She really didn't want to take this on right now. But she felt she had to. It seemed like part of the fight for Manuel's life.

Angelica straightened and set her jaw. She would be prepared for her four o'clock meeting with Jack O'Hare. Brushing her finger across the mouse pad, she rolled the cursor down to the first file . . . "Recent Court Cases—Prayer in School."

The Tuesday morning traffic on the Anillo Periferico skirting Guadalajara had been horrendous. Traffic lights and speed limits were treated as minor nuisances by the Mexican drivers.

Having grown up far from the city, where walking had been the primary mode of travel, Antonio found the driving as challenging as it would be for any American tourist. Every time he visited, he rented a compact car because it made it easier to maneuver in and out of the traffic while abiding by the Mexican rules of the road. The speed limit was the rate of speed the cars around him were traveling. A yellow light meant speed up, a red light meant look left and right before speeding up. He soon got the hang of it and by the time he reached Highway 15 on the northwest side of the city he was beginning to feel like a native. Still, he welcomed the lighter traffic on the interstate that would take him to his family.

As the kilometers stretched behind Antonio, the buildings and businesses that had crowded the roadside disappeared. Soon he began to recognize the silhouette of the hills and mountains, the expanse of a field, the bend of the road.

As he rolled down the window, the scent of the air stirred memories. The bonds that the poverty and hardship of his childhood had forged still linked him to his family and friends. The success he'd found in America had not diminished that. It was a part of who he was, and he embraced it.

He'd come to visit his family four times since he'd married Angelica, twice with her and the children. He was a patient man and Angelica had probed the depths of that patience both times. Though she was polite and kind to his family, and deferential to his culture, her privileged upbringing showed itself in a hundred ways, silently condemning all who observed it.

The way she carefully stepped down the rutted path that led to his mother's front door, dusted her chair before she sat in it, or frowned when a chicken scurried across the dirt floor of his mother's home was not lost on anyone. Least of all his mother. Had it not been for the children, she and Angelica would have found no common ground. He sighed. He adored his wife, but his mother deserved respect. It was

140

a difficult balancing act for him. Thankfully, this time it would not be an issue.

The steeple of the church in Santa Cruz del Astillero came into view. Antonio grabbed his hat from the seat and pushed it down on his head. A stranger in a rented car would be spotted immediately by the locals, and he didn't want his surprise spoiled by word reaching his family's home before he did.

Looking from side to side, Antonio shook his head in amazement. The town had grown dramatically since he last visited. The development of Club Guadalajara's hotel and restaurant nearby brought jobs and money to the little town, and now it occupied both sides of the highway. A Minisuper and the bus stop next to it marked what would be considered the "downtown." Some of the buildings even had power lines connected to the poles that edged the highway.

Antonio turned west onto the third dirt road after the bus stop. He dropped the car into second gear as he navigated the rocky, rutted lane past rows of tightly packed adobe huts. Dust filtered through the car's open window. He slowed down.

Children kicked a soccer ball along the side of the street. A woman crossed in front of him, a baby on one hip, a bag of vegetables on the other. A radio played somewhere in the distance. Antonio began to whistle as he bounced along toward the outskirts of town.

Soon the rutted road became a narrow path. He continued west, a lone traveler. About a mile from town, he saw a long adobe-brick wall on his right. He stopped the car, letting his eyes rest on the arched gateway in the center of the wall. Hesitating, he glanced in the direction he'd been driving . . . no one knew he was coming. His eyes returned to the opening in the wall. This was a good time to visit his

141

grandmother. Each time he'd visited Mexico he made it a point to pay his respects to her and read a Bible passage at her graveside.

He put the car in park and got out. After opening the trunk, he unzipped his valise. Then he felt around the side pocket and found his Bible. He tucked it under his arm and started down the trail that led to the cemetery.

As he passed under the arched entryway, he took off his hat. Being careful where he walked, he made his way to her gravesite and knelt beside her marker. All her grandsons had pooled their money to give her a proper headstone. One of the few in the cemetery.

Her years on this earth had been hard. She, like all his family, had lived under a tree most of her life, with little to wear and less to eat. She had accepted God's provision as sufficient, always seeking His face and not His hands.

She'd spent a number of months living in America with them when Angelica had been expecting Manuel. When the doctors told Angelica their son might be born with Down syndrome, his grandmother prayed for a healing. But believing every child is born perfect for God's plans and purposes, she prayed not for the child but for the heart of man.

He traced her name with his fingertip. Maclovia Regosa. *. . . born perfect for God's plans and purposes.*

The truth of his thoughts swept through him.

His grandmother, living in a remote part of Mexico, poor and illiterate, had come to know the God of the universe. And He had used her. He had sent her to America.

Antonio sat back on his heels as vignettes of the past flashed through his memory. Manuel's impact on Benito, the man who at first had rejected his disabled grandson, then grew to love him deeply. The effect of the child on their marriage, first threatening to destroy it, then drawing

142

them close. The healing of Angelica's heart, not toward her son, but toward the God she had questioned . . . and even cursed.

The old woman's prayers had not gone unanswered.

He felt as though he'd been looking at the underside of a tapestry. A jumble of color and knots and threads. Now, for the first time, he was being allowed to see the perfect pattern woven on top. That had been Maclovia's view. She prayed for God's vision and work, not man's.

Antonio leaned forward, resting his forehead on her marker. If only she were alive today. If only she could have written down all God had taught her.

Sitting up, he took his Bible from under his arm and opened it.

A breeze kicked up, fanning the pages.

He chose a verse at random from the column before him. "Therefore know this day, and consider it in your heart, that the Lord Himself is God in heaven above and on the earth beneath; there is no other."

Antonio stared at the words. *There is no other.*

The words spoke directly to his heart. He was not operating in a random world. There were no coincidences if one was in the will of God. He recalled the events that had brought him to Santa Cruz del Astillero. The doctors had said a match would most likely be found among the Mexican people. But it had been more than that. When he'd been alone in the truck, on the side of the road in Valle de Lagrimas, and he'd asked Jesus to help him, he felt with certainty that he should come to Mexico. The same sense of assurance came to him again.

He began to see with clarity that if a blood match were found for Manuel, it would not be the result of testing a thousand people at random. It would be the result of the hand of God bringing that one perfect person into the thousand.

He understood the importance of the moment. He hadn't stopped on an impulse to visit his grandmother and take his Bible to read by her graveside. Instead, God had chosen this specific time to meet with him, and then used what was at hand to speak to him.

He rose and slowly walked back to the car. If only Maclovia were here to pray for her great-grandson now. Prayer held the greatest hope for Manuel to be set free from the cancer.

Antonio started the car and continued toward the grove of trees now visible in the distance. He began scanning the fields, hoping no one would see him. It had been four years since he'd been home and he wanted to surprise his mother. As he neared the grove, the path he was driving on disappeared entirely. He parked in a patch of shade and got out.

He could have walked the rest of the way blindfolded. A short distance to his right was the river, twenty minutes by foot to the north were the hills where food could be hunted, and within two hours by horseback were all the people who had made up his world before he left for America.

He heard children laughing. The trees weren't dense, and to his right he saw two little girls and a boy running barefoot, chasing one another. They caught sight of him and stopped. Their faces filled with surprise. He turned and began walking, slowing down as he approached his mother's "house."

There were three plastic chairs by the front door. Behind them was a big barrel with a lid on it. How many times had he filled that barrel with water? Rocks were scattered about the yard and a makeshift fence protecting a large plot of dirt had been lashed together on one side of the house. On the other side stood the old jacaranda tree.

144

He saw her.

His mother had her back to him. She was hanging clothes on the tree's branches. Her long gray-streaked hair was pulled into a ponytail at the base of her neck. She was wearing a tattered print skirt that hung just below her knees and a man's plaid work shirt.

Antonio's heart swelled with love for her.

"Mother."

She turned, her eyes widening in wonder.

He began to run. "Mother."

She stretched her arms toward him.

Bending down he scooped her up, holding her close. He could feel her tears on his neck.

Finally, he set her down and kissed her leathery cheek.

Stepping back, she looked around his shoulder. "Where's your family, son?"

"They couldn't come this time. Anica is in school. There is a lot going on—"

"*Hola!*"

Antonio turned at the voices behind him. Two of his sisters and the children he'd seen playing stood a few yards away. "Concha. Chayo."

Within moments his sisters had their arms around his waist, the children standing back, shyly watching the *tío* they'd heard about but didn't know.

Antonio knelt, facing them. "Hello, little ones." He patted his knee.

The littlest girl approached him cautiously, and soon the others followed.

Lifting the little boy to his shoulders, and taking his nieces by their hands, he walked to the plastic chairs by the door. "Where is Papá?"

145

He set the children down and pulled the chairs out for his mother and sisters.

"He left for Texas after the rains last year."

His father had worked at the Texas ranch for years. The *patrón* was a good man who had helped his father get a visa years before. Antonio, Angelica, and the children had visited there once.

His father made a thousand dollars a month keeping the big horse facility clean and supervising all the other Mexicans who worked there, and he sent a large part of that money home every month. Still, except for the square adobe hut his mother had his brothers build, and the two rooms she later added to it, she still lived very much the way she had when Antonio was growing up. Her life now centered on the raising of her grandchildren.

Someone shouted in the distance. "Antonio?"

A smile spread across Antonio's face. He knew who it was even before he saw his childhood friend Ricardo emerge through the trees into the clearing. Antonio strode toward him, clasping Ricardo's extended hand in both of his.

Word was out. Over the next few hours, family, friends, and neighbors poured into the front yard of Elena Regosa de Perez, some on bicycles, some on horseback, but all with smiles on their faces and questions on their lips. Wanting to know everything about the *campesino* who had achieved the American dream that most had pursued, but all had failed to find.

As evening approached, the working men found their way to the gathering. Antonio's brothers arrived one by one, bringing wives and children with them. Soon a fire was lit and a bucket of water for coffee put to boil. Nearby rocks became chairs and the talk turned from the present to the past.

Ricardo stood. "Where is your guitar, *amigo?*"

Antonio shrugged. It had been almost a year since he'd sold his guitar to buy Angelica's anniversary ring. "I haven't played for a long time."

He'd seen the guitar he had as a boy inside his mother's house when he visited in the past. It hung on the wall next to the table that held a picture of Jesus, a crucifix, and several candles.

Someone called out, "Play for us."

God had given him the gift of music. When he'd lived in the fields he'd played at weddings and funerals, for fun and even for food, and many times for gatherings just like this one.

Suddenly, his mother was at his elbow, putting the guitar in his hands.

People began to clap and cheer.

As they settled down, Antonio pulled the guitar to his chest and closed his eyes. Waiting to hear the music.

He strummed a chord.

A hush fell over the crowd around him.

He felt a tender ache in his heart. These were his people. This was the land of his birth. He turned and looked at his mother. She stood straight, her shoulders back, her chin raised. She did not care for the things money could buy. He was her recompense, the fruit of her labor.

Humbled by their request and grateful to return to his roots, he began to play. As his fingers moved across the strings of the guitar, they released a melody so sweet and pure that even the sounds of nature quieted as the music filled the air. For the next measure of time Antonio paid tribute to his past. And as the rhythmic flow that came as naturally to him as breathing began to pulse through him, he abandoned himself to the moment. His fingers flew and the sound of the guitar seemed to resonate from the hills.

When he finished, there wasn't a sound but the whisper of the evening breeze.

Moments passed. A young woman began to clap her hands and sing. The man next to her joined her. Antonio strummed his guitar lightly, following along. His brother stood and took his wife's hand. They began to dance. Another couple followed. Soon the children joined in, the mood becoming light. And so the evening passed.

Eventually, people began to leave. Children were sleepy and animals needed to be fed.

With most everyone gone, Ricardo clapped Antonio on the back. "I've missed you. You shouldn't stay away so long."

Antonio smiled at him.

"I can't blame you, man. If I had my papers, and a job in the United States, I'd never come back here." Ricardo slowly shook his head. "I've seen your wife. You were born under a lucky star, *amigo*."

Antonio could see the discontent in Ricardo's eyes that came from not being able to see beyond one's circumstances. He felt compassion for his friend.

"It's true. God has poured out blessings on me." He took a deep breath. "But it isn't like you think. I'm here because I've got to find someone—"

"Ines?" Ricardo's face grew serious. "Are you talking about Ines?"

Antonio's heart began to pound. Ines had been gone for fifteen years. And though Antonio had not seen Ricardo often since moving to America, his friend had never mentioned her name in all that time. "What are you talking about?"

"Last week. My wife was very sick. I took her to the

Cruz Roja in Guadalajara to see if they could help her. I saw Ines there."

Antonio's eyes widened. This was God's providence. But why was she there? "Was she hurt?"

"I don't know, I didn't have time to talk to her because my wife was so ill. Ines asked me to tell you that she wanted to talk to you. I told her you lived in the United States and I asked her if we could meet later. She said no, she would be leaving. When I left, I think I saw her sitting with a lady out front. Maybe one of the missionaries. She had a Bible in her lap."

Antonio's heart soared. It was critical to find every member of his family that he possibly could and have them tested for a blood match to Manuel. To get a lead on his sister's whereabouts this soon was surely the hand of God.

Antonio grabbed Ricardo's shoulders and looked into his face. "You have no idea how important it is that I find Ines. Maybe she goes there often." Antonio's stomach clenched . . . maybe she worked the streets nearby. "Maybe someone there knows her."

Ricardo shook his head. "No, I don't think so. She said she was leaving."

Antonio straightened. "What do you mean, leaving?"

"She said she lives in Mexico City."

"Thank you for agreeing to meet with me." Angelica extended her arm across the principal's desk.

Jack O'Hare gave her hand a perfunctory shake and seated himself.

Angelica looked around the office. "Do you mind if I sit?"

He gestured toward a chair.

She pulled the chair to the desk and sat down. "As you know, Anica and Jimmy Shultz want to start a club."

The principal's face was expressionless. "So I've heard."

She cleared her throat. "I know you have concerns about them meeting during the lunch hour. I've talked to Jimmy's father about it and I think we've come up with a good compromise."

Principal O'Hare coolly narrowed his eyes. "And what is that?"

"We thought the kids could meet *after* school in the auditorium. Maybe once a week."

"And what would they be doing at those meetings?"

Angelica knew the unspoken question was, "Were they going to be praying?" She thought for a moment. She didn't want a confrontation. That wouldn't solve anything. "Anica's talked about a number of things the kids would like to do. She thought at the first meeting they could all make cards for Manuel."

The principal's shoulders relaxed and his face softened. "That sounds fine." His manner warmed. "Well, this is a pleasant surprise. I'm glad we understand each other. That's a very appropriate alternative to prayer."

The politically correct words slapped Angelica in the face. "I don't think Anica and Jimmy were thinking that making cards would be an alternative. It would be in addition to prayer time."

"As a school we can't endorse children meeting and praying under the guise of a club." The tone of the principal's voice hardened. "I thought I'd already made that clear."

"We're not asking the school to endorse this."

"It's still against our policy. If you want to help your daughter form a club that includes prayer, I suggest you do it at your home."

150

"Mr. O'Hare, having it at my home would make it extremely difficult for many of the children to participate."

"Actually, Ms. Perez, I think in the long run you might find it will make it *easier* for the children to participate."

"And exactly what do you mean by that?" Angelica sat back in her chair and folded her arms. She had come to the meeting hoping to work with Jack O'Hare. Compromise where possible and find common ground.

The principal's eyes darkened. "I know there are parents here who will not like the idea of having a forum for prayer at our school. And to be perfectly honest, I support their position. I see it as my job to keep a neutral environment here for all the children. We don't want to offend anyone."

She held his gaze. "There's nothing neutral about your position."

The principal leaned forward on his desk. "Look. Save yourself a lot of trouble. You may remember last year one of the students tried to start a Bible club. Hugh Bris's mother contacted the ACLU and they got involved." He lowered his voice. "There was legal action."

Jimmy's father had reminded Angelica of the incident when she'd spoken with him. She was embarrassed to admit she knew little about what had happened, even though both her children attended the school at the time. She was very busy with her own life . . . it hadn't seemed important. But today, during the long quiet hours with Manuel, she located and spoke with Mary Andrews, the mother of those children. "Actually, I'm quite familiar with that incident."

Surprise flickered across the principal's face, but his eyes didn't leave hers. "I don't recall ever speaking to you about it."

For a moment, a feeling of déjà vu settled over Angelica. When she'd worked as a public defender, she'd sat across from many clients who, after giving her their version of events, had registered the same kind of surprise when she presented them with the evidence. She decided to do now what she had done then. She asked a question she already knew the answer to. "And what kind of legal action was there?"

Jack O'Hare blinked.

His mouth quirked. "Uhhh. Well."

Angelica let him flounder a full minute before she spoke. "There was no legal action. Even though that's the impression the school gave the community. The ACLU didn't file a suit and stop the club. They intimidated the parents of the child, and the parents withdrew the request."

"I really can't help how the media portrayed what happened." The principal's voice became defensive. "The action the parents took was a decision they came to on their own."

A rush of anger rose within Angelica. Mary Andrews had told her the call from the ACLU had frightened them to death. The Andrews family had never been in a court or before a judge in their entire lives. And even though they felt passionately about a need for a Bible club at the school, they didn't want to cause a lawsuit to be filed against the school district.

"Well, Mr. O'Hare, I've come to my own decision. And here's how I did it." She leaned forward and rested her arms on the desk. "The Supreme Court's decision in the *Westside Community Schools v. Mergens* completely resolved the issue of equal access to secondary schools for Bible or prayer clubs. And their ruling in the *Good News Club v. Milford Central School* did much the same for elementary schools, regarding adult-led, after-school programs. So I've decided to be that adult for Anica and Jimmy. We have our rights. And I know what they are."

Angelica couldn't help thinking about the conversation she'd had with Anica the night Antonio left for Mexico. *There's going to be a prayer group for Manuel, Mr. O'Hare. And if you don't like it, you can take it up with the Holy Spirit.*

Angelica's cell phone rang. "Excuse me." She opened her purse, flipped the phone open and glanced at the screen. The phone number had a prefix from the hospital. "Hello."

"Angelica, it's Mom. Manuel got a temperature right after you left and it's still rising. I think you'd better come."

10

ANTONIO OPENED HIS eyes.
The unevenness of the bed, the coarseness of the pillow, the starkness of his surroundings, disoriented him. As he sat up, confusion turned into clarity.

He was in his mother's house, in the little room built onto the back. A long wedge of sunlight where the wall should have met the ceiling said it was morning.

His thoughts turned to what Ricardo had told him the night before. Ines was in Mexico City.

He swung his feet off the side of the bed. Resting his elbows on his knees, he cupped his face in his hands. Why had Ines been at the hospital Cruz Roja? Apparently, she wasn't hurt or sick.

He huffed a sigh and stood. There would be no chance of finding her now, and equally discouraging, her son was probably in Mexico City with her. That meant, including Antonio's father, there were at least three members of his family who could not be tested. He took a deep breath; there was no point in dwelling on it. He would spend the morning working out the arrangements with the bank, Banorte, in Guadalajara, as his father-in-law had instructed him. He looked at his watch. It was a little after six.

He walked to the corner of the small room, picked up his suitcase, and tossed it on the bed. After unzipping the bag, he took out a pair of slacks and a polo shirt. He dressed quickly and combed his hair. Then found his toothbrush and razor, stuck them in his back pocket, and walked out to the front yard.

His mother was in her kitchen. A three-sided shed with adobe tiles for a roof she'd had built between the jacaranda tree and her new home. Her stove was a brick pedestal that housed a fire under a large grate. The shelter built around it was a privilege only a woman with a working husband and five working sons could hope for. She was making tortillas.

As he approached her, he noticed the circles under her eyes. They'd talked late into the night. His brothers Elias and Moises, and his friend Ricardo, stayed after everyone had left. Antonio told them the reason for his trip.

His mother cried. The men pledged to give their blood.

"Good morning." Antonio walked around the stove and kissed his mother's cheek, flushed from the heat of the fire. "You look pretty this morning."

She wiped her forehead with the back of her hand and a smile spread across her face. "Breakfast is almost ready."

"I'm starved." He eyed the steaming tortillas on the grate. "But I want to go wash up first."

"Then go." She shooed him away. "It will be ready when you come back."

"Who's that?" He pointed behind her. As she turned to look, he snatched the biggest of the golden brown disks and ran.

This was something he had done many mornings when he was growing up, and his mother loved it when he repeated

155

the mischief during his visits. There was something about the ritual that brought their shared past into focus, validating that life without looking through the lens of Antonio's new life in America.

Antonio turned and faced her. With a dramatic flourish, he laid the tortilla on his hand, rolled it up, and took a big bite out of it. Then turned on his heel, walked to one of the buckets by the front door, grabbed a bar of soap from it, and headed to the river.

It was good to be home. In a strange way, he felt more capable of helping Manuel here than he had in America. Talking the night before, he'd learned that the driver who bussed the workers from Santa Cruz del Astillero to the Club Guadalajara was married to the sister of Ricardo's wife's cousin. Ricardo said he would talk to the driver about transporting people to Guadalajara when it was time to start the testing. Antonio knew there would be no issues about insurance, liability, union wages, overtime, or forms to sign, which in America Angelica would have had to handle. The only issue that might arise would be if the bus broke down, and then it would be a matter of opening the hood and waiting for someone passing by to stop and help fix it.

As Antonio started down the bank to the river, he noticed a young woman kneeling by the water directly in front of him, washing clothes. She raised her head as he approached.

Antonio nodded to her. *"Buenos días, señora."*

She looked at him a moment. "You are Elena's son visiting from America, no?"

Antonio put his hands in the pockets of his very American slacks. *"Sí."* He tilted his head. "And you are?"

She lowered her eyes, looking at his feet. "Juanita Rivera de Lopez."

Antonio felt heat in his cheeks. She was showing him deference. To her he was an important, rich man. He glanced at the shirt she had spread on a large rock, ready to scrub. The pocket was torn and buttons were missing. Her dress was too large for her and she had no shoes. He squatted beside her. "Who is your husband, *señora*?"

Her gaze didn't leave his feet. "Mario Lopez."

"Mario whose family lives in the canyon?"

She nodded.

"I know his father." Antonio gave a sharp half nod of his head. "A very good man. I saw him last night at my mother's house."

She peeked at him from the side of her eye and nodded.

"He told me his sons are doing well. He's very proud of Mario." He stood. "It was nice to meet you."

Turning away, he walked along the river's edge. He wanted to find a spot where the water pooled among the rocks. Finally, he stopped. Taking the soap, he lathered his face, then he took his toothbrush and razor from his pocket and squatted by the pooled water. He shaved as best he could and brushed his teeth.

When he finished, he jogged up the bank, through the trees, and back to the house. He put the razor, soap, and toothbrush in his room, then joined his mother in the kitchen. She had a baby on her hip. The child was fussing and her cheeks were flushed.

Antonio glanced at the baby. "Who is this?"

"You missed Teresa. She stopped by while you were gone. This is her granddaughter." She wiped the baby's nose with the edge of her blouse. "She has a bad cold. I'm watching her while Teresa goes to town."

With her free hand, his mother ladled a big portion of eggs and beans onto a plate and handed it to him. Then she took a cloth and stacked hot tortillas on it. When she finished, she gathered up the corners, making a sack, and handed it to him. They both walked to the jacaranda tree and sat down.

His mother cradled the baby in her arms. "Teresa said she went to the bus stop with her husband this morning. He's working at Rancho Contento. And she heard that you were here."

Antonio took a tortilla and scooped up some eggs with it. Teresa was one of his mother's closest friends, and he knew the woman well. Teresa's mother had grown up with Maclovia. The families had lived in the area for a hundred years and the relationships went back for decades.

"I told her that my grandson is very sick, and that you are here because he needs our help. I asked her if she would donate blood for him." She lifted her chin, then waited a moment as if to give her next words a proper entrance. "And she said she would do it."

Listening to his mother, Antonio suddenly realized that when he'd tried to simplify the explanation of Manuel's situation the night before, she had not understood about the matching. That Manuel not only needed blood to be donated, but that the blood must be typed, and the donor would need to be a part of a continuing process.

Antonio could hear the relief in his mother's voice as she spoke of her closeness with Teresa and how it was fitting that she be the one to save Manuel's life. How she had told Teresa if anyone in her family ever needed blood, the favor would be returned.

He put his tortilla down. The simple story his mother told of finding the perfect donor to save Manuel drove home to him the complexity of the task he faced. He closed his eyes, realizing his brothers too had probably not understood the commitment a donor would have to make. And how

158

could they? The people here knew nothing of the sophisticated medical procedures available to almost everyone in the United States.

"Mother, I'm glad Teresa wants to help. But remember, I told you the blood would have to be tested."

His mother smiled. "I know, son. But now that won't be necessary. Teresa is as close as family."

"If being close were enough, I would give my blood." Antonio tried to reason with her. "It's more complicated than that. The blood must be tested by doctors. That's the only way to know the blood will be good for Manuel." He searched his mind for something familiar to her that he could use to explain the situation. But he was at a loss.

He rehearsed some phrases in his mind, but then realized he was thinking in English. He didn't know the Spanish translation of peripheral blood stem cell, haplotype, or any of the medical terms he'd heard so many times during Manuel's illness. He put his plate down, leaving most of his breakfast. If he couldn't make his own mother understand, what was he going to tell everyone else?

"Thank you for breakfast, Mother." Antonio rose. "I'm going to the bank in Guadalajara, and then I'm going to visit the hospitals and ask them about blood testing. I'll be back later."

"Be sure to tell them that Teresa wants to give her blood."

The feverish baby began to cough. His mother laid the child in her lap and quickly took off the baby's tiny knitted socks. Gathering spit in her mouth, she pressed it on the tips of her fingers, then rubbed it on the baby's feet. She began to whisper prayers over the child.

Antonio watched her.

She was treating the child for a sore throat.

159

Angelica whispered a silent prayer over Manuel. The antibiotics had been dripping since the night before, but Manuel's fever had not come down.

"Good afternoon."

Angelica jumped. "You startled me, Dr. Dorak. When you were here earlier, I thought you said you were leaving for the day."

"I got Manuel's latest blood work back."

Angelica's stomach tightened.

"His white blood count is still very low."

"And he isn't eating." Angelica looked at her son's flushed face. "Even when he was, he threw it up."

She fought a sense of panic. Why couldn't things turn around? If only Antonio were here. She longed to feel his arms around her, reassuring her it would work out. How was she going to get through this alone? Trying to keep Anica's life on an even keel, trying not to burden her parents any more than she already had, trying to keep the household running—it was all too much. *God, where are You?* She took a deep breath. "Did the blood cultures show anything?"

"Not yet. But a fever like this is not uncommon, and it may take a few days before we know if there's an infection in his blood. We'll keep treating him as if he had one. Just in case." He hesitated. "You doing okay?"

No. She was not doing okay. Everything seemed to be crashing down around her. She looked at the doctor.

The compassion and care she saw in his eyes touched her. There was something about him, something she didn't understand, but it calmed her. The intense feeling of hopelessness and fear that had gripped her vanished.

"Am I interrupting?"

Angelica saw Tex standing in the doorway with a bouquet of balloons. "Not at all." She stepped around the doctor and gave Tex a hug. "It's so good to see you."

Taking the balloons, she said, "This is Dr. Dorak, Manuel's oncologist. He was just filling me in on the latest test results."

Tex shook the doctor's extended hand. "I can wait out in the hall until you're finished."

"No, that's not necessary." Angelica turned to the doctor. "Was there anything else?"

"No, but I'll let you know as soon as there is." He smiled at the two women and left.

Tex raised her eyebrows. "Wow. He's a nice-looking man."

"Single, too." Angelica smiled at her mischievously.

"Well, keep that in mind, girl." Tex winked at her, then tiptoed to Manuel's bedside. "Is he sleeping?"

"Yes, praise God for that." Angelica tied the balloons to the foot of the bed. "He has terrible sores in his mouth." She glanced at her friend. "He's on morphine for the pain."

Tex's eyes began to tear up.

Angelica took some tissues from the box on the table at the end of the couch and handed them to her. "He's got a fever and they can't find out why. His white blood count is so low that he can't fight whatever is causing it. If this infection can't be stopped . . ." The two women's eyes met.

Angelica gestured toward the couch. "Let's sit down."

She sat, her legs curled under her, facing Tex. "Thank you so much for coming. Without Antonio here, it's so much harder."

Tex nodded in sympathy. "That's one of the reasons I stopped by. I thought maybe I could be of help."

Angelica waited for her to continue.

161

"I've been praying for Manuel since you first told me the cancer had returned. This morning, during my prayer time, I got a very strong impression that I was to ask you if I could be of more help."

Angelica's lips parted in surprise.

"As you know, I live alone. My life is very simple, and I consider being a teacher my ministry." She looked toward Manuel. "I feel every one of these precious little ones is given to me by God to be loved, nurtured, and taught." She turned her gaze to Angelica. "And maybe this time, for something more."

She reached across the couch and rested her hand on Angelica's arm. "I want you to know I'm available to help you any time you need me, in any way I can. Grocery shopping, staying at the house, staying here, whatever helps, that's what I want to do."

Angelica felt as if a huge weight were being lifted from her shoulders. Her thoughts flashed to her critical, accusatory prayer, *God, where are You?* Looking at the sweet face of Tex Gaynor, she knew. He was in the hearts of His people. "I don't know what to say."

"Well." Tex tilted her head. "You could start by saying what would help you most."

With the prospect of help in front of her, Angelica allowed herself to express some of the feelings she'd kept at bay. "The thing that bothers me the most is how disrupted Anica's life has been. I hardly get to see her, and when I do, I'm so distracted I can't give her the attention she needs."

"How about if I fill in for you here some of the time? I'm usually finished at the school by three thirty, and my weekends are open. That would give you more time for her."

"That just seems like too much of an imposition." A second thought occurred to Angelica. "What if Manuel calls for me and I'm not here, or an emergency arises?"

Tex patted her hand. "That could happen any time you're not here."

Angelica was well aware of that and had thought about it many times. Trying to come up with contingency plans for all those scenarios was part of the stress she was living under. She looked away for a moment as a wave of anxiety washed through her.

Manuel knew his teacher. It wouldn't be like having him wake up to a stranger. . . . Still. "I don't know, Tex. It just doesn't seem right that my problems should infringe on your life."

"Let me explain something." Tex straightened. "When I felt the Lord calling me to this, I understood what it could mean." She chuckled. "Knowing the Lord as I do, and the different calls He's put on my life over the years, I almost started by asking you if you had a spare bedroom."

She winked at Angelica. "Do you?"

Angelica put her hand on her chest. "You really are serious about this, aren't you?"

Tex gave a sharp nod of her head. "You bet."

A peace that passed her understanding settled over Angelica. This woman had come to her offering the support she desperately needed . . . and wanted. She began to share with Tex her deepest fears and concerns. As the hour passed, the women realized the idea of Tex staying with Angelica at the house until Antonio returned was, by far, the best one.

"How about if I stay with you and Anica during the week and stay at my own place on the weekends? I can take her to school and pick her up at the O'Connells on my way to your home. Then she and I can start dinner."

163

"You have no idea how wonderful that sounds." Angelica reached across the couch and gave Tex a hug.

Tex shushed her. "I'm looking forward to it. Now tell me, what happened at your meeting with Jack O'Hare yesterday afternoon?"

"Before we really got to finish, my mother called to tell me Manuel had developed a fever and I rushed back here. But basically I told him the law is on our side."

Tex looked surprised. "Is it? All I've ever heard is that you have to keep church and state separated. The school won't allow the mention of Jesus or God in the classroom, I know that for sure."

Angelica sat back and folded her arms across her chest. "Well, that may be the case during school hours, but I've done some research, and we are well within our rights to have a prayer club after school. There's been a lot of misinformation put out in the media about it. The groups that want to take God out of the public discourse have been very successful getting their side of the story out. They'd have you believe that if you want to offer any faith options to kids at school, you'll cause a lawsuit."

Tex nodded. "That's what I've heard."

"They're trying to use intimidation to further their agenda. But I'm not easily intimidated and I plan to go ahead with helping Anica set up a prayer club for Manuel. In fact, the few minutes I had with Anica after dinner last night, we talked about making a flyer she could hand out. But first I need to find out from Principal O'Hare which room and which day we can have the meeting."

"You could certainly use my classroom. No one meets there."

Angelica sat forward. "That would be perfect, since most of the kids will be from his class. I'll call Jack O'Hare about

164

it, then write him a note confirming that phone conversation. Since he's been so hostile to the idea, I think I'd better create a paper trail just to keep things documented."

Tex rose. "Well, honey. I've got some things to do. Did you want me to start staying with you two girls tomorrow night?"

Angelica stood, and the women hugged again. "That would be just great."

Tex limped across the room toward the door.

As she watched Tex leave, Angelica was overcome with gratitude. The woman had come here offering all she had to give, and asking nothing in return.

Suddenly, Jesus's words to Philip came to her mind: "He that hath seen Me hath seen the Father."

Dr. Dorak's calming touch passed through her thoughts.

Angelica couldn't help but feel that in much the same way, today she had seen Jesus.

Sitting back down on the couch, she picked up her purse, took out her cell phone, and called the school.

"Has Jack O'Hare left yet?"

"One moment, please."

The principal came on the line.

"Mr. O'Hare, this is Angelica Perez, Anica's mo—"

"Yes?"

"I'm sorry we didn't get to finish our conversation yesterday, but I'd like to go ahead and arrange a day and place that the prayer group could meet."

She waited for a response.

The silence on the phone spoke volumes.

Angelica continued. "I was speaking to Mrs. Gaynor and she said her room was available."

"How is Ms. Gaynor involved in this? She's a school employee."

Angelica winced. She shouldn't have mentioned Tex. Was Jack O'Hare going to target her now, harass her in subtle ways and make her life miserable?

"She's Manuel's teacher and it just seemed like his home-room would be a logical place to start."

Angelica again waited for his response.

"I've done some checking, Mrs. Perez, and I've decided to allow you to have your club. After school. But there will be a fee to use the room."

"A fee!" Angelica tried to keep the anger from her voice. She knew of several clubs that met at the school after regular school hours, and she'd never heard of them being charged a fee. "The Boy Scouts meet there, the Sign Language Club, what about the Homework Club? Do you charge them fees?"

"We're looking at that now."

The implication was clear. They were going to charge the prayer club a fee, and if that meant they would have to charge all the other clubs fees, they would do that. Leaving the impression that the prayer club was causing the problem. Next, parents would be saying, "Until there was a prayer club, we were able to use the school facilities without charge."

Angelica measured her words. "When will you know how much the fee will be?"

"Probably not until the next school board meeting."

A delaying tactic. "What do you mean by probably?"

"I thought I'd check with the other districts and see how they've handled it."

Angelica thought she might do the same. "What has the process been for other clubs that are using the school now?"

"What do you mean?"

He wasn't going to give an inch. If she didn't know the

right question to ask, then he would let her flounder. "I mean what is the process to start a club? Do I need to fill out a form, go before a committee, or what?"

"There's an application form called Request for Use of School Facilities."

"And where would I get that?"

"Here in the office."

"Are the instructions on it?"

Again, telltale silence. Then an abrupt, "Yes."

Angelica ignored his obstinacy. "Thank you for your help. I'll get the form, and please let me know when the school board will be holding their next meeting."

"Very well."

Angelica closed her cell phone and sank back into the couch. She chewed on her lower lip. She felt like she was entering a battle.

And Jack O'Hare had just fired the opening shot.

Antonio snapped his cell phone shut and pressed it against his cheek. He knew his wife well. And even though they'd talked only a short time and she'd said nothing to alarm him, he sensed that things were not going well. Manuel had made little improvement, and the doctors still didn't know what was causing his fever. The one piece of good news was that Tex Gaynor was going to be staying with Angelica. He hadn't liked the idea of leaving Angelica at such a troubled time. Even though she was strong and capable, she was still his responsibility. He dropped the phone on the passenger seat, leaving it plugged into the lighter socket so it would charge.

He turned his attention back to the traffic on Avenida Vallarta. He should have left Guadalajara earlier and avoided the

167

rush hour, but the more he got done today, the less he would have to do tomorrow. He'd found Banorte easily, and met with the bank manager. They called Benito and confirmed the first part of the money had already been wired.

Antonio smiled, remembering the look on the bank manager's face as he realized the amounts of money that were being transferred. Antonio knew his Spanish had told the educated Mexican that Antonio was a poor *campesino*, and the man had treated him with cool indifference when Antonio first inquired about the account. But by the time the manager got off the phone with Benito, he somehow perceived Antonio's true value as a fellow human being and spoke glowingly of their common heritage. Even noting they shared the same last name of Perez. A horn blasted behind him, urging him through a red light.

The search for a lab had been far more difficult. He first went to Cruz Roja because he found out from Ricardo approximately where it was and he said they'd drawn his wife's blood. And, Antonio had to admit, deep down he hoped by some wild twist of fate, or the will of God, he might see Ines there. He hadn't.

He even went as far as to ask if there were any missionaries working that he could talk to. A Sister Maria was located. But she had never heard of Ines or Cirocco Perez. "I'm certain I would remember a name like Cirocco," she said, then wished him luck.

She also gave him the names and general directions to other hospitals in the area, but he soon found trying to drive the unfamiliar streets and find parking was not only impossible, but dangerous. Buses, cars, pedestrians, and even horse-drawn carts all seemed to be vying for the same piece of pavement. Finally, he parked near San Juan de Dios and flagged down a cab. He worked out a deal with the cab driver, who, for a hundred American dollars, spent the rest of the day driving Antonio where he wanted to go and waiting for him until he was ready to leave. At the Hospital Metropolitano a doctor in the emergency room directed him to a private laboratory nearby.

As the city disappeared behind him, Antonio's thoughts turned to his conversation with the lab director, Dr. Montoya. Antonio had explained the situation as best he could. Fortunately, the doctor spoke English and seemed to go out of his way to try and help. He understood the urgency, and when Antonio gave him the papers Dr. Cohen had sent, he excused himself and took them into his office. Antonio heard him talking on the phone, and when he returned he told Antonio he thought they would be able to work something out, but he wanted to talk to Dr. Cohen and Dr. Dorak first. He suggested Antonio return the following morning. They set an appointment for ten o'clock.

One good thing Antonio had learned was that the test wasn't going to be as expensive as it was in the United States. Dr. Montoya said it would be two hundred fifty dollars. That was a savings of a hundred dollars a test.

But there was one other thing the doctor had said that Antonio had not thought about before. He told Antonio there were "ethical considerations." Antonio was not sure what the term meant. He'd heard Angelica talk about ethics when she was a public defender, and he understood that it meant to do what was right. He found that if he treated people as he wanted to be treated, it seemed to work out pretty well. But the doctor had explained that some people would feel like they had to donate because they were friends or relatives, or because they felt they had to try to save Manuel, when in fact they did not want to donate their blood. He said there were many reasons someone might feel that way, and they should not be pressured. It had to be each person's choice, made of their own free will.

Antonio released a deep sigh. The doctor's caution about ethics now made Antonio feel even more burdened to do a good job explaining exactly what donating was and what it would mean if a match were found. Still, there was no way most of the people would understand anything about the medical procedure. He understood it only in the most basic way himself. Yet he didn't want to discourage anyone from volunteering. It was critical that he get as many people as possible to test.

As he rounded a curve ahead of him, the steeple of the church in Santa Cruz del Astillero came into view. His brows drew together. *Dios, I do not want to bring dishonor to myself or my family. I will have to trust You to make a way.*

He slowed down as he entered the little town. One thing was for sure, he needed to make some kind of announcement, and the sooner the better. Otherwise information would go out by word of mouth, each person adding their own thoughts as word spread, complicating an already difficult task.

He scanned both sides of the street, his gaze drifting to the Minisuper and bus stop. A vignette from his last visit home flashed through his mind—standing at the counter, talking to a *señora*, the head of the family that owned the store.

He made a quick turn, pulled into the flat dirt area in front of the business, parked, and got out of the car.

He hadn't crossed the threshold when he heard, "Antonio! I've been waiting all day to see you."

The short, round woman with a silver front tooth bustled around the counter with her arms extended. He bent down and hugged her.

"I must be the last person on your list," she chided him

good-naturedly, putting her hands on her wide hips. "I've been worried sick about your boy. What happened in Guadalajara today? I told Filipo, who drives his bus to the big sports field every morning and every night, he'd better be planning some trips to the city or don't come in here looking to buy cigarettes on credit. Or his tequila either." She pointed her finger at Antonio. "You make him give you a fair price too."

A broad smile spread across Antonio's face. This was the hub of Santa Cruz del Astillero. And Celerina Gomez was the center of the hub. Everything that happened in the area made its way in, and then out, of the Minisuper.

"*Señora*, I need your help."

"Of course. Of course. Tell me." Her bright eyes sharpened. What the old woman lacked in education, she made up for in savvy.

"Wait a moment." She put her finger up, then shouted an order to her grandson who was standing by the cash register. "Bring him a crate out of the back, and put it next to my chair."

Within moments Antonio was sitting on a box next to Celerina's big chair, right inside the front door.

"Now tell me, boy, what is it?"

Antonio told her of his reason for the trip, and as best he could, explained his desperate search to find a blood match for Manuel. "I need you to tell people there will be a meeting at the plaza Friday night. I will explain everything then."

The old woman's face had sobered as he spoke and her dark eyes searched his. She nodded. "I will do that."

Antonio rose and tipped his head to her. "I will be at the plaza Friday night."

He turned and walked outside, head bowed, deep in

thought. He still had no idea how he would explain to the people about peripheral blood stem cells or haplotypes.

"Antonio."

He raised his head. "Ricardo. What are you doing here?"

"My brother-in-law's car won't start." Ricardo pointed to an ancient Ford with its hood up. "Can you give us a hand?"

Antonio shrugged. He didn't know much about old cars. "Sure, I'd be glad to help. But it's been a long time."

Ricardo slapped him on the back. "Buddy, if you're planning to stay here awhile, you'd better learn. There isn't a man around here, young or old, who doesn't know how to fix a car." He winked. "Even some of the women know how."

Antonio was only half listening. Knowing how to fix a car was one thing. But how did you explain how to fix a little boy with cancer? How was he going to explain stem cell transplantation to the people of Santa Cruz del Astillero?

C IROCCO ROLLED TO a stop at the corner where he usually turned to go to Diego's food stand. He looked down the street toward San Juan de Dios. He couldn't face his friend. He felt ashamed he'd allowed the man's generous donation to be stolen. Crossing the street, he continued north.

He'd been to see Mama Rose only once since that day. She cleaned his cuts and bandaged his arm. She begged him to stay with her, but he couldn't do that. He couldn't bear to listen to her talk about Jesus.

He'd been a fool to think Jesus cared about him. He tossed his head and clenched his jaw as he remembered her praying for him just before he'd left for the bus. If Jesus really loved him, He would have had a bus coming down the street just as he hit the pavement. It would have been better that way. He continued north.

It had been a week since the incident. And he'd avoided all the places where he thought he might run into the boy who pushed him. It wasn't that he was afraid. It had just been bad luck. If the boy hadn't surprised him, he could have held his own. Still, he didn't want to go where there was bad luck. And that included the public toilets. He'd have to find another place to work.

He continued to push himself along the sidewalk, looking at the storefronts and doorways, places he could return to late at night, when he was tired . . . when no one was around.

He'd been scouting new areas every day. There were certain things he needed, access to trash, a park nearby, and people with money in their pockets. He'd never been this far north until yesterday. And yesterday he made some money here.

As he neared the Hospital Metropolitano, the sidewalks became crowded and he slowed down.

He wheeled around to the front of the hospital and took a position at the same spot he'd sat the day before. It was a small jut in the wall, out of the way, but visible to people walking on the sidewalk. He had a clear view up and down the street, and as soon as he had enough money to get by for a few days, he was going to look for work.

Cirocco took a deep breath and began to search the faces of the people passing by. Hunger gnawed at his stomach. To keep himself from starving, he would use the only thing he had been able to salvage from the street where he'd crashed. He extended his hands, anxiously waiting for the sound of a coin hitting the tin cup.

Antonio walked along the foothills behind his mother's house, slowly waving his hand back and forth.

He had his cell phone screen tilted so he could see it. Every once in a while a bar would appear. He'd stop and slowly rotate the phone, hoping to catch a signal strong enough to make a call to Angelica. Finally, standing atop a broad boulder and leaning a little to the right, he saw two bars. He dialed all the numbers and pressed Send.

She answered.

"Angel, can you hear me?"

"Not as well as the last time you called. That was great. It was like you were right next door."

He smiled. He wished he were. "I was on the road in Guadalajara then. Reception is good anywhere in the city. How's Manuel?"

"Better. His fever is down and he's starting to eat. The doctor said he might even be able to come home a few days before his next round of chemo starts. How did the meeting go yesterday morning with the lab? Dr. Dorak told me he had a good conversation with the director."

Antonio had been present during the conversation. "They're going to be able to do about twenty-five tests a day and they found another lab that can do about twenty."

"How many volunteers do you have?"

"I'll know tonight. I've asked people to come to the plaza in Santa Cruz this evening so I can explain everything."

"Tex and I will be with you in spirit."

"Is Anica there?"

"She's right here, jumping up and down."

"Daddy? Daddy?"

Antonio closed his eyes. "Yes, precious."

"Are you coming home soon?"

"As soon as I can. How's school?"

"Oh, Daddy. We're going to have a club. The Mighty Warriors. We're going to meet after school and I'm helping Mom. She might give a . . . a . . . presentation." Anica delivered the important word with precise enunciation.

Antonio smiled, remembering the conversation they'd had in the van on the night he'd left and Anica's earnest question,

"What if the rules are wrong, Mom?" Apparently his strong-willed wife had decided the rules *were* wrong. He raised his eyebrows at that thought. Heaven help Mr. O'Hare.

"I'm proud of you, honey. Prayer changes things." Antonio heard Angelica in the background telling Anica to say good-bye.

"I'll pray for you too, Daddy. Bye."

He heard Angelica take the phone. "Antonio, call me after the meeting tonight, even if it's late. Tex and I will be praying for God to move."

"I will. Please call your father when we hang up and tell him I will be going back to the bank today to see if the second transfer of funds came in."

"I'll let him know." She lowered her voice. "Antonio, they still haven't found a match in the registry."

The tinge of panic in her voice was wrenching for him. "I won't give up. I will find a match for our son." His voice became husky. "I love you, Angelica."

"I love you too. Call me tonight."

Antonio closed the phone and stood for a moment gathering his thoughts. He stepped down from the boulder to the rocky dirt of the hillside. Then he dropped to his knees.

There, beneath the clear blue sky of Central Mexico, he petitioned the God of the universe. Not with words of despair, but as one father to another. He did not want his son to die.

As thoughts of Manuel surged through him, he allowed the Spirit to search his heart, to perceive the deep emotion he could not find words for, and to make intercession for him with groanings which could not be uttered.

As he prayed, he suddenly realized the enormity of God's sacrifice, suffering His own Son to die.

Antonio dropped his head to his knees and beneath that

176

arc of truth, he knew with certainty that for a season, there would be a trial of his faith, but that the outcome was known by God. And the victory would be His.

As time passed, he felt encouraged and strengthened, and a sense of assurance settled over him.

He rose.

With renewed faith, tempered by a sobering truth, he walked slowly to his car. He needed to find Filipo, the bus driver who took the workers to Club Guadalajara each day.

Antonio drove the short distance to Santa Cruz and began to drive up and down the rutted streets. Since he'd arrived, he'd seen the old school bus parked in different locations, sometimes at Ricardo's, sometimes at the Minisuper, sometimes at the local bar.

Filipo's pride in his job as the official driver for Club Guadalajara's workforce was evident. He'd painted the bus with the black-and-white pattern of a soccer ball, though Antonio had to admit, his first thought was of a Holstein cow. Then Filipo had hand lettered Club Guadalajara on both sides and across the back in bright yellow.

Going through the back streets, Antonio worked his way up to the main road. Turning onto Highway 15, he spotted the bus about a quarter mile ahead parked on the shoulder of the road that led into the village. He hoped the bus had not broken down. He drove the short distance and pulled around behind it.

As Antonio approached the bus, he saw the doors were open and a thin young man with slicked-back hair was perched on the driver's seat. His shirt was open and a big gold-colored cross hung from his neck. Antonio thought of Celerina's caution about paying a fair price. *"Hola!"*

177

A quick smile appeared on the driver's face. *"Buenos días."*

Antonio stepped up into the bus and extended his hand. "I am Antonio Perez."

"Oh, yes. Ricardo's friend." The man shook Antonio's hand. "How are you?"

"I am well. You must be Filipo?"

"Sí."

Antonio looked down the length of the bus. "Would it be possible to talk to you about doing some business?"

"Sit. Sit." Filipo jumped up, grabbed a rag from his back pocket, and dusted off the first seat across the aisle.

Filipo was clearly ready to do business. Antonio suddenly knew why the bus was parked so prominently at the entrance to Santa Cruz del Astillero.

He resisted the urge to get directly to the point, as he would have done in America. Instead, he asked Filipo about his family and spoke of their mutual friendship with Ricardo. Finally, Antonio sat back and casually swung his arm across the top of the seat.

"Ricardo told me you work for Club Guadalajara."

Filipo nodded.

"May I ask what your schedule is?"

"I take the people at six o'clock in the morning and I bring them back at six o'clock at night."

"Is your bus available for rent during the day?"

Filipo clicked his tongue. "The bus is usually busy during the day."

Antonio recognized this as part of the negotiating and chose not to point out that he had seen the black-and-white bus parked all over town during the days since he had arrived.

"I see." He hesitated, giving Filipo's declaration of the

178

many demands put on his bus respectful consideration. "My son is very sick in the United States, and I am hoping to find some volunteers to donate blood to him. But the work must be done at a laboratory in Guadalajara. I need transportation for the volunteers, so I might need your services these next few weeks."

"I heard something about that." Filipo ran the rag around the face of the steering wheel. "Where in Guadalajara is this laboratory?"

"Downtown, near the Hospital Metropolitano, just north of San Juan de Dios."

Deep concern appeared on Filipo's face. "That's a very long way." He paused. "What day did you want to go?"

"It isn't just one day. I am hoping many people will decide to help. It could be many days."

"Many long trips to downtown Guadalajara?" The thought seemed to distress Filipo greatly. "I don't know, *amigo*. My bus is old. She needs new tires."

Antonio pursed his lips at the troubling information. "I understand."

Moments of silence passed. Antonio knew the next one to speak would lose the advantage. He chewed his lower lip.

Filipo gazed out the window.

Antonio drummed his fingers on the seatback.

"How long would I have to wait there?"

"I'm not sure. It will depend on how many people are having their blood drawn. I'll know a lot more after tonight."

"Exactly how far is this laboratory from San Juan de Dios?"

Antonio dropped his hand from the back of the seat and leaned forward. "I have to go to a bank near there this morning. Why don't we drive in together and you can see for yourself."

Filipo gazed at him intently and then shrugged. "Sounds good to me. But I don't have much gas."

"You could ride with me."

Filipo looked out the back window that framed Antonio's rental car. "It would be good if I had gas."

Antonio chuckled. Apparently Filipo knew how American drivers fared in city traffic.

"How much gas do you need?"

"About two hundred and twenty pesos' worth."

Antonio took his wallet from his pocket and took out a twenty-dollar bill. "Deal."

By the time they reached the bank, they had come to an agreement about the bus. Antonio would pay a flat fee of twenty-five dollars for each round trip to Guadalajara, regardless of the number of passengers.

Filipo waited for Antonio while he met with the bank manager. When Antonio returned, they decided to continue on to the laboratory. The lunch hour traffic was heavy, but Filipo proved to be a very skillful driver, steering the bus in and out of traffic fearlessly.

Antonio pointed toward the lab. "It's up there on the corner, on the left."

Filipo began guiding the bus to the middle of the street for a left-hand turn. Horns honked all around them. Filipo stepped on the gas, then the brake, working his way to the intersection. As they approached, it became clear that it would be impossible to park anywhere on the streets that bordered the lab. Filipo glanced at Antonio. "When I bring the people, I'll have to park."

Antonio stood and dropped the window next to his seat and stuck his head out the opening. He looked up and down the busy street. "Let's turn around. I have an idea."

Filipo crossed himself, then cut the steering wheel hard right.

Antonio fell backward, catching himself with the seat-back.

The bus plowed forward, avoiding the left turn, and crossed the intersection on a red light.

"Are you crazy?" Antonio grabbed the metal bar in front of him.

Filipo looked at him with perplexed surprise.

Antonio took a steadying breath. "Take the next right and get back on the main street, going back the way we came."

Antonio directed Filipo through a series of turns. They ended up in front of a building near the lab. The street was lined with taxis and cars. "I saw this when I was here yesterday. This will work just fine. Cars are stopping here letting people out all day long. You can let us off at the lab and when we're finished, we'll meet you back here. It's only a few blocks."

Filipo craned his neck, looking over the long hood of the bus, down the line of cars. "Where are we?"

"Hospital Metropolitano."

"Come on, Anica," Angelica shouted. "Turn off the television. It's almost five o'clock." She looked at Tex, who was across the table from her, writing in a spiral-bound notebook. "I got a lot of calls made this afternoon from the hospital. The prayer chain at the church and almost everyone in my Bible study group has been notified that we're going to start praying in one accord at five. With the time difference, that should be about when Antonio will be speaking at the plaza.

I asked that they just cover him in prayer and ask God to bring that one person. God knows who it is."

Tex nodded as she wrote.

"And there's another thing." Angelica hated to voice it. It seemed like borrowing trouble. It was the one thing she and Antonio had not talked about in any depth. It was something that was not an issue yet. But it would be, if a match were found. And it could be an obstacle as hard to overcome as finding the blood match itself. "The person has to have a visa."

Tex groaned as she started a new line and wrote a few more words. "I hadn't even thought about that. I'll put it on my list right now." She glanced at Angelica. "I like to pray in detail. I like to speak to the Lord very specifically, and when possible, pray His Word." She ran her finger down the list. "Plane on time. Smooth flight. Rental car available. Rest well at night." Angelica could see Bible verse references scattered throughout.

Tex set her pen down. "It's going to work out. You know, there are several teachers at school who always ask about Manuel and let me know they are praying for him. I told them what was going on and that we'd be praying tonight. They're joining us too." She clucked her tongue. "In fact, four of us sneaked out of the teachers' lounge at lunchtime and met in the staff bathroom to talk about it. The administration is so hostile toward Christians that we didn't want to take a chance of being overheard."

Angelica frowned. "It's ridiculous you're made to feel that way. You have every right to speak about your faith on your own time."

"It seems like that's the way it should be, but we need our jobs, and don't want to rock the boat."

"Well, I'm hoping the Mighty Warriors Club will help

182

educate the parents and teachers that schools aren't 'religion-free' zones."

"Did Jack ever get back to you about a day and time?"

"No. But I had the school office email me the application form they require if we want to use the school facilities." Angelica smiled. "And I filled it out and submitted it. It'll end up on Jack O'Hare's desk Monday. That puts the ball in his court."

"Angelica, I admire you so much for not backing down. It's spiritual warfare, you know."

Angelica considered Tex's words for a moment. "You saying that made me think of Maclovia, Antonio's grand-mother. Now there was a woman who knew how to pray." The memory of seeing Maclovia praying, surrounded by a circle of light, flashed through Angelica's mind. "She died about ten years ago. Right after Manuel was born."

"Did she ever get to see him?"

"Do you mean, did she know he has Down syndrome?" Tex nodded.

"She was living with us at the time." Angelica's voice softened at the memory. "When I was pregnant, and we knew there was a strong possibility that Manuel would have Downs, we were devastated. But Maclovia prayed for a healing." Suddenly Angelica's eyes teared up.

"Of course," Tex whispered.

"Not for the healing of our unborn child, but for the heal-ing of our hearts." Angelica lowered her eyes. "I can't believe I felt that way then. I dreaded his birth. I . . . I . . . there was a time I didn't want him." A thought flashed through Angelica's mind. "You don't think that has anything to do with this, do you?"

Tex's face filled with concern. "What are you talking about?"

"Maybe this is some kind of punishment for not wanting him."

Tex rose and hurried around the table. She put her arm around Angelica's shoulders. "You mustn't think such a thing—that's right from the pit. You love Manuel."

"Mommy, why are you crying?"

Tex straightened and Angelica quickly wiped her cheeks. "Oh. I didn't hear you come in. It's nothing, honey. I was just sad for a minute. Here, sit by me."

Anica sat on Angelica's right, and Tex went back to her chair.

Angelica smoothed her hand across the top of her Bible. "Maclovia always said that she waited on the Lord when she prayed. She never just started praying. She would sit and wait until she felt His presence." She looked first at Tex, then at Anica. "Shall we do that?"

Anica nodded her head excitedly.

Tex smiled in agreement.

Angelica reached for Anica's hand. "When you feel His presence, just begin to pray." She could see the kitchen clock next to the refrigerator. "It's almost five. That's seven o'clock in Mexico. There are over a hundred people who have agreed to pray with us, wherever they are, right now." Angelica bowed her head.

"Wait, Mom."

She looked at her daughter.

"How will I know when God is here?"

Angelica raised her head. "Um." She glanced at Tex. "Uh. Well, you'll just know." She tightened her grip on Anica's hand and bowed her head again.

Only a few minutes had passed when Angelica felt Anica wiggle out of her chair, while still managing to hang on to Angelica's hand. Angelica lifted an eyelid. Anica was craning

184

her neck, looking around the kitchen area. After a moment, she sat back down.

Angelica closed her eyes. It had been a long time since she had really felt the presence of God. Her life had been so busy, so much had happened. Lately, her prayers were frantic and demanding, coming from a place of fear. How *did* you really know if you were in God's presence?

She turned her head slightly and peeked at Anica. Her daughter's eyes were tightly closed, a look of innocent expectation on her face.

Oh, to have the blind faith of a child. Angelica returned to her quiet contemplation.

Minutes passed.

She heard Anica whispering. A hopeful call. "Jesus?"

The scent of roses began to fill the room. Angelica opened her eyes and raised her head.

Tex's eyes met hers.

Both women slowly turned toward Anica.

Anica, eyes closed, face flushed with excitement, whispered, "He's here!"

She clasped her hands together in front of her chest. Her face grew serious and a line formed between her brows. "Please help my daddy."

Her face contorted, and a tear slipped down her cheek. "And don't forget to make my brother well again."

Antonio stood on the steps of the church that faced the plaza, watching people arrive. Someone had brought chairs out from inside the church, and Antonio's family sat behind him. His mother smiled and waved at people she spotted in the crowd gathering before them. Being seated in a place of prominence had its responsibilities.

Antonio looked at his watch. 6:10. He nodded to Teresa as she stepped past him to visit with his mother, with the baby who'd been so sick in the crook of her arm. The child looked at him with bright eyes and a toothless grin.

Most of the people had come as families and had brought baskets or bags of food. Many had dressed up. Little girls wore frilly dresses and lacy socks; little boys wore collared shirts. It touched Antonio that his neighbors were honoring him in this way. He was sure they didn't understand exactly why he had called them together. They knew only that a father feared for the life of his son.

Antonio glanced behind him. A chair had been added, and Teresa sat next to his mother.

Antonio saw Lorenzo, the man who made and sold *churros* every Friday and Saturday night, roll his cart up to the far side of the plaza. Antonio's stomach growled at the thought of the hot doughy cylinders rolled in sugar and cinnamon. He hadn't eaten since breakfast.

Señor Cardoza, who had let the children ride his burro on Sunday afternoons when Antonio was a boy, walked up the steps and shook Antonio's hand. Behind him was *señora* Salazar, who had shared the milk from her cow with his family many times over the years. She approached Antonio shyly and, after asking permission, spoke a blessing over him. A stream of people came, some he recognized, some he didn't, but all seemed to know his son was gravely ill and wanted to hear how they could help.

And he wanted to tell them. But how could he explain peripheral blood stem cell transplantation to them? He had thought of nothing else since he and Filipo had returned from Guadalajara. He even tried to talk about it with Filipo, who nodded his head and waited for Antonio to finish, then

186

quietly said, "If you give your blood to someone else, you might not have enough for yourself."

Antonio watched as the plaza filled, but instead of the excitement he thought he would feel, he found himself fighting a growing sense of panic. Everything was riding on what he was going to say. The Banorte account—$350,000. Money borrowed from Regalo Grande. The extraordinary effort that the lab director had put forth, with numerous calls to Dr. Dorak and Dr. Cohen, and even finding a sister lab to help with the testing. Angelica left alone at home shouldering the entire burden of Anica and Manuel's care. The loss of income from his business while he was gone. All of it done with the expectation that he would be able to find a large number of volunteers to be tested, and if a match was found, bring that person to the United States to save Manuel's life.

Doubt snaked through his stomach and up his throat. For the first time, it occurred to him he might fail. His hands felt clammy.

Maybe it wasn't necessary that everyone understand the whole process. Dr. Cohen had said that the chances were small that a match would be found. Why worry about anything beyond a blood sample? If there was a match, he could worry about it then.

Dr. Montoya's voice echoed in his mind, *ethical considerations*. He'd said the people should not be pressured. It had to be each person's choice, made of their own free will. He called it "an informed decision." But Manuel's life was hanging in the balance. Wasn't that more important?

Suddenly something occurred to him. Why hadn't he thought of it before?

Whoever matched would be going to America. That's what he could tell them. That's how he could start his talk. Downplay the details and point out that this could be one way to get to the United States legally. It was true. He had to get a visa for the donor. They respected Antonio and viewed him as a wealthy and important man. They would volunteer with no questions asked, hoping it would lead them to America. They'd probably think they might be able to find a way to stay and work. He wouldn't tell them that, but if they thought it . . .

The plaza was full. He was going to have to get started. Antonio turned around to look at his family sitting behind him. As he did, his gaze passed across the open church doors, which drew his eye and gave him an unobstructed view of the altar and the statue of Jesus on the cross.

His heart began to pound and he felt shaky. The image sparked the memory of the prayer he had prayed on his knees that morning, after talking to Angelica. One father to another Father.

He dropped his head to his chest.

He couldn't do it. It would be wrong.

The church bells began to ring. It was seven o'clock.

He turned and faced the plaza. His eyes swept the crowd. As he tried to think of what to say, a persistent thought pricked in the back of his mind like a fiery dart. . . . Maybe he *should* go ahead and say whatever he needed to, so they would volunteer.

He pushed the thought away. He couldn't do it.

As the seventh ring of the bell faded, Antonio saw someone waving at him from the base of the church steps.

Ricardo. Black grease smears on his face and hands. He must have come from working on his brother-in-law's car.

His brother-in-law's car.

"There isn't a man around here, young or old who doesn't know how to fix a car. Even some of the women know how."

188

Suddenly, Antonio knew exactly what he was going to say. The obvious simplicity of the idea made him wonder why he had been blind to it. He began to formulate his speech. . . . *You wouldn't put a car engine into a truck, they wouldn't match. . . . Every car is made a certain way and needs certain parts to make it run.*

The idea was perfectly tailored to the people before him. Why hadn't he thought of it sooner? How had it come to him now?

Cirocco vaguely listened to the bells of a nearby cathedral ringing in the seventh hour as he moved along the sidewalk. His mind was on the bus he'd seen that morning driving by the Hospital Metropolitano. It was black and white with big yellow letters. Club Guadalajara. That was the sports club outside the city, where all the famous soccer teams practiced. He and Diego had talked about it many times. Diego said he'd driven by it once right after it was built, and that it was behind guarded gates.

Cirocco had watched the bus pass by, then turn and go behind the hospital. Wondering if a famous soccer player had been injured and was being brought in, he wheeled his board around to the back of the building. But the bus stopped for only a moment, picked up some people, then moved on.

He'd played soccer as a boy. As he pushed himself along the sidewalk, the memory awakened something deep within him. . . . *His feet pounding through the grass, eye on the ball, a touch, a jog, now running, now looking, his mother cheering. Joy.* He set his palm down on something sharp and snapped his hand back in pain. Stopping, he examined the cut, then wiped his hand on his pants and continued down the sidewalk.

Diego. He hadn't seen him since the accident, though each time Cirocco passed the corner where he used to turn to go to the food stand, it stirred a longing for the man's friendship. The bus sighting would have provided a topic of conversation for days.

Cirocco slowed the board down. It had been another good day at the Hospital Metropolitano. He ran his hand over the bumpy bulge in his front pocket. Actually, he'd done better than he ever had on the streets he'd left. Maybe he could save up the money to replace what Diego had given him. Then the man would not think him a fool for not defending himself, or worse, pity him. He would tell Diego he decided to wait to go to America until he had more money saved. Diego would nod and think him wise. They could be friends again.

He brought the board to a stop at the corner. He looked down the street toward San Juan de Dios. His stomach growled. They could be friends again.

12

Antonio stepped out of the lab and stood on the busy city sidewalk. It had been two weeks, and no one had matched. Not his mother, or his brothers, or his sisters. Nor any of the 632 people tested so far. He shoved his hands in his pockets and began to walk.

The lab had told him in the beginning they could not report directly to him. If a match were found, they would be contacting Dr. Dorak and the laboratory in California. But through the days he'd spent at Laboratorio Centro, he began to ask Dr. Montoya from time to time, "Do you think you'll be calling Dr. Dorak today?" And the doctor began to answer him, "I'm sure you're the first one Dr. Dorak will call if I do." And so the exchange let him know there was no news. Today it had been no different.

Still, the outpouring of goodwill and concern from his friends and neighbors had exceeded his wildest expectations. Word had even spread to nearby villages and there was no shortage of volunteers. But the life-saving blood was not among them.

One of his sisters had carried the same rare haplotype he

did, but without the rest of the match it was meaningless. Somehow that news had seemed more foreboding than finding no match at all.

As he approached the park, he crossed the street, then walked across the grass and sat down beneath a tree. Angelica would be waiting for his call. He hadn't spoken to her since Friday.

On Friday she'd given him some very good news. Dr. Dorak had ordered another biopsy prior to starting the second round of chemo, and it showed Manuel was responding to his treatment. That development was a huge relief and renewed Antonio's optimism. Until he'd arrived at the lab this morning and inquired about the exact number of tests that were done. Hundreds and hundreds and still no match.

He opened his cell phone, took a deep breath, and dialed. Angelica answered on the first ring.

"Good morning, Angel." He braced himself, anticipating her next words.

"Any news?"

Antonio leaned against the tree. "Not yet."

The phone was silent, condemning him.

"Antonio, I'm getting scared. I'm praising God that the biopsy showed Manuel's blast count coming down. But if his cancer goes into remission when this round is finished, we're going to only have the time it lasts to do the transplant."

"I know, Angel. There are lots of people here willing to test, and I will keep bringing them to the lab as long as the money lasts." If only he could do more. "Did you get in touch with my dad in Texas?"

"Yes, Dr. Dorak is arranging for him to test there. Isn't there anything you can do about finding Ines and her son?"

"There are over thirteen million people living in Mexico City." He tried to keep the frustration from his voice. But

Angelica asked him about Ines every time they talked. "How is everything else? How are Anica and the Mighty Warriors doing?"

Angelica's voice brightened. "We had our first meeting last Thursday. I sent Jack O'Hare a detailed letter citing specific court cases, and I guess he consulted with whoever he consults with. On Wednesday we got the approval. About twenty kids came."

Antonio smiled. This was the Angelica he'd married. "And what did you do at the meeting?"

"The kids made cards and they picked a Bible verse to memorize."

"What was it?"

"Romans 8:28."

Antonio was familiar with the verse. . . . *And we know that all things work together for good to those who love God . . .*

He continued, "How are your mom and dad?"

"Between helping me and keeping the ranch up for showings, they're busier than they want to be."

Antonio hadn't wanted to ask her about the sale of the ranch because he knew it was a subject that still upset her. And during his conversations with Benito about Banorte, he'd not wanted to ask because it was really none of his business. Still, the huge amount of money being spent on the testing was something he thought about often. And beyond that, what would happen when the money ran out?

They spoke for a few more minutes, then, mindful of the cost, they said good-bye.

Antonio sat silently. Angelica was distancing herself from him. Isolating herself. He could feel it. It was in the tone of her voice, asking questions she already knew the answers to, omitting things that would keep them connected, like details of her day-to-day life in his absence. This was how his wife handled extreme stress. He'd gone through it with her during Manuel's first illness. He stood, his heart heavy. He needed to do more. Maybe he would ask the bank manager if he would consider donating blood.

As Antonio walked back to the lab, he looked at the faces of the people around him, wondering if one of them had the life-saving blood. Was it the short woman in front of him with the baby on her back . . . the young man walking toward him, moustache trimmed, starched white shirt under a suit coat . . . the beggar looking in the trash?

Only God knew.

Mark Dorak hoped his words gave some comfort to Angelica.

"I won't take any more of your time, Doctor." Angelica rose. "It was just that after talking to my husband this morning . . . I don't know, I mean they've tested hundreds of people. I just thought maybe you could give me some perspective." She gave him a tired smile. "And you have. Thank you."

He'd seen the scenario a hundred times before. The drawn face, the carefully chosen words. When it was a husband and wife, the man usually did the talking, abandoning all pretenses, defaulting to his most basic instincts, to protect his wife. Somehow believing that by asking the questions he made it easier for her to hear the answers.

A woman alone was hard to watch. Wanting to be strong, but not made for it. Mother's love, visceral and raw, rendering her helpless. Trying to ask her questions in a reasoned and measured tone while her eyes begged him to say her child would be all right, wanting him to validate her hope.

194

He watched Angelica leave the room. Then got up, closed his office door, and slowly walked to the window. She'd asked him about tissue typing, and he explained it again. Then she asked him about how the National Marrow Donor Program processed the requests they received, and he went over that once more. Then she asked about the testing in Mexico. He lowered his eyes. She asked everything except what she really wanted to know. Would a match be found for her son? And at an even deeper level, had God forsaken them?

His gaze drifted to the mountains in the distance. He walked a fine line regarding his responsibilities in caring for his patients and their families. He felt God had put a call on his life to do this work and he sought God's guidance in deep prayer each morning. Yet there was an ethical line between doctor and patient that he could not cross. Not all patients wanted to be held up in prayer, though this was clearly not the case with the Perez family.

He'd observed Angelica in Manuel's hospital room, holding his hand, singing to him, praying over him. The gifted young woman seemed not only to endure the situation but to embrace it with quiet dignity, and it touched him deeply. But since her husband had been gone, she seemed to change. Not only had she lost weight, she seemed to be drawing inward, as though looking for the strength that had sustained her, but not finding it. He had seen it happen before. In a very real way the cancer had spread, it had metastasized into doubt that now threatened her faith.

He knew her pain. He'd been with Jeremiah on his long downward spiral, when his short, boxy fingers let go of his mother's hand for the last time. His almond-shaped eyes open, observing death as he had life, innocent, accepting. It seemed so unfair. He was a child and had done nothing to cause his illness. And doubly so because he had Down syndrome.

Yet it was through that journey Mark learned God's ways were mysterious and unfathomable to the mind of man, but perfect and self-evident to accomplish His purposes. Mark was more committed now than he had ever been to walking the long, dark road of pediatric leukemia with his patients and their frightened, anxious families.

Dr. Dorak looked beyond the mountains to the endless blue canopy that arched above them . . . a reflection from a crystal sea.

"For with You is the fountain of life; in Your light shall we see light."

Antonio waved good-bye to Filipo and got in his car. He hadn't been able to shake the anxious feeling that had settled over him while he was talking to Angelica earlier in the day. He started the car and headed toward his mother's house. As he passed the cemetery, he glanced to the backseat. His Bible was still there from when he'd stopped to visit Maclovia's gravesite that first day. When he reached the grove of trees near his mother's house, he parked, picked up his Bible, and got out. Then he walked down to the river.

He hiked along the riverbank until he came to a stretch where the water pooled among the rocks. Finding a flat spot under the nearby trees, he sat beside the still waters. The early afternoon sun angled through the leafy branches, and a light breeze played in the grasses around him. He set his Bible in his lap and rested his elbows on his knees.

He had to do more. His family was depending on him. The testing would continue for another few weeks, and God willing, a match would be found. But if not, then what?

His gaze drifted to the river. Staring vacantly, he searched his mind for ideas, a direction to go. Anything.

His eyes refocused as a bird swooped down in front of him, landing a few feet away. It grubbed in the rich earth beneath the tree, snapping up a morsel here and there.

Antonio watched, a thoughtful smile curving his mouth. "You don't worry, do you? God gives you what you need when you need it."

The bird tilted its head back and forth, observing him with a bright, beady eye.

Then it flew away.

He picked up his Bible and opened it.

Angelica had said that she and Anica were memorizing Romans 8:28. Angelica probably already knew the verse by heart. He turned to it in his Bible.

"And we know that all things work together for good to those who love God, to those who are the called according to His purpose."

Antonio laid the Bible down. He frowned as he considered the promise within the verse. Really nothing had worked together for good. Manuel's recovery from AML had not lasted. The national registry had not yielded a donor. No one in his family had matched, nor had anyone in his community.

This troubled him greatly. He knew God's Word was truth and God kept all His promises. Therefore, the problem must lie with Antonio.

He looked at the verse again. *To those who love God.* Did he love God . . . really love God?

Maybe this was the problem. He began to search his heart, seriously reflecting on his feelings about God, his actions toward Him.

He'd learned of God early in his life. His mother and

197

Maclovia had taught him about the Creator. Life seemed so simple then. They trusted Him to provide what they needed. And He had.

Antonio knew nothing of God's rules and penalties until after he married Angelica and learned to read. He used the Bible to help him practice his reading. In fact, he recalled that Jesus said, "If you love Me, keep My commandments."

Keep My commandments.

Had he?

Antonio began to silently recite the Ten Commandments. They were one of the first parts of the Bible he'd committed to memory.

He'd put no other gods before God. He'd never taken the name of the Lord in vain. He didn't believe he'd even thought such a thing. He'd honored his father and mother. He'd never committed murder or . . . adultery. He felt heat in his cheeks.

He'd never stolen anything or coveted anything. . . . His heart started to pound.

Yes he had.

He had coveted the life in America. And because of that, he had broken the law.

But he'd asked God's forgiveness for that long ago, and had bowed before God in repentance, staying there until he felt released. He would never forget that moment. It felt as if a weight were lifted from his shoulders. God would not punish him now. He was forgiven.

Antonio continued to think about the meaning of keeping God's commandments, and though he was able to identify some areas where he'd faltered, he knew in his heart that he had tried to please God. And he believed in his heart he did love Him.

Antonio picked up his Bible and read the verse again.

"And we know that all things work together for good to those who love God, to those who are the called according to His purpose." This time he noticed there was a little mark next to the word "purpose." He looked at the bottom of the page for the comment. "Purpose, the Greek word 'prothesis' meaning a setting forth. The word suggests a deliberate plan, an advance plan, a design."

God's purpose . . . His plan . . . His design. What exactly was God's plan?

Antonio stood and began to walk along the river's edge. Whatever God had in mind was for his and his family's best good, of that much he was sure. That was the nature of God.

He had definitely felt God's leading to come to Mexico. It had only been lately, when the days dragged by and no match was found, that he began to doubt. And then this morning on the phone with Angelica, he sensed she was beginning to lose hope. That had troubled him deeply. He clenched his jaw. He was the spiritual head of his house. It was his responsibility to be strong. He needed to stay partnered with God and keep the faith. Nothing was impossible.

A match would be found. Somewhere. Maybe one of the people yet to be tested . . . maybe his father . . . or Ines . . . or her son.

He stopped. He was going to look for Ines. Someone had to know something about what had happened to her. Why she had moved. Exactly where she had moved.

He turned around and strode to the car.

He would go to Santa Sophia.

Benito watched as Sandi Greer lifted a stack of documents from her briefcase. The attractive, middle-aged woman was the broker and owner of Associated Brokers and Company. He'd chosen her to list the ranch because of her reputation for handling high-end properties in the area. She closed her briefcase, pulled her chair closer to the desk, and smiled at him. "I think this is something we can work with. They've offered the full price of three million five hundred thousand dollars."

Benito leaned back in his chair and folded his arms. "Let's hear about it."

"A Town and Country Realty agent, Stacy Carson, brought me the offer. She said these people are moving back here from northern Idaho. They'd moved up there to be close to their only daughter and grandchildren, but the winters are just too hard and they're moving back."

"Have they sold their house?"

"Not yet. My understanding is that it's on the market, but it's valued far less than this home. They're selling some other properties they own to make this move. That's why they're asking you to carry a first trust deed. A seventy percent loan, interest only, for a year."

Benito pursed his lips. He'd planned on being cashed out so he could pay off the existing first loan on the house and the second loan he'd put on it for the testing in Mexico. That would still leave some for a substantial amount of his outstanding debts and a down payment on another home. He pulled his calculator in front of him and entered the figures. After the loans and commissions there'd be enough left for a down payment on another home, but that was all. Although the first trust deed would give him an income of about $150,000 a year. He'd been selling assets over the past several years to keep things going, so the income would be a welcome change. Still, taxes would have to be paid on it. "Carrying that loan is not my first choice. I would much rather have a straight sale and be cashed out. Then I'd have a good down payment on something else and still be able to make investments that would give a better return."

"I agree. But when I listed the property I understood you to say that you were very motivated. I thought this might be something you'd want to consider."

Sandi Greer's manner was professional and her presentation of the offer made him feel like it did have potential. "How long of an escrow do they want?"

"They'd like to wait until their house in Idaho sells and closes."

Benito dropped his hands to the desk and leaned forward. "So you're saying I'd be taking my property off the market while they try to get their house sold?"

"It's up to you."

"This house hasn't been on the market that long, and this is the first offer. I say let's wait."

Sandi thought for a moment. "There is one other strategy to consider."

Benito waited for her to continue.

"You could counter this offer, accepting the terms, but reserving the right to continue to show the property. If an offer with a faster, cleaner close comes in, you can notify these people. At that point they would have to perform or cancel. On the other hand, if nothing better comes in, you still have them on the back burner and if their house in Idaho sells, they'll close on this. That gives you two chances to sell."

Benito sat back in his chair and steepled his fingers under his chin. He really didn't want to carry that big note. He needed cash. "I'll give them two weeks to get something going on the house in Idaho. If they don't have an offer up there by then, we can talk about extending."

The reality that he could end up with the ranch sold and

201

his equity tied up in a trust deed, leaving him little cash to work with, suddenly hit him. His stomach churned. He shouldn't have waited so long to put the ranch on the market, but he'd hoped his stock investments would come back, he'd hoped interest rates would rise and he would be able to get a better return on the other investments he had . . . he'd hoped he wouldn't have to sell the ranch. But he did have to sell it and the clock was ticking on his financial obligations.

"Draw a counter offer."

Sandi pulled a pad of forms from her briefcase. "I'll need your wife's signature."

"I have her power of attorney. She's never bothered herself with our finances."

Sandi glanced around the well-appointed office. Her gaze returned to him. "I'll need a copy of the power of attorney for my file."

"I'll get a copy for you."

Gen didn't need to know the details of the sale. He'd sheltered her from the ups and downs of their finances for their entire married life. He weathered the crash of the stock market in the nineties, the financial crisis caused by the FDA's refusal to approve his drug Thrombexx, and the termination of his career as a heart surgeon after the car accident. And he would get through this.

He released a deep sigh. But never before had he had so little cash to work with and so few options available to get it. If this was the deal he ended up having to take, and a lump sum of money were needed for any reason, it wouldn't be possible for him to come up with it.

Sandi Greer's voice broke into his thoughts. "Sign here."

13

IT WAS MIDMORNING by the time Antonio turned off the highway toward the scattered village of Santa Sophia. He hadn't been to the town in almost thirteen years, just before he'd left for America. He'd always gone without his parents' knowledge, walking through the hills and fields to the little town to visit Ines, and then that last time to tell her he was leaving. But he didn't find her that day, only her son, Cirocco, staying with a neighbor.

As the potholes deepened on the rutted dirt road that connected the sparsely populated area to the main highway, Antonio resigned himself to the fact that the rest of the trip was going to have to be made on foot. He drove the car onto a level spot well off the road and turned it off. Then he got out of the car and locked it.

When he returned to the road, he scanned the area. There was no one in sight. He began to walk west, just another *campesino* on his way to or from somewhere. His thoughts turned to finding his sister.

Coming to the place he'd last seen her seemed like a logical starting point. Still, finding the general area was easy; finding the exact location she'd lived was another matter entirely. It had been over thirteen years since he'd last been to Santa Sophia, and in the past he walked south from Santa Cruz, finding his way by using familiar landmarks of ridges and agave fields that all locals recognized. He continued to look right and left, hoping to find something familiar from which he could get his bearings, the curve of a hilltop, an outcropping of rocks. He remembered there had been a large cluster of mango trees near the small house where she lived.

And what about her son, Cirocco? Ricardo said he'd seen Ines, alone. That could mean Cirocco had stayed in Mexico City, or . . . Antonio caught his breath. Maybe Cirocco still lived here. He was certainly old enough by now. Maybe his mother had come to Guadalajara to visit him! Antonio quickened his pace.

He'd walked perhaps twenty minutes when he spotted a travel trailer tucked beneath the branches of a tree. He angled off the road and headed toward it. As he approached, the front door opened and an old man, unshaven and wearing a T-shirt, staggered out. *"Hola!"*

"Good morning." Antonio answered him in Spanish. "I'm hoping you can help me."

The old man's eyes wandered lazily over Antonio's work shirt and worn, dusty pants. "What you want?"

"I'm looking for my sister, Ines Perez. She used to live here."

The man snapped his head back. "I've lived in this trailer for twenty years, my friend."

"I meant she used to live here. In Santa Sophia."

The man's face relaxed. "Oh. Well, you're not actually in Santa Sophia." He pointed west. "It's 'bout four kilometers that way."

"As I remember there were a lot of mango trees near her house. Is there a place like that near here?"

"Lots of mango trees?" The man's lazy eyes drifted closed.

Antonio waited.

"Yeah. But it's on the other side of Santa Sophia."

That sounded right. He'd never actually gone into the town when he visited Ines because he came through the hills, away from the highway. That would have meant he was on the far west side of town. He tipped his head to the man, turned, and left. He jogged back toward the dirt road, a wave of excitement rippling through his stomach.

Antonio jogged, then walked, as he hurried toward Santa Sophia. He saw a few people as he made his way, a father and son herding a flock of goats, a young boy on a bicycle, two women carrying buckets of water. Each time he spoke to them, he asked if they had known Ines Perez or her son, Cirocco. Each time he was answered with a curious stare or a polite shake of the head.

It was after noon when Antonio finally began to see some modest structures clustered together, their appearance marking the presence of a town. There seemed to be no center like there was in Santa Cruz, just the dirt road he'd been traveling on, but now bordered by a long row of open buildings. A marketplace of sorts.

He walked along, looking at the tables, seeing everything from produce to car parts. At each table he stopped and asked about his sister and nephew. No one knew anything. The answers were cautious, guarded. This was expected, he was a stranger in town asking questions about one of their own. At one point he bought a gearshift knob to create some common ground with the vendor. But the man had nothing to tell him, other than to confirm there was a large grove of

205

mango trees "that way," past the broken fence post, then right up a hill, and waving his hand back and forth added, "in there."

Antonio continued west, glancing at the surrounding terrain, but somehow it just didn't look right. The hills were familiar but different. It had a disorienting effect on him. As if he were in the wrong place.

A young man with a big sack balanced across his shoulders cut across the road in front of him. Antonio called to him. *"Señor."*

The young man stopped. *"Sí?"*

"Is this Santa Sophia?"

The man grinned. *"Sí."*

Antonio guessed the boy to be about eighteen or twenty. "My name is Antonio Perez." He extended his hand.

The young Mexican shook it. "I am Che Salinas."

"Do you know Cirocco Perez?"

The young man's warm smile disappeared and his face darkened. "No." The single word ending the conversation.

Antonio felt a chill.

The boy turned on his heel, leaving Antonio staring after him.

For a moment Antonio considered following the young man, wanting to question him about his strange behavior. But the thought made him uneasy. He didn't know the people of Santa Sophia or their secrets. If he could find the neighbor who had cared for Cirocco, she might be able to help him. If not, he would make it his business to find Che Salinas later. He picked up his pace, continuing west, looking for the broken fence post.

After a few more questions of passersby, Antonio found the piece of broken wood with wire dangling from it, and the hill that had been mentioned. He continued on, looking for familiar terrain.

It still didn't feel right.

He gazed into the distance. Mangos! And a low, open shed.

He began to run, his eyes searching through the trees, hoping he would find someone who knew something about Ines or Cirocco.

As he approached, he saw the shed was a home. There was a water barrel by the door and several chairs scattered about. He looked through the opening, into the hut. Seeing no one, he stepped back. Just then a woman emerged from around the corner of the house.

Her eyes widened and her hand flew to her lips.

"I'm sorry I frightened you." Antonio clasped his hands behind his back and took a step away from her.

She was stunningly beautiful. Her long black hair and flawless dark skin quietly deferred to her deep blue eyes. He took another step back.

She dropped her hand to her side. "Who are you?"

"I am Antonio Perez."

"Why have you come to my father's house?"

"I am looking for my sister and her son. Is your father here?"

She hesitated. "He is nearby . . . with my brothers."

Antonio took another step back.

"Who is your sister?" she asked, caution in her voice.

"Ines Perez."

The young woman furrowed her brow. "I don't know her. Why would she be here?"

"I think she used to live near here." He looked across the hills. "I'm just not sure. It's been a long time, but I must find her." He continued with his story and told of Manuel's desperate situation, though he skipped the details of Ines's past.

The girl waved him toward the front of the shack and pointed to a plastic chair. "Here, please sit." She moved past him. "She lived near here?"

"Yes, I think so." He shifted in his chair. "I remember the mango trees near her house. Thick like this. They were within a kilometer of her house." He glanced at the countryside. "But somehow this doesn't seem like the same place."

"My father sells the mangoes when they ripen. He planted many of these trees."

Antonio's heart sank. This was not the right place.

The young woman continued. "There was another place where many mangoes grew. More than this. But lightning started a fire there and burned up everything. That was many years ago."

Antonio straightened in his chair. "How many years ago?"

She thought a moment. "I was very young then. Maybe ten years ago, maybe more."

Antonio stood. "Where exactly is it from here?"

The girl explained that if he went back down to the dirt road and continued until the road ended, then looked straight ahead, he could see the spot. Now, just low brush and few trees.

This had to be the answer. He thanked her profusely and headed back to the dirt road. Feeling a sense of urgency, he started to jog again. It was already midafternoon. Once he reached the general area, he didn't want to be searching on foot after dark for the house. People had been shot for less.

When Antonio reached the end of the road, he looked straight ahead. No longer looking for clusters of trees, he focused only on the ridgeline. A sense of vague familiarity passed through him. He started up the rise, continually looking north toward Santa Cruz del Astillero, hoping something familiar would catch his eye.

And it did.

An outcropping of rock and black shale.

For the first time since he'd arrived, he knew where he was. He quickly made his way to the rocks.

As he recalled, he was about fifteen minutes from the house where Ines had lived. He could find it now, though he would have to pay close attention to where he was walking. Things still looked very different than he remembered.

It suddenly occurred to him, what if the houses had burned too? He clenched his jaw. If they had, he would deal with it then. He pushed the thought away, turning his attention to the ground just ahead of him. Before long he began to scan the land below him hoping to glimpse a rooftop.

He angled down the hillside just as he had years before. Mango trees. He could see a few scattered below him. Memories sparked within him as he quickened his pace.

Down from what must have been the fire line, he saw some rooftops. He stopped, dusted himself off, and continued to the first house. Hurrying past it, he saw the hovel Ines had lived in, and next to it the hut where he'd last seen Cirocco. Antonio walked toward the neighbor's house. A woman was putting wood on a fire. She rose as he neared. Her eyes narrowed slightly, but she didn't speak.

Antonio spoke first. "Good afternoon, *señora.*"

It was her. She'd aged dramatically, but it was definitely the woman who'd been caring for Cirocco the last time he came to see Ines. "I am Antonio Perez, Ines's brother." She continued to observe him. "Cirocco's uncle."

As recognition dawned in her eyes, her face broke into a

smile. She stepped toward him. "Welcome. Welcome." She wiped her hands on her skirt, then hugged him. "Come, sit down." She pointed to the ground next to the fire. "Let me get you some coffee." She rushed into the cabin.

Antonio brushed away some bark and pebbles with his foot and sat.

There were two pots sitting on a large, flat rock on the edge of the fire. He could smell *mole*. His stomach growled.

The woman returned with a ceramic cup, cradled proudly in her palms. She dipped it into the smaller of the pots, wiped the bottom of it with the edge of her skirt, and handed it to Antonio. She sat beside him. "How is Ines? I always hoped she would come and visit me after she left."

Antonio took a sip of the strong coffee. "I was hoping she had stayed in touch with you and you could tell me how to reach her. Not long after I was here, I went to the United States. I haven't seen her since then."

The woman clucked her tongue. "No, she never came back here after Cirocco died."

Antonio looked at her, stunned. "What?"

"She never came back after he died."

"What are you talking about?"

The woman looked puzzled.

"When did he die?"

Concern darkened her face. "I'm sorry. I assumed you knew."

"I know of nothing after that day I last saw you."

As the hour passed, the woman told Antonio what she knew. How Cirocco had been tormented by the local children because of his mother's "job." And tragically, one day, trying to escape them, he had fallen down a canyon. When he was found, he was near death. Somehow Ines managed to get Cirocco to the Cruz Roja in Guadalajara, where he died.

Antonio's stomach churned and his heart ached. The fortunes of darkness had followed Ines from Santa Cruz to Santa Sophia. "Where is he buried?"

She shrugged. "I don't know. Ines never returned."

"How did you find out Cirocco died?"

"After months passed and Ines didn't come back, it became known. After that, it was seldom spoken of." She frowned. "Many felt, though it was a terrible thing, it was an accident. It was better that the other children involved forget."

Anger flashed through Antonio. Just forget about a child who lost his life, and the mother who loved him? No wonder Ines had moved to Mexico City. Perhaps when Ricardo had seen her, she had been in Guadalajara visiting Cirocco's grave. Had he had a proper burial? Did his grave even have a marker?

"I'm sorry." The woman rested her hand on Antonio's shoulder.

Antonio looked at her. "I am sorry for you too. I know you loved Ines and Cirocco."

Her eyes reddened.

Antonio sat in silence trying to sort through his anger, sadness, confusion . . . guilt. He should have tried to stay in touch with Ines on those few visits he'd made home over the years.

He took a steadying breath. Although he couldn't change the past, he could do what he should have done a long time ago. He was going to tell his mother and father that he stayed in touch with Ines after she'd left home. That no matter what had happened, she was their daughter, and it was their grandson who died. Then he would go to the Cruz Roja and find out what had been done with the body. There must be records of some kind.

He stood. "My car is a long way from here and I want

to get back to it before it gets dark." He reached down and helped the *señora* up. His stomach growled.

"Wait one minute." She hurried into the hut.

He looked around him, suddenly conscious of the extreme poverty the old woman lived in. The two battered pots, the rocky ground where they had been sitting, the chipped cup she'd served him coffee in.

This had been *his* life when he was a boy.

He took out his wallet, removed several bills, and folded them into a tight wad. He reached down, poured out the coffee he'd been drinking, put the money in the cup, and set the cup upside down where he'd been sitting. He straightened.

The woman emerged from the doorway holding a cloth folded into a sack. "Take this with you." She placed it in his hands.

He could feel the tortillas in it. "Thank you." He put his arm around her and kissed her cheek. "Thank you very much." He turned and started down the slope.

When he reached the bottom, he looked over his shoulder. The old woman was still waving. He raised his hand in a final good-bye.

As he retraced his steps to the car, he mulled over all he had learned about Ines and her son, trying to piece things together. Ricardo had seen her at the Cruz Roja just the week before Antonio arrived from the United States. She was visiting with a woman that Ricardo thought might have been a missionary. Why would she go to the hospital so many years after her son's death? Ricardo said she told him she lived in Mexico City, so it didn't make sense that she was seeing a doctor at Cruz Roja. Was the missionary her friend? There had to be a connection somehow.

He raised his eyes toward the evening sky. "*Dios*, with Your help, I will find her."

By the time Antonio reached Santa Cruz, he'd decided he would talk to his mother about Ines this very night. But there was always a steady stream of people in and out of her house and he wanted to talk to her privately. He parked the car and made his way through the trees.

He could hear voices and the squeals of children as he approached the front yard. Two of his sisters-in-law, one brother, and several nieces and nephews were gathered around the kitchen visiting while his mother cooked.

They all ate together, and he managed to sidestep their questions about what he had been doing all day, knowing they assumed he'd been in Guadalajara at the lab. As the night deepened, they said good-bye and returned to their own homes. By the time he was alone with his mother, the moon had risen high overhead.

His mother turned her chair toward him and looked directly in his eyes. "Where were you today, *mi hijo*?"

Antonio felt himself blush. It didn't matter what his age, she was still his mother. And somehow she sensed that there was something on his mind.

He stood, reached over, and took her hand. "Come. Let's take a walk."

As they strolled toward the river, Antonio spoke to her about how much he loved and esteemed her and his father, how much he was enjoying this time with her, and how much he appreciated the sacrifices they had made all their lives to provide for him.

When they reached the water's edge, he cleared a spot, and they sat down.

"Mother." He hesitated. *Dios, soften my words.* "I want to talk to you about something." *Please prepare her heart to hear me.*

She nodded and folded her hands in her lap.

"I want to talk to you about Ines."

His mother turned her face to the river.

An evening breeze suddenly swept through the trees around them.

He continued. "When she lived in Santa Sophia, before I left for America, I went to see her . . . more than once." He hesitated. "She had a son, Cirocco."

The shadowy moonlight revealed his mother staring straight ahead.

"I went to Santa Sophia today, hoping to find them, to ask them to have their blood tested."

Though his eyes were on her, he did not perceive any reaction.

"But I learned that she has had much trouble in her life and she has moved to Mexico City. I want to try and find her."

Still, his mother did not speak.

"I want to ask you to forgive her, so I can feel free to find her and bring her here, back to her home." He took his mother's hand in his. "Can you forgive her, Mother?"

His mother turned to him, tears streaming down her face. "Oh, my son, how many days I have thought of her, how many times I have forgiven her, how often I have prayed God would bring her back to me."

Antonio brushed the tears from his mother's face.

"And now to learn God heard my prayer and even more, she has a precious son. Yes, yes, find them and bring them here." His mother's face was a mixture of joy and sorrow.

If only they had talked before, years before.

Antonio blinked rapidly and pulled his mother to his chest. He raised his chin and closed his eyes, steeling himself. He had to tell her about Cirocco. Even now the seeds of love for her grandson were rooting in her heart. "Cirocco died."

His mother began to tremble.

There by the river Antonio endured his mother's pain as she wept for the years of separation from her daughter and for the grandson she would never know.

Things had not worked out. They had not "worked together for good." The door was closing on finding a match for Manuel. Deep down Antonio knew his blood relatives were the greatest hope he had of finding the exact genetic match.

He held his mother, stroking her hair as she sobbed. She would forever grieve over the lost opportunity to heal the broken relationship with her daughter and her grandson. Ines could not be found in Mexico City, one person among thirteen million. It was impossible.

And not even God could bring Cirocco back to life.

14

ANTONIO ROLLED DOWN the car window to let in some fresh air. He hadn't slept well. He drifted between thoughts, then dark dreams of Dr. Montoya saying no match had been found, *señor* Perez saying the Banorte account was empty, and crowds of faceless people walking through the streets of Mexico City.

Then, while eating breakfast, his mother had announced she wanted to come with him to the Cruz Roja. He rolled his eyes. After taking her to the lab for her blood test, he'd sworn he would never drive with her in Guadalajara again. And today he needed to go to the lab and the bank, and he didn't know where his inquiries at the hospital would take him. The thought of her riding in the car as he made his way through Guadalajara made him cringe.

He hated arguing with his mother, and in this case he couldn't tell her his reasons for not wanting to take her. It would be disrespectful to say he had enough to worry about without her acting like a frightened old woman who'd never been to the city. He released a deep sigh. He hated arguing with his mother because—he looked at her in the rearview mirror—he never won.

"It seems like you are driving fast." His mother strained forward.

"I'm driving the speed limit."

He'd made her sit in the backseat, then strapped her in with a seat belt. She was a small woman, not even five feet tall, and he thought it would keep her from constantly grabbing his arm and leaning over him to look at the speedometer. As long as she didn't think of putting the top of the seat belt behind her back, she wouldn't be able to see the dashboard or reach him while he was driving.

He glanced in the rearview mirror again. God bless her. She clearly considered this a special outing and had dressed for it. A black scarf draped over her hair, and a red sweater beneath an orange cardigan. The sleeves of the cardigan were too long, so she'd rolled them back to her wrists. She had on a green skirt and beige knee socks. Instead of sandals she was wearing black plastic shoes. Antonio had never seen them before. He guessed they were kept in a box, in a plastic bag, stored somewhere in the house known only to her. He and Angelica had given her things over the years, only to find she never used or wore anything they sent. The gifts were carefully preserved in plastic or boxes, only to be brought out and displayed when she had company from the village. He grinned.

His stop at the lab was brief. He double-parked and convinced his mother to stay in the car and wait. Dr. Montoya's cordial greeting told him there was no news. He then picked up the bill for the previous week's testing and left.

As he drove to the bank, he heard only two stifled screams and one loudly whispered prayer for protection from the backseat. When they arrived his mother insisted she accompany him in, even though he explained he wouldn't take more than a minute to authorize the payment of the lab

217

bill. Having become familiar with the seat belt latch while he was in the lab, she jumped from the car before he turned off the engine. Oblivious to the van that swerved to miss her opening door.

Dios, watch over her. Please.

Antonio held the bank door open for her. She strode through it and stopped, waiting for him. Then she slipped her arm through his, threw her shoulders back, and surveyed the bank lobby.

He walked with her to a row of chairs. "Mother, could you wait here? I'll just be a moment."

She looked at him with surprise. "I want to meet this man. You said his last name was Perez, and he told you he might be a relative."

Antonio drew a deep breath. "That's true." He hesitated a moment. The lobby of the bank was no place to argue with his mother. He turned and walked with her on his arm, to *señor* Perez's office.

"Good morning." The bank manager rose.

Antonio shook his hand and introduced his mother.

He took the bill from the laboratory out of his pocket and handed it to the manager. "Please transfer funds in this amount to the Laboratorio Centro account."

The manager nodded and took the piece of paper.

Antonio turned and stepped toward the door. His mother didn't follow. Looking over his shoulder he saw her gaze was fastened on *señor* Perez, her brows knitted and her mouth in a firm line. "Mother?"

She looked at Antonio.

"So good to meet you, *señora*." The manager smiled at her politely.

She nodded, stepped toward Antonio, and slipped her arm through his as they exited the building.

After helping his mother into her seat belt, Antonio got in the car, started the engine, and pulled out onto the street, heading for Cruz Roja.

"He's a relative," came the announcement from the backseat. "He has your grandfather's nose."

"You think so?"

"I'm certain. I watched him closely and not only that, but he sits like your uncle Eduardo."

Antonio kept his eyes on the road and his thoughts to himself. He'd heard the whispers about Eduardo's effeminate mannerisms over the years.

"That's your father's side of the family."

Antonio looked at her in the rearview mirror. There wasn't any reason to think that the well-positioned banker, *señor* Perez, was related to them . . . other than the fact that it would raise one's status considerably in the fields near Guadalajara. But there was no point in arguing with his mother. "It's possible. Who knows?"

An imperturbable assurance settled on her face. "*I* know." She lifted her chin. "Wait until I tell Celerina at the Mini-super that the manager of that important bank thinks he's our relative, and I met him and it's true." She didn't appear to notice the horse and cart that cut Antonio off as he turned down the block to Cruz Roja.

Antonio found a place to park near the hospital. As he guided his mother along the busy sidewalk to the building, the sobering reality of the task before him came into focus. Had Cirocco died while in the hospital? What kind of records would be available? Would any of the doctors or nurses who had cared for him so many years ago still be working there? It had been only a few weeks since Ricardo had seen Ines talking to a woman with a Bible. Who was that woman and what did she know?

219

Antonio and his mother walked through the front door of the hospital, and Antonio stepped up to the counter. He explained to the woman behind the counter that he was inquiring about the death of Cirocco Perez. He gave her as much detail as he could. She asked him to take a seat and said she would try to find someone who could help him.

An hour passed. No one spoke to him. He approached the counter and asked again if someone would be able to help him. The woman was polite, but indicated that she had left a message for one of the administrators. And since Antonio did not have an appointment, it would take time to find someone to help him. Antonio sat back down.

People came and went as Antonio and his mother sat in the lobby of the hospital. Each time he saw a missionary or any woman with a Bible he would ask her if she knew Ines Perez. No one did.

Though he was directly in the line of vision of the woman behind the counter, she made no eye contact with him. He thought about speaking to her again, but he didn't want to annoy her. Another hour passed.

Finally, a man appeared and called his name. He stood and walked toward him. "I am Antonio Perez."

He shook the man's hand.

The man adjusted his glasses. "How can I help you?"

Antonio repeated what he had told the woman behind the counter.

The man looked as if he were hearing it for the first time. "Wait here, I'll try to find someone to help you."

"*Señor*, I've been waiting for hours. Do you keep the records here? Will someone be able to find them today or should I come back?"

"Please, wait here, *Señor* Perez, I will try to find out." The man turned and left.

Antonio slowly walked back to his seat and slumped into it.

His mother patted his leg. "Son, you are so impatient." She grinned at him. "Americano."

Antonio folded his arms across his chest. It was true. He had forgotten how slowly things could move in Mexico. But that didn't make it right. Why couldn't things work out for once? The time wasted here could have been better spent talking to people in his town about donating blood. Finding where Cirocco was buried wouldn't necessarily bring him any closer to finding Ines.

He looked at his mother, sitting with her hands in her lap, waiting to find out what had happened to her grandson. Antonio huffed a sigh. This was the right thing to do. Another hour passed.

People started to move through the lobby. Apparently, it was a shift change. Antonio watched as people filed out and in through the front doors. He looked at each one, trying to discern which ones might be missionaries.

He leaned forward in his chair. A familiar face.

Sister Maria!

Antonio jumped from his chair and ran toward her. "Sister. Sister."

Several women looked his way.

"Sister Maria."

Reaching her side he grabbed her arm. "I am Antonio. Remember me? We spoke a few weeks ago. I asked you about Cirocco and my sister Ines."

They stepped out of the way of the people moving through the lobby.

Recognition flashed across her face. "Of course. Yes. How are you?" She began to shake her head. "Surely, this is of God."

Antonio drew back. "What do you mean?"

A smile broke across her face. "After you left, I couldn't stop thinking about that unusual name Cirocco. I thought if someone had worked with him, they might remember that name. So I began to ask around." She put her hand on Antonio's arm. "A woman who has volunteered here for years took care of him. I told her you were his uncle and you were looking for him and your sister. She said she knows Ines. In fact, Ines was here recently and—"

Antonio couldn't believe what he was hearing. "What's her name?"

"Well, I have always known her as Rose, but I think that's a nickname. I—"

"Is she here now?"

"I don't know. I—"

"I need to speak to her right away. Cirocco is dead. I just learned of this yesterday and I want to find out—"

The sister's hands flew to her lips. "Dead! How terrible." Her eyes began to tear. "I don't think she knows anything about it. She said she'd seen him only once since that boy pushed him and caused the accident."

Anger surged through Antonio. He had not understood that one of the children in Santa Sophia had pushed Cirocco, only that they had chased him. No wonder no one in the town spoke of it. He was glad his mother could not hear what was being said. "I'm sure my sister would have told this Rose about his death. How can I find the woman?"

Sister Maria took a tissue from her sleeve and dabbed her eyes. "She usually volunteers here in the afternoon and evenings. I'll go look for her." She hesitated a moment. "I'll leave it to you to break the news to her."

Antonio took his seat by his mother.

"Who was that?"

He debated how much to tell her. He didn't want to get her hopes up by telling her he thought this Rose woman had been in touch with Ines. "Her name is Sister Maria. I came here before, when I was trying to find a lab to do the testing, and asked her about Ines and Cirocco. She said there is someone who works here who might be able to help us."

His mother's face brightened.

About twenty minutes had passed when Antonio saw Sister Maria hurrying toward him. A large woman, carrying a Bible, was close behind.

"This is Rose."

Antonio tipped his head toward her. "I am Antonio Perez and this is my mother, Elena."

The two women shared a smile.

"I was hoping you could tell me how to get in touch with my sister, Ines."

Rose grabbed his hand in both of hers. "How wonderful to meet you. Yes, Ines was here just a few weeks ago." Rose's eyes filled with compassion. "She came to see Cirocco."

Relief flooded through Antonio. "I thought maybe she was here to visit him." He dropped his voice. "We want to visit him too. We were hoping you could tell us where he's buried?"

Rose's face froze. "What do you mean buried?"

"I learned yesterday that he died."

"Died where?"

Antonio heard a note of panic in the woman's voice. Surely Ines had told the woman who had helped care for him. "Died here. He was in a terrible accident. Or I thought it was an accident." He looked at Sister Maria.

Rose's eyes narrowed and she took a step back from Antonio. "No, it wasn't an accident. He was pushed. And he was badly cut up and bruised but he wasn't killed."

223

"His neighbor in Santa Sophia told me he died."

"Santa Sophia!" Rose paused. "It's been at least twelve years since he lived in Santa Sophia."

Antonio nodded. "I know. That was the last time I saw him."

Relief flooded across Rose's face. "There is some kind of a misunderstanding. Cirocco was at my house only a few weeks ago. He was in an accident on the street. I wanted him to stay with me until he recovered, but he wouldn't." She shook her head. "He's always been independent like that."

Antonio turned to his mother. Tears were streaming down her face. He pulled her close to him. Fighting tears himself, he turned to Rose. "He's alive?"

"I'm sure he's alive." A trace of concern passed through her eyes. "I haven't seen him lately, but that's not unusual."

Antonio suddenly felt weak in the knees. "You said Ines visited him a few weeks ago."

"She comes to see him a few times a year." Rose hesitated, looking around the lobby. "Do you think we could take a walk to the park? It isn't far."

Sister Maria excused herself. Rose, Antonio, and his mother walked to the nearby park. Along the way, Rose told them of the accident that took Cirocco's leg and the second accident that happened when he was leaving for the United States. As they passed the public toilets, she explained how he lived on his own and made enough money to get by, refusing help from anyone.

When they reached the park, they sat on the low wall that surrounded the fountain.

Cirocco's story was wrenching. It would almost have been easier if Rose had confirmed that Cirocco had died from the fall in Santa Sophia years before. "Why would he choose to live on the streets instead of with his mother?"

Rose looked at him, not speaking. For a moment, he thought she wasn't going to answer his question.

"It's a very sad situation all the way around." She seemed to be weighing her words. She glanced at his mother.

Antonio took his mother's hand. "You can speak freely to us. We know about Ines." He patted his mother's hand. "And we love her."

Rose set her Bible in her lap and wiped her eyes.

"Cirocco and Ines were shunned by the people of Santa Sophia. The children there taunted and ridiculed Cirocco because of his mother's 'work.' It got out of hand and eventually led to the tragic accident that almost cost him his life. Ines has never forgiven herself. She still tells me, if it weren't for her, he would have his leg." Rose stroked the cover of her Bible. "I helped care for him after his surgery." She smiled. "He's the one who first called me Rose, Mama Rose. . . . He was a fighter. God had blessed him with a strong will to live. But as he grew stronger, and it became clear that he would survive, Ines started to separate herself from him. Eventually she met a man and moved to Mexico City with him. That hurt Cirocco deeply. She visited Cirocco once after that. Her lover was with her." Again, Rose seemed to consider her words. "He made it clear he didn't want Cirocco with them."

Antonio caught his breath. "In front of Cirocco?"

Rose nodded. "Ines told me it was the worst moment of her life. Cirocco told her he hated her. They have never spoken since that day."

"I thought you said that Ines comes to see him a few times a year."

"She does, but he's never known about it. She watches him from a distance, and it tears her up every time. Over the past few years I've asked him from time to time if he'd like to see

225

his mother—I did that this last time she was here—but he always says no or changes the subject. She helped pack the lunch I sent with him that day he left for the United States. But of course, he had no idea. She went back to Mexico City right after that."

"Can you get in touch with her?"

"I do have an address, but over the years, it seems sometimes she gets my letters and sometimes she doesn't."

Antonio tried to absorb everything he'd heard. This situation must not be allowed to continue. Ines and her son should be reunited, and if the man in her life didn't like it . . . he would deal with that if it became necessary. He looked at Rose. "Will you write to her and tell her we are looking for her. That we love her and want her to come home?"

"Of course."

"Where is Cirocco now?"

"I wish I knew. I haven't seen him since I bandaged him up. That was weeks ago."

Antonio drew a deep breath. "Let me tell you what brought me here."

He told Rose about Manuel and how his illness had been the reason for the trip and how Antonio regretted that it had taken Manuel's illness to get him involved in finding Ines and Cirocco. "I should have tried to find her years ago."

He looked Rose in the eyes. "Thank you for all you've done for them. I see why Cirocco called you Mama Rose. You *were* like a mother to him." He smiled at her. "I feel like you're part of our family . . . Mama Rose."

His mother nodded. "Thank you, Sister."

Mama Rose put her hand on Antonio's leg. "The important thing is you're here now. We'll find him."

Antonio pursed his lips. "Where does he usually work?"

"He used to work at the public toilets around here and

San Juan de Dios. But when he didn't come to see me and let me check his bandages, I went out looking for him. I've been to all of the places that he used to go to. The first place I went was to Diego's. He's a very nice man who has helped Cirocco out from time to time. But he didn't even know Cirocco hadn't gone to the United States."

"When was the last time you looked for him?"

"It's been about two weeks. As I said before, it's not unusual for him to stay away for months."

Antonio stood. "Then let's start by going back and re-checking every place you've been."

"We'll start at Diego's tomorrow." Mama Rose looked at Antonio and his mother. "Can we pray first?" She reached for their hands.

Antonio bowed his head as Mama Rose prayed.

"Jesus, I thank You for bringing us together. I ask You to walk with us as we look for Cirocco. We know You work all things together for good . . ."

Antonio raised his head a few inches and glanced at Mama Rose.

Did He? Things had not worked out for Cirocco or Ines. No match had been found for Manuel. The money at the bank was dwindling. Antonio's stomach churned.

And time was running out.

Cirocco rubbed his arms. They ached from holding up his cup for hours on end. His early success at Hospital Metropolitano had waned, and he was thinking of moving on. But first, he wanted to talk to Diego about it.

When Cirocco had first come to Diego's food stand after the accident, Diego listened to Cirocco's story and told him there was no need to pay the money back. That Cirocco should keep the money he earned and continue to save for the trip.

Diego's wife changed Cirocco's bandages and even brought him clean clothes and a shoe to wear on his foot.

They spent hours talking about the bus from Club Guadalajara, and why it would be at the hospital almost every day. How some famous player must be getting treatment. How they probably were on to something no one else in the world knew.

Diego wiped his counter one last time. "Well, *amigo*, I should go home. Sleep here tonight if you like."

Cirocco smiled and gave a quick half nod.

"Diego, I'm thinking of going farther north to look for work."

Diego pushed his stool under the counter. "Why don't you give it a little more time?"

Would a little more time make any difference? He didn't want to be a burden to Diego. He didn't want to burden anybody.

Diego looked at Cirocco and smiled. "I'd miss you. And who'd sample my food and who'd keep an eye on that Club Guadalajara bus?"

Cirocco drew a deep breath. Maybe Diego was right. He thought for a few moments. It wouldn't hurt to wait another couple of weeks.

"Okay. I'll wait. But on one condition. You promise that if Mama Rose comes looking for me again, you'll tell her you haven't seen me. That I moved north."

15

ANGELICA WINCED AS she listened to her father giving Dr. Dorak a critique of Manuel's response to chemo. She studied the kind doctor's face as he stood patiently waiting for her father to finish.

The muffled sound of her phone caught her ear. She raced for her purse and pulled out the phone.

"Hello." Angelica caught her breath. It was Antonio.

She listened as he told her about meeting Mama Rose, and all he had learned.

"Dad."

Her father turned to her.

"Antonio thinks they've found Cirocco."

Her father stepped beside her.

"Will you talk to him today?" She tilted the phone from her ear so her father could hear her husband.

Antonio explained the plan he and Mama Rose had made.

She knitted her brows. "Well, it shouldn't take long to find him if the woman's a good friend. Call me the minute you know something."

"I love you, Angelica."

Benito jumped away from the phone and turned toward Dr. Dorak.

Angelica grinned at her father's retreating back. She lowered her voice. "I love you so much. I hope you'll be home soon."

After saying good-bye, Angelica slowly shut the phone and faced the two men. Her father was examining his thumbnail.

"There's been over a thousand people tested and no one has matched, so I'm trying not to get my hopes up. But Tex and I were just praying about that this morning. And . . . And I just feel this is answered prayer."

"Grrrampa?"

"It's good news, Angelica." Benito quickly stepped to Manuel's bedside. "Hey, buddy, I was just about to leave." He brushed Manuel's hair from his forehead. "I'll see you tonight."

"My crown."

Benito looked at Angelica. "It's over there on the table at the end of the couch."

Angelica picked up a worn paper crown. Smoothing the band into a circle she brought it to him. "Where'd you find this, Dad?"

"It's been up at the house. Manuel left it there the last time he was at the ranch. He's been mentioning it, so your mother and I hunted for it yesterday."

Angelica held the crown out in front of her, pricking the points to make them stand up. "It seems like a hundred years ago that Anica made this for him." She handed it to her father.

Benito bent over, lifted Manuel's head from the pillow,

and gently eased on the crown. "There you go, my man." He stepped away and gave a deep bow. "At your service."

Manuel lifted his thin arms. "Hug Manuel."

Benito carefully worked his arms around the child, holding the little boy to his chest with a tenderness that was reserved for his grandson. Her father closed his eyes, his face a mixture of concern, longing, and sadness. It was obvious to Angelica, of the two, her father was receiving the greater blessing. She pressed her lips together.

"Grandpa will be back soon. I've got to get home." He stood and looked at Angelica. "We're having a showing today."

"No news from the people in Idaho?"

"Not yet, and I'd just as soon get another offer with more cash down so your mother and I can start looking for a place to move. As it stands, we're considering renting for a while."

"It'll work out, Dad."

Her father moved toward the door. "Wish you could come by. Pasha paces up and down the fence every afternoon. He remembers when you used to come up a few times a week."

"I'll try, Dad. If we get through with dinner early, maybe Tex, Anica, and I can come up later." She took the chair next to Manuel.

"Hope you do, it would please your mother." He turned toward the doctor. "Good day." He left the room.

Angelica slowly shook her head. "It's hard to believe there was a time that getting up to the ranch to ride my horse was my biggest worry."

"Is the ranch nearby?"

"It's in the Sonoma Mountains. Twenty-five acres. I grew up there. It has a nice horse facility."

231

"How much is it?"

Angelica tilted her head. "Over three million. You interested?"

Dr. Dorak grimaced. "I guess not." He chuckled. "I've been looking for property in this area to open a camp for kids with cancer."

"You've mentioned that before." Angelica took Manuel's hand in hers. "Regalo Grande is the most beautiful place in the world. There's a live stream that runs through huge old oaks. And you have a view to eternity from just about every place on the ranch. There's an arena and barn and guest quarters and acres of rolling hills. You could easily have a hundred kids there."

The sweetness of the memories touched her deeply. She paused.

"I grew up there. I was pretty much raised by a wonderful man named Poppy. Well, that wasn't his real name, but that's what I called him. He was an awesome Christian. He seemed to have a direct line to God. I still miss him." She became aware of the empty ache in her heart that always returned when she thought of Poppy. "When the ranch is gone, that connection to him will be gone too. That's something I have no control over. My father feels he needs to sell the ranch and it's his to sell."

She turned her thoughts back to the present. "I wish it would work for you. Nothing would please me more than to see a bunch of kids enjoying themselves there." Her eyes reddened. She pulled Manuel's hand to her lips and kissed his fingers.

Why did things have to be this way? Why couldn't she make things better? Would Manuel ever run and play on the ranch again? She squeezed her eyes shut, letting her lips linger on Manuel's precious fingers.

As she settled back in her chair, Dr. Dorak gently changed the subject. "So Antonio found his sister and nephew?"

"Well, not exactly, but he found a woman named Rose who has known them for years and he thinks now he'll be able to find them. Since we found out his dad didn't match, they're the only relatives left to be tested." She leaned forward in her chair. "Do you think the chances are good?"

Dr. Dorak pursed his lips. "The best chance would be of a relative or someone in the community having one parent whose origins were out of the area Antonio grew up in. According to what Antonio has said, most of those people have lived there for generations. But don't forget, the National Marrow Donor Program is still looking. They may find a match."

Angelica turned back to Manuel. Seeing he'd fallen asleep, she carefully removed his crown. "I can't imagine Manuel asking my father for this." Turning it back and forth, she looked at it, her eyes narrowing slightly. "You know, Doctor, I just remembered, that afternoon we drove down here to meet you. Manuel asked for this crown then. He was sitting in the backseat and he said, 'Crown.'" She paused. "When I asked him if he'd left the crown at Grandma's, instead of answering, he pointed at the seat next to him. It was odd. He waved his hand as if he were trying to reach for something. But of course, the crown was at my parents'."

Dr. Dorak looked at her as if he wanted to say something, then seemed to reconsider. "We'll keep good thoughts about Antonio's sister and nephew." He turned to leave the room.

Angelica stood. "Dr. Dorak, was there something you wanted to tell me?"

He paused and looked at her. His eyes drifted to the paper crown. Finally, he spoke. "No, nothing."

She frowned as he turned and left the room. Did he know something he wasn't telling her?

Cirocco scooted out from under Diego's food stand. He tilted his head back, squinting at the sun. For the first time in a long time he'd slept well, and he was surprised to find morning was well under way. People were moving along the sidewalks on their way to work. He grabbed Diego's stool and pulled himself up. Resting his arms on the counter he surveyed the street, taking in details, wanting to remember this place that had been the closest thing to a home he'd had since he left Mama Rose.

He'd decided he wasn't going to wait a few days, as Diego had suggested. He was going north. Diego should be arriving soon and he'd tell him of his decision, then be on his way.

Cirocco scanned the street, lingering in the moment, enjoying the beautiful morning and the promise of a fresh start that lay before him. His eyes widened.

It was her.

Pretty pink lips, straight white teeth, and the young boy skipping in front of her. A smile spread across his face. Maybe she would look his way and smile. He started to raise his hand.

His smile froze. His heart began to pound.

Just a few steps behind her was the boy who had pushed him into the street and stolen his money. Cirocco dropped behind the stand.

"Hey, stump boy."

He pushed himself onto his board.

Dread seized him. He began to sweat.

He craned his neck around the corner of the stand. The boy was running toward him. Dropping his hands to the

234

ground, Cirocco shoved himself away from the stand and began rolling down the sidewalk. Glancing over his shoulder he saw the boy close behind and beyond the boy, in a blurred freeze-frame, the face of a young woman, pink lips parted, looking in his direction.

"Hey. Got any money?"

Cirocco could hear the boy's feet pounding behind him.

Cirocco twisted away from a stinging slap on the side of his head.

He arched his back, trying to keep his head down as he pumped against the sidewalk.

As his tormentor grabbed Cirocco's shirt collar, the boy's fingers scratched Cirocco's neck.

Cirocco felt his board slowing. He reached around behind his back and caught the torn cuff of one of the boy's pant legs. Giving it a pull, he felt his shirt collar being released. The boy stumbled.

The board began to wobble. Cirocco struggled frantically to keep it from tipping.

He could see the intersection in the distance. Morning traffic was heavy.

Thoughts darted through his mind like the tongue of a snake. He couldn't win. He was worthless. No one wanted · him. Then quick, crisp, clear . . . there was a way out.

He pressed his hands to the pavement, pumping hard, the boy's feet pounding behind him.

The intersection was directly in front of him. He gave himself a final thrust forward as the curb approached. Then, he sat up straight, closed his eyes, and raised his hands into the air, surrendering.

Vignettes of his life appeared to him. Present in his mind collectively, yet individually. A series of still shots. Each understood with emotion rather than thought . . . his mother's face, a spring day in his childhood, the sound of his feet as he ran. A lifetime compressed into a single moment . . . crystal clear, then fading . . . Mama Rose holding him, praying for him.

A shadow of light. The scent of roses.

Set me free.

He heard his name being called. "Cirocco. Cirocco."

A vice gripped him around his chest.

His eyes flew open as he found himself pulled up, standing beneath a gaze of compassion, chest to chest with a man.

The man's dark eyes, filled with concern, searched his.

Cirocco blinked in confusion. He could hear Mama Rose's voice. "Is he all right?"

Nothing fit.

A small crowd gathered around him. His tormentor was nowhere in sight.

Mama Rosa was beside him. "Thank God, you're all right." She brushed his hair away from his face.

Cirocco felt himself being lifted into the man's strong arms. He felt like a child. He'd never been held by any man.

The man's kind gaze rested on him. Then he kissed Cirocco's sweaty forehead.

A surge of emotion swept through Cirocco. He had never experienced such a loving touch.

He turned his face into the man's broad shoulder and wept.

The morning sunlight filtered into the little room through the crack between the wall and the roof. Antonio quietly raised himself from the dirt floor and squatted beside the bed. Cirocco was still sleeping.

Antonio shook his head. If he and Mama Rose had arrived

236

at Diego's food stand one minute later, he might never have had the chance to meet his nephew. Just as they turned the corner from the main street, Mama Rose joked about how it seemed as if someone were parting the traffic for them. Then she saw Cirocco careening toward them.

Antonio had stopped in the middle of the street, raced to the sidewalk, and grabbed Cirocco just as he was speeding by. Diego arrived shortly after that, and Antonio explained he was Cirocco's uncle and would be taking Cirocco to Santa Cruz del Astillero. Antonio and Mama Rose put Cirocco in the backseat of the car, and then the three of them drove to the Cruz Roja.

Though Mama Rose rescued the board from the street, Antonio asked her to try and find a pair of crutches for Cirocco since there weren't many paved streets in Santa Cruz. After she did, Antonio and Cirocco left, finally arriving home in the early afternoon.

Antonio smoothed the blanket over Cirocco's shoulders. His nephew hadn't talked much, and Antonio perceived that the boy's heart was as scarred as the stump of his leg.

When he'd called Angelica the night before to tell her they found him, her parents were in the hospital room with her. They had all rejoiced. And she gave him more good news about Manuel's progress. It wasn't until he lay down and drifted to that vague and unburdened place between waking and sleeping that he was robbed of his joy.

He lowered his eyes as the thoughts that had plagued him during the night returned to him. The only reason he had looked for Cirocco and Ines was that Manuel needed a blood stem cell transplant. Until then, their lives hadn't seemed important to him. He had gone to America years ago and made a good life for himself. It was not until Manuel's

237

life hung in the balance that he thought of looking for his sister and nephew. And he deeply regretted it.

He looked at Cirocco, studying his thin face. Even in sleep his brow was creased, his mouth turned down. No rest for him, not even in his dreams. How many people had disrespected the boy, stolen from him, used him? And now he was going to learn that even his uncle wanted something from him. His blood.

Antonio felt a weight on his shoulders. *Dios, forgive me that I did not reach out to them years ago, for their sake alone. Instead of now, only to help myself.* He felt ashamed to ask Cirocco to take the blood test.

Antonio rose, fished his razor, soap, comb, and toothbrush from his bag, and shoved them in his pockets. He turned toward the door.

"*Tío?*"

Antonio looked toward the bed. "So, you've decided to wake up?"

The boy gave him an awkward smile, as though his lips were unfamiliar with the expression.

Antonio sat on the edge of the bed and took Cirocco's hand in his. "Ready for some breakfast? I think I smell tortillas."

The boy pushed himself into a sitting position and glanced around the room.

Antonio squeezed Cirocco's hand. "Your crutches are outside." Slipping from the bed, he squatted with his back to Cirocco. "Come on." He patted his shoulders. "Put your arms around my neck, and we'll go get them. Then we'll wash up and go see what your grandmother has waiting for us."

Cirocco pulled himself onto Antonio's back and Antonio carried him to the front yard. As they emerged from the

238

house, his mother called to them from the kitchen. "Are you ready to eat?"

As they neared her, she clapped her hands. "My son and my grandson, I am twice blessed today."

"We're going to wash up. We'll be right back."

"*Tío*, give me my crutch."

Antonio laughed. "You don't weigh more than a couple of sacks of grass seed. I will carry you."

"No." Cirocco's voice was tinged with anger. "I want to take myself there."

Antonio set him down and brought him his crutches. Cirocco took only one.

Stumbling and slipping through the trees, Cirocco managed to get himself to the river.

As Antonio shaved, he watched Cirocco lower himself to a rock and then splash water on his face.

Antonio rinsed his face, then wet his hair and ran a comb through it. He stood and walked to Cirocco.

From the adolescent shadow above Cirocco's lip, Antonio guessed the boy had never used a razor. "Looks like you need a shave."

The boy eyed the razor for a moment, then gave a quick half nod of his head.

"You have to let me help you. You could cut yourself." Antonio waited for his answer.

Cirocco's eyes narrowed slightly. He looked at the razor again. "Okay."

Antonio knelt beside him and lathered Cirocco's face. With careful, gentle strokes, Antonio shaved the boy's face.

When he'd finished, Cirocco rinsed away the remaining soap, and using his crutch, got out of the river.

Antonio put his hand on his nephew's shoulder. "I need to talk to you."

Cirocco stiffened, his eyes became guarded.

Antonio moved away from the river to a flat spot. "Here, sit."

The boy hobbled to the spot and lowered himself to the ground.

Antonio searched his mind for words. Finally, he decided keeping it simple was best. "I need your forgiveness."

The lines across Cirocco's forehead deepened.

"I should have looked for you and your mother years ago. I'm sorry."

The boy's face was void of emotion, and he said nothing.

Antonio waited, hoping that Cirocco would reveal his thoughts. But as the minutes passed, Antonio realized the boy was not going to speak. Antonio rose and began to walk up the riverbank.

He had not gone far when he stopped and looked back. Cirocco was still sitting on the rock.

Their eyes met. Moments passed.

Cirocco lifted his arms toward Antonio.

Antonio walked slowly back to him. Then he turned and squatted, his back to Cirocco.

The boy wrapped his arms around Antonio's neck. As Antonio stood, Cirocco wrapped his leg around Antonio's waist.

Antonio began to climb the bank.

Thank You, Dios.

Cirocco could not believe he was riding on the big black-and-white bus that went to Club Guadalajara.

While they were eating breakfast his uncle had said he was going to Guadalajara, and Cirocco asked if he could come. When his uncle had driven to Santa Cruz and parked next to the bus, Cirocco was stunned. He learned that this wasn't the bus the players used, but the one that carried the workers from Santa Cruz to the club every day. And now it was taking his uncle and some other people to a hospital, or something like that. His uncle didn't explain it exactly. He just said it was work he had to do. Cirocco assumed it must be Hospital Metropolitano because he'd seen the bus there so many times.

Cirocco looked at the driver in front of him. Filipo was his name. The man had told him he saw the soccer players at Club Guadalajara almost every day. And then Filipo said maybe Cirocco could come with him one morning on his run to the club.

Cirocco pressed his head back into the seat and dropped his arms to his sides. He couldn't believe it.

He looked across the aisle at his uncle. This was a good man. A very good man. And important too. After breakfast Antonio had changed his clothes. The shirt was quite fine. It was knit and instead of a row of buttons down the front it had only a short opening at the neck with three buttons. You pulled the shirt over your head. He'd seen them before on the streets of Guadalajara, but always from the ground looking up. He never actually touched one.

He smoothed his hand across his chest. Now he was wearing one.

He observed that Antonio buttoned only one of the buttons on the front of the shirt. Cirocco quickly unbuttoned all but one of his. Then he drew a deep breath and straightened, turning to the window beside his seat. From his high vantage point, he looked down at the cars on the road next to the bus as they neared the heart of the city.

Thoughts of the day before played across Cirocco's mind.

He had been stunned when his uncle asked Cirocco to forgive him. Antonio had said, "I need your forgiveness." *Need*. Why would someone *need* forgiveness? Especially from him. He was not his uncle's responsibility. Still, when his uncle said it, Cirocco couldn't deny it touched him. And it frightened him. He felt that by responding he was allowing Antonio to cross a line somehow. A line Cirocco had drawn around himself to establish a safe place, where no one could hurt him. But then he remembered Antonio carrying him to the car. It was safe to let Antonio in.

As he glanced at his uncle again, he felt something in his heart. Something he didn't understand.

The bus stopped in front of a building, and the passengers filed out onto the sidewalk. Cirocco hopped down the steps of the bus behind his uncle, then using his crutch, he followed the others into the building.

His uncle immediately went into an office with a man, and a nurse called someone from the group.

Cirocco took a seat with the other people who'd come on the bus. He still didn't know exactly what his uncle's business was. He spoke to the woman next to him. "Why are you here?"

The woman folded her hands in her lap. "Antonio's son is very sick, and I am going to see if I can help him."

Antonio had spoken of his family during the short time Cirocco had been with him and said his little boy was in the hospital in the United States. But Cirocco didn't really understand all that Antonio said about it. English words sometimes got mixed in. Cirocco knew only that it troubled his uncle deeply. And that troubled Cirocco. "What is wrong with his son?"

"He is dying."

Cirocco's heart started to pound. "Dying?" His uncle

242

hadn't told him anything like that. His uncle was a man of courage to carry such sadness without showing it.

The woman explained that the little boy needed new blood and that the people who worked here could take a sample of a person's blood and test it and find out if it matched the little boy's. If it did, that person would be able to help him get well.

Cirocco clenched his fist. "I want them to test my blood."

The woman shrugged. "I don't know. You'll have to talk to the nurse."

Cirocco rose and hobbled to the counter. "I want you to test my blood."

She smiled at him. "Are you next?"

He swallowed hard. "Yes."

Cirocco followed the woman into a small room where she asked him questions and he answered them. Then a second woman poked him with a needle. After his blood was drawn, the first woman gave him a paper with a number on it and told him how he would be notified if he was the match. He put the paper in his pants pocket and returned to the chair he'd been sitting on.

As he sat watching the people go forward and into the little room, he hoped they did not match. He wanted to be the one to match.

As he waited for his uncle, he reflected on all that had happened over the past two days. His *tío* had been so good to him. How could he ever repay the man?

A grin pulled at his lips. He would not tell his uncle that they had taken some of his blood.

He would wait and surprise him.

16

Antonio snapped the cell phone shut and jumped off the rock, the excitement in Angelica's voice still ringing in his ears. Manuel's condition was continuing to improve and Dr. Dorak thought Manuel would soon be well enough for the transplant.

Angelica had also said that the news of Manuel's improvement had given the Mighty Warriors Club quite a reputation around school and new children joined at each meeting. Everyone wanted to be part of Manuel's recovery—except the principal who, it was rumored, was quite upset about the whole thing. And Benito had told him that their senator's office was working with the American Consulate in Guadalajara to be sure that a visa could be obtained if a donor were found. Antonio had managed to be upbeat and optimistic. But nothing could have been further from the truth. He hadn't told Angelica that Cirocco hadn't agreed to be tested. That he tried to talk to the boy several times about Manuel and how sick he was and how finding a blood match could save his life. But every time he brought the subject up, Cirocco seemed disinterested or tried to change the subject.

Antonio finally decided it was best to drop it for the time being. Even if Cirocco were tested, it didn't mean he would match. And just as upsetting was the fact that the money in the account at Banorte was nearly gone. Most likely this would be the last week of testing.

He walked to his car. It was Monday and all the tests taken the week before would be reported this morning. He drove to town and rode with Filipo and the day's volunteers, of which there were only nine, to the lab. His thoughts were on Ines. Mama Rose had written to the address in Mexico that she'd used before. But there was no guarantee that Ines would even receive the letter. If she did, she would know Antonio was looking for her and needed her help. But if she didn't, he would have no way of knowing. How long should he stay in Mexico waiting to find out? He shook his head. Nothing seemed to be working out.

Filipo stopped the bus and opened its doors. Antonio dreaded going into the lab and hearing no match had been found. He waited as everyone got off the bus, then followed them into the building.

The director's office door was open and the director was at his desk talking on the phone. Antonio took a seat, waiting for him to hang up. Sitting with his gaze on the floor, he sorted through the troubling thoughts that presented themselves in an endless procession.

"Antonio!"

He raised his head. Dr. Montoya was standing in his office doorway.

"I didn't know you were here. I was just on the phone with Dr. Dorak and Dr. Cohen." The lab director smiled and put his forefinger to his forehead. "I think I'm going to hear your cell phone ring."

Antonio's mouth dropped open. He started to stand, then

245

sat back down. Suddenly, all the sounds around him seemed to be background noise. He couldn't focus on anything. The next thing he knew, he was shaking Dr. Montoya's hand and the doctor was shouting, "Answer your phone. Your phone is ringing."

Antonio jammed his hand in his pocket and pulled the phone out. Fumbling, he almost dropped it. He finally got it to his ear, but he couldn't hear anyone.

Dr. Montoya gently took the phone from him, turned it around, and put the earpiece on Antonio's ear.

"Antonio?"

"*Sí. Sí.*"

"I'm standing here with your wife and father-in-law. I wanted to let you know a potential matched donor has been found for Manuel."

Antonio turned in a circle, then dropped into his chair. "What will happen now?"

"After the donor is notified, Dr. Montoya will meet with the person and confirm their desire to donate. If that person agrees, then we'll do the next phase of testing. That testing will be for the presence or the past presence of infectious diseases like HIV, hepatitis C, and syphilis. We'll also need to give a complete physical exam and have a general history done. But the first step is to get the potential donor's consent. Dr. Montoya said the person gave minimal contact information."

Antonio was having trouble absorbing what he was hearing.

"Antonio?"

It was Angelica's voice. Suddenly, Antonio was overcome with emotion. He leaned forward with his elbows on his knees, still listening to his wife's excited voice. "We've really got a chance to beat this thing now." For the first time in a long time, Antonio realized he was smiling. "Manuel has been improving and the timing couldn't be better. God's timing is perfect. Praise God." Tears caught in her words.

Benito's voice replaced Angelica's. "You did it, son. I'm proud of you. As soon as you have the name of the donor, the hospital will fax a request for a temporary visa to the American Consulate so you can bring the person here. Senator Evans's office has assured me there won't be any problems."

Antonio stood. "I will take care of it. Can I talk to Manuel?"

"Daddy?"

Antonio's heart soared. Manuel's voice sounded so strong. "I sure miss you. Daddy's coming home soon to help you."

"Manuel miss Daddy."

"I love you, buddy. I'll be home soon."

Angelica took the phone. "What do they mean, minimal contact information?"

He'd picked up on that too, and knew exactly what it meant. The donor didn't have an address. Just like his mother didn't have an address. But in the beginning, Dr. Montoya told him the lab would handle contacting the donor. That Antonio was not allowed to know who the donor was until the person gave their consent. "It means they don't live in town."

"You mean like your mother?"

He could hear the excitement leave her voice. "Yes, but the lab has ways of contacting them."

"What if they can't?" Her tone had become concerned.

"Don't worry, they will."

By the time they hung up, he knew she would have no peace until the person had agreed to the donation.

247

Dr. Montoya put his hand on Antonio's shoulder. "Let's go into my office."

The lab director sat behind his desk.

Antonio sat in a chair across from him. "Exactly how will you contact the donor?"

The director looked at the file that was open on his desk. "Well, this donor didn't give an address or phone number, just the name of the nearest town. As you know, many of the volunteers didn't have addresses, but nearly all were able to give some kind of contact information, a relative, or a business. There were a handful who gave only the town name. In those cases they were told their identifying number would be posted at the plaza of their town within ten days of the day they were here. This one is Santa Cruz del Astillero and the blood was drawn last Wednesday, Thursday, or Friday."

Antonio stood. "Give me the number. I can post it today and I can stay at the plaza and ask people to help us find the person."

"Antonio, please sit down."

Antonio felt a wave of uneasiness. "Yes?"

"It's very important that you don't pressure this person. This is a decision that they must make on their own. They need to know what they're consenting to. And they have the right to say no."

"Why would someone come in here and give their blood and then not want to help Manuel? I am sure that they will be happy when they find out."

The doctor gave a slow nod. "I know it seems odd, but it happens. Sometimes people change their mind or become frightened. There can be many reasons."

Antonio sat staring at the doctor as he tried to imagine such a thing happening. "That is not going to happen, especially not in my town. I am sure of it."

The doctor handed Antonio a form with the number 1133-1027 printed in large bold type at the top. "It's going to work out."

It was all that Antonio could do not to gather everyone together and tell them to go back to the bus so he could return to Santa Cruz and post the number at the plaza. But in light of what Dr. Montoya had told him it would be best to finish whatever testing that the remaining money would allow, even though he knew the chances of finding a second match were close to zero. He kept the news to himself while he waited until the last person had his blood drawn and the entire group made the short walk to the waiting bus.

As soon as Filipo closed the bus doors and pulled away from the curb, Antonio stood and announced the good news. "But the testing today is still important. Thank you so much." He held up the form. "Here is the number: 1133-1027. I'll be posting it at the plaza. Be sure to tell everyone you know who donated last week to go check."

Excited chatter erupted on the bus and Filipo sounded the horn for three long blasts.

Antonio sat looking out the window as the bus headed back to Santa Cruz. His mind was spinning. Posting the paper at the plaza seemed too chancy. What if it blew down, what if the person came and didn't see it? Maybe he could make copies and post them all over.

Still, it would be best if he sat at the plaza. Many of the people didn't read and write. And though most would recognize the number they were given, they might not know what to do. No matter what the lab director had said, the person with the number would be far more likely not to respond because they didn't know what to do, than because they'd changed their mind. He chewed his lower lip, he knew these people. Forms and numbers were not how they communicated.

He caught his breath. Celerina's Minisuper. He would post the number there and have Celerina tell everyone who came in. By tomorrow word would have spread not only through Santa Cruz but probably beyond.

And he would sit at the plaza and watch for people. That way, if they could not read the form, he could tell them what they needed to do. That would not be pressuring. That would be helping them.

The bus hadn't come to a full stop when Antonio grabbed the lever and opened the doors.

He burst through the entrance of the Minisuper, nearly tripping over Celerina, who was sitting by the door. "We have a match!"

She clapped her hands together. "Wonderful." She stood and shouted through the store. "Someone matches Antonio's boy, Manuel."

Everyone in the store crowded around. Antonio held the form above his head, slowly turning from side to side so everyone could see it. "This is the number, 1133-1027. It belongs to someone who went in last week on Wednesday, Thursday, or Friday. I'll post it on the church door at the plaza tomorrow. Please tell everyone you know to come here for information."

"Violeta." Celerina called to her granddaughter who was working behind the counter. "Come here." The young woman came forward.

Antonio showed her the form.

Celerina tapped the big numbers on the top of the paper. "Write 1133-1027 on every receipt. Tell people to check their numbers. And put that number on a piece of paper and tape it to the front and back of our door."

"*Señor.*"

Antonio glanced over the crowd, trying to see who was speaking.

"*Señor.*" A short man, unshaven and in tattered clothes, made his way from the middle of the group of people. "I have the number."

Antonio's heart began to pound. Could it be possible?

People stepped to the side as he made his way through.

The shoeless man stopped in front of Antonio. He was gripping a soiled slip of paper. He held it up so Antonio could take it.

Antonio's hand was shaking as he looked at the number. 0634-1010.

The steel edge of disappointment cut through his stomach.

This was going to be the problem. These people just didn't understand. Dr. Montoya's words echoed through Antonio's memory. *Sometimes people change their mind or become frightened.*

Looking at the man's hopeful, upturned face, Antonio suddenly realized that this was what Dr. Montoya had been referring to. The potential donor didn't have an address. The person was probably a *campesino* from the surrounding area. It was not this man, but most likely it was someone just like him, or his wife, or his child. Had the number matched, would the man have wanted to go through all the testing? Could someone who couldn't read numbers have even understood what he was consenting to? The sobering reality of the situation became clear. The excitement of only moments before vanished.

Suddenly, Antonio realized he was glaring at the man.

He quietly drew a deep breath. "I'm sorry. That is not the

251

number. Thank you for volunteering to help." He reached for the man's hand and shook it.

Antonio straightened and looked around the store. "Thank you all for everything." He turned to Celerina. "I'll be at the plaza tomorrow if you learn of anything."

Antonio left the store, walked to his car, and headed to his mother's house. They would be excited to hear the news. He pushed away the doubts that nagged him. He needed to stay positive. Things were more hopeful than they had been. That's what he needed to think about.

Antonio pulled the car into the grove of trees. He reached across the front seat and retrieved the form with the number on it. He folded up the paper, put it in his front pocket, and got out of the car. As he started toward his mother's house, he saw Cirocco sitting beneath one of the trees in the direction of the river. He had a donkey tethered to a rope he held in his hand.

Ricardo had gotten the animal from someone on his wife's side of the family. The donkey was blind in one eye and old. He'd brought it to Cirocco a few days before and told the boy he could keep the donkey as long as he fed it. Antonio had teased Cirocco, telling him now he had wheels.

Cirocco and the little donkey were inseparable. Watching the boy pet and talk to the animal had touched Antonio. The boy continually brushed its gray coat with his fingers, picking the tiniest specks of leaves or brush from its body, speaking to it as if it were a dear friend. And the little donkey, that Ricardo had warned could be obstinate, seemed content to have Cirocco climb on its back, picking its way among the rocks, carrying Cirocco carefully around the fields. Even now, Cirocco was fully absorbed watching the donkey eat, seemingly unaware of Antonio's presence. "*Hola*, Cirocco."

Cirocco started. "I didn't see you drive in."

Antonio walked over to the boy and sat beside him. "I had some very good news today."

Cirocco's face lit up. "What happened?"

"I found out at the lab that someone who donated blood last week is a match for Manuel." Antonio took the form out of his pocket and unfolded it. "I'm going to be posting this at the plaza." He glanced at Cirocco.

Cirocco turned his face toward the donkey. "Oh."

Antonio hated to push the issue. Cirocco was again making it clear that he didn't want to discuss the subject. Antonio folded the form, took out his wallet, and tucked the paper in with his money.

Time was running out, and there was no guarantee that he would find the person with the matching number. He needed Cirocco's help. Dr. Dorak and Dr. Cohen had both said a relative was the most likely source of a match. He released a deep sigh. He might as well ask his nephew straight out. "Cirocco, would you mind being tested? I can explain to you how it works. It's kind of like when a car needs a certain part."

Cirocco looked at him with surprise. "A car?"

The look on the boy's face made Antonio realize that the young man probably knew nothing about cars.

Antonio spent the next few minutes explaining about peripheral blood stem cell transplantation in terms he thought the boy would understand. He told Cirocco how Manuel needed a certain kind of blood and how if someone had that blood and shared it with Manuel, Manuel would live. When he finished he smiled at Cirocco. "Well, what do you think? Would you be willing?"

Cirocco's face was a mixture of concern and fear. "No."

253

Cirocco lay in the bed staring at the ceiling. He could hear his uncle's steady breathing. He looked to his right, at Antonio sleeping on the floor next to the bed, his back to Cirocco.

Cirocco wiped the tears from his face. This was a good man. He closed his eyes, seeking that moment when Antonio had lifted him from the careening board and held him. He had revisited the feeling a hundred times since it had happened. No one had ever held him like that. He returned his gaze to his uncle, wanting to go to him, to lie down next to him and feel Antonio's strong arms around him again, wondering if that was how a father held a son.

But that would be wrong to do. Antonio wasn't his father, and Cirocco would be nothing but a burden to him. Just as he had been to his mother and Mama Rose. No one could ever love him. He was a cripple and a beggar. His life was worthless and always would be . . . unless he died.

His uncle had tried to talk to him several times about donating blood, and he'd delighted in ignoring him, planning how he would surprise Antonio if he was the match. The more he rehearsed the moment, the more convinced he became that he was going to be the one. He imagined how he would tell his uncle. When the time came, he would ask Antonio to invite all the family to the house for an announcement. And everyone would come. Some would probably bring friends and neighbors with them. Everyone would be wondering what the announcement was. He would be sitting in the white chair by the front door and the people would look at him, wondering what important thing he knew. Then, after a while, he would clap his hands. Everyone would be quiet and all eyes would be upon him. Then he would ask his uncle to come forward. He would tell the people what a good man his uncle was. And then he would make his announcement. Everyone would cheer and Antonio would lift him up on his big shoulders and carry him around the yard.

But this afternoon had changed everything.

Antonio had explained in detail what would happen to the person who had the matching blood. He said a tube would be put in the person's arm and his blood would go through a machine and then be put back into the person's other arm.

Cirocco had seen the machines that pumped blood. When he was in the hospital and they'd cut off his leg, the boy in the bed next to him had bled out. That's what they called it. He heard the doctors say, "He bled out before they could get him here." And they hooked up bags of blood and tried to put blood back into him. But the boy died. You couldn't do that. You couldn't put blood back into someone.

He wiped his cheeks with the back of his hand and set his jaw, angry at his cowardice. This was a worthy thing. A right thing. And he was going to do it.

He would give his own life to save Manuel.

He slowly drew a deep breath, then quietly sat up in the bed.

He'd watched Antonio put his wallet on top of his suitcase before lying down. When Antonio had sat beside him with the paper that was going to be posted at the plaza, Cirocco tried to see if the numbers were on it. But his uncle held the paper open only an instant, then put it in his wallet.

Cirocco slipped off the left side of the bed and crawled to the suitcase. He looked toward Antonio, then silently picked up the wallet and put it in his mouth. Gripping the wallet with his teeth, he crawled slowly across the floor, through the front room, and outside into the moonlight. He stood

255

and hopped to the jacaranda tree where the donkey was tied. He dropped to the ground.

He took the wallet from his mouth and opened it. He could see the folded paper to the side of a thick wedge of money. American money. Cirocco took the money out, the folded paper dropping away, into his lap.

There were several hundred-dollar bills.

A night breeze stirred the branches of the tree.

Smoothing his hand over the top bill, his eyes lingered on the stack of money.

He carefully put the money back into the wallet, then opened and closed the billfold several times, pretending he was about to pay for something. His shoulders slumped. He set the wallet down and picked up the piece of paper. He closed his eyes, remembering the number the nurse had given him. 1133-1027.

He held his breath and opened the paper.

1133-1027.

His heart began to pound. He was the match.

Instantly, everything seemed different. Seeing the number on the paper wasn't like seeing it in his imagination. The number was big and black and intimidating. It shouted a final, decisive truth. He was the match. No one else. If he told Antonio, there would be no turning back.

His eyes darted to the wallet. He could see the corner of one of the bills sticking out. That was a lot of money. It was more than enough for bus fare to America. He could go to America tonight. He cut his eyes to the donkey. The main road wasn't that far.

He put the wallet in his mouth and pushed himself up. He hopped next to the donkey and balanced against him. He took the wallet from his mouth and folded it into his chest.

He would go to America and then . . . and then . . . and then what?

As the moments passed, the stark reality that was his life came into focus. He had no future. He would always be a burden to someone. His life had been over long ago, he just hadn't seen it. He was never going to America; he was never going to get a leg; he would never have a family . . .

"Cirocco?"

It was Antonio, walking toward him from the house.

"Are you okay?"

The warm concern in his uncle's voice filled him with shame. He turned toward him. "I'm okay."

Antonio stopped a few feet from him and his eyes drifted to the wallet. The crease in his brow deepened.

"I'm the match." He spit the words out, still fearing he might swallow them. "I'm the match for Manuel." He extended the wallet toward Antonio.

His uncle stood, staring at him. "What do you mean?"

"I wanted to surprise you and I saw that you put the paper in your wallet. I took the wallet to see if I was the match . . . And I am."

"What are you talking about? You've never had your blood drawn."

Cirocco explained what he had done and how he had done it. "I want to help your son."

Antonio stepped toward him and embraced him. He could feel his uncle trembling.

"Cirocco, you will never know what this means to our family. We will never be able to repay you."

Then Antonio dropped to his knees.

Cirocco heard his uncle whispering. "Praise to You, *Dios*. Praise to You."

A twinge of anger corkscrewed in Cirocco's stomach. What

257

did God have to do with this? Cirocco had made the decision on his own. God had never done anything for him. Except take away his leg, his family, and his life.

Leaving him without hope or a future.

Angelica heard her Bible fall from the nightstand as she reached for the phone in the darkened bedroom. Instantly awake, her heart was pounding. Had something happened at the hospital?

"Hello?" Holding the phone to her ear, she struggled out of the bedcovers and dropped her feet to the floor.

"Cirocco is the match and I'm bringing him home."

Angelica sat stunned, a sea of emotions flooding through her. "Cirocco is the match? Is that what you said? Cirocco is the match?"

"I'm bringing him home as soon as everything else that is required is done."

Angelica dropped the phone. She began to shake uncontrollably. Somewhere deep in her core, a racking sob began to work its way out through silent, choking heaves. Putting her hands over her face, she surrendered to the weeks of emotions she had not permitted herself. Now unrestrained, pain and joy seemed inextricably woven together. She couldn't focus, hope and hell vying for her attention. Flashes of words and scenes from the hospital, Dr. Dorak's office, and her private thoughts cascaded over her.

Cirocco is the match.

Her husband's words cut like a blade through her, slowly displacing everything else . . . *Cirocco is the match.*

Still sobbing, Angelica slid from the bed to the floor. "Thank You. Thank You." Retrieving the phone, she put it to her ear. "Thank you. Thank you."

"It's going to be okay, Angel." Her husband's voice was husky. "Everything will be okay. I'll be home soon."

The sound of Antonio's voice began to calm her. With her eyes closed she breathed it in, letting it nourish her. He spoke of his love for Manuel and her, and God's unceasing faithfulness to them. As the moments passed, she felt her strength returning.

Slowly, she rose, turned on the light, and sat on the edge of the bed. "Why did you wait until the middle of the night to call me?"

Antonio explained how, when he'd awakened and found Cirocco was not in his bed, he went outside and saw Cirocco with the wallet. He told her he felt ashamed because his first thought had been that maybe the boy was stealing money, when actually Cirocco was trying to find out if he was the match.

"Angel, I should have looked for him before now. I knew my sister's situation. He's my flesh and blood and I should have tried to help him."

"Maybe we can help him now."

"I've been thinking about that ever since I found him. And now that he's coming home with me, I'm going to do everything in my power to help give him hope and some kind of a future."

The earnestness in her husband's voice touched Angelica. "We will. And I'll talk to my father about it too."

"I was thinking we could look into getting Cirocco a new leg. Maybe it would even be possible to get him a permanent visa."

She could hear the excitement in his voice, then the line went silent for a moment.

"Maybe he could live with us, even work for me."

"Antonio, it would be wonderful to have someone from

259

your family be part of our life. Cirocco could even take English as a Second Language classes at the community center like you did. We'll talk more about it when you get home."

They spent a few more minutes going over the life-saving news again, and then said their good-byes.

Angelica shut the phone off. She began to key in her parents' phone number, then she stopped.

Putting the phone down, she rose and walked quietly to Tex's room.

She touched Tex's shoulder and awakened her. "Tex," she whispered softly, not wanting to frighten the woman. "Antonio just called."

Tex sat up.

Angelica told Tex all that had happened. "Will you pray with me?"

"Of course."

The two women kneeled on the floor by the bed. Angelica reached for Tex's hand.

Tex prayed from her heart, thanking God for all He'd done and all He would do. Speaking out the promises of His Word and reaffirming her faith that His Word is Truth.

When she finished, Angelica waited for a moment. Everything still seemed unreal. Manuel was going to get the peripheral blood stem cell transplant he so desperately needed. She felt profoundly grateful, but words escaped her.

Finally she whispered, "Lord, I pray, that through this You will be glorified and the name of Jesus will be praised. Amen."

The two women rose and hugged. Angelica returned to her bedroom and called her father at the hospital, and her mother at home, to share her news.

By the time she finished talking to her parents she wasn't

sleepy. She picked her Bible up off the floor and climbed into bed with it. Leaning against her headboard she opened the book to the spot where she'd placed her bookmark. Isaiah 55.

Seeing the page, she realized it had been weeks since she read in bed at night. Before Manuel had gotten sick, it had been a nighttime ritual. She quickly uttered the little prayer she always said before reading. "God, show me what You have for me."

She started at a random verse. "'For My thoughts are not your thoughts, nor are your ways My ways,' says the Lord."

Her eyes narrowed slightly, creasing her brow, and she felt a little twinge of uneasiness. She frowned and flipped back into Proverbs. Again, she glanced down the page, her gaze stopping on a passage she'd marked. "Trust in the Lord with all your heart, and lean not on your own understanding."

For some reason the words did not comfort her as they always had.

She understood that a blood match had been found, and that Antonio and Cirocco would be home soon. She understood that her son was going to get well and their lives would be made right again.

She snapped the Bible shut and threw it on the nightstand.

That's what she understood.

17

THE LAST TWO weeks had been a test of faith. Waiting for the test results that Cirocco needed, to be cleared as a donor, had taken over a week. Getting Cirocco's Mexican passport had been easy. Getting his visa had been much more difficult. If it hadn't been for Senator Evans's office, they might still be waiting for it to be issued.

All the uncertainty had made booking a flight in advance impossible. The first available flight had been one to San Jose del Cabo in Baja, California, then a six-hour layover before their connecting flight to Los Angeles and then Sacramento.

"Did you hear that? That's the landing gear." Antonio spoke to the back of Cirocco's head. "We'll be setting down in San Jose del Cabo soon." The boy had had his nose pressed to the airplane window ever since the ocean had come into sight.

Everything was coming together. Manuel had improved dramatically, and Dr. Dorak had said Manuel could be prepared for the transplant as soon as the donor arrived. Angelica called it God's provision. And it was. A tiny stab of guilt pricked Antonio. He had doubted God so many times during the search for the blood match. And still, God faithfully overcame each obstacle. Now that it was over, he realized the ordeal had strengthened his faith and truly deepened his relationship with the Creator.

Antonio glanced at Cirocco. The young man had no faith in God. This troubled Antonio greatly because he knew Mama Rose had spoken to Cirocco many times about God's love, and still Cirocco hardened his heart. Several times over the past few weeks it had occurred to Antonio to talk to Cirocco about the importance of having a personal relationship with Jesus Christ, but Antonio hadn't. The time just never seemed right. Now certainly wasn't the time. The plane was landing. Antonio reached over and tousled the boy's hair. "Love you, man." And though his nephew didn't turn around, Antonio smiled. He would talk to Cirocco about Jesus when things had settled down.

The only thing Antonio had not been able to accomplish before he left was establishing contact with Ines. She answered Mama Rose's letter, but Antonio had to leave before Ines was able to return to Guadalajara. At least she knew he was looking for her. And now that he was able to reach Mama Rose through the church where she lived, he felt sure he would be reunited with Ines before long.

As the plane hit the runway, Cirocco turned toward Antonio, his face flush with excitement, his eyes wide, and his mouth forming a silent O.

The plane taxied to a stop. Antonio grinned at him. "Time to unfasten your seat belt."

After the other passengers had disembarked, the flight attendant brought Cirocco his crutch. The two men made their way through the terminal to the front of the building.

Antonio's stomach growled. "I'm starved, how about you?"

Cirocco gave a sharp half nod of his head. "I thought you'd never ask."

"First I'll call Angelica and let her know we're here and things are on schedule. Then we'll go eat."

Antonio sat down on a step and Cirocco plopped down next to him. Then Antonio took out his cell phone and entered Angelica's phone number. She answered on the first ring.

Antonio closed his eyes, savoring the sound of her voice. "Just thought I'd let you know we're here in San Juan del Cabo," he said in English. "You'd better start getting dressed for our anniversary dinner."

Angelica blew a kiss through the phone line. "I was just thinking about that. And ya know, I don't have a thing to wear."

The intonation of her voice sent heat crawling up Antonio's neck. "How is Manuel?"

Angelica laughed. "He's doing great. Remember his invisible companion?"

The one-sided chattering had started shortly after Manuel had been stricken with acute myeloid leukemia the first time. Antonio smiled. He knew that Angelica had secretly thought Manuel was talking to his angels, but the nurses said it was probably a reaction to all the medication. "Of course."

"Well, he's back. I left the room for a few minutes yesterday and when I returned, Manuel was giggling and pointing."

Manuel was giggling. *Praise You, Dios.* "Is everything else okay?"

"Everything is fine here. We're just waiting for you and Cirocco."

"Would you like to say hi to him?"

Antonio handed the phone to Cirocco, who held it gingerly between his finger and his thumb.

Cirocco nodded into the phone.

Antonio elbowed him. "Speak. You have to speak."

Cirocco nodded to Antonio.

After a moment, Cirocco handed the phone back to Antonio.

"Well, Angel, what did you say to him?"

"I just said we appreciate him so much. But you know my Spanish isn't that good. He didn't say a thing."

Antonio glanced at Cirocco. His nephew was watching a pretty girl get out of a cab. "I don't know, Angel. He just doesn't seem happy. You'd think a trip like this would be beyond his wildest dreams, but something seems to be on his mind. Still I don't feel like I should question him about it. After we get home, maybe you can help me figure it out."

"I can't wait to meet him."

They spoke for a few more minutes, Antonio telling her they would go through Immigration in Los Angeles, and then fly to Sacramento. Then he said good-bye . . . taking advantage of the fact that Cirocco couldn't understand a word of English.

After hanging up, he slapped Cirocco's leg. "We've got about six hours to kill, *amigo*." Suddenly it occurred to him, Cirocco had never been outside the Guadalajara area. In the plane, he hadn't been able to take his eyes off the ocean. "Come on, let's take a taxi to San Juan del Cabo and get something to eat. Then after that, we'll still have time to look around town."

As they left the airport, Antonio quizzed the taxi driver about where the locals ate. He didn't want to go to the tourist area.

The taxi driver took them on a twenty-minute drive and finally stopped in front of an open-air building in a poor section of town. Antonio could see a plane landing in the distance and realized the driver had taken the "scenic route" and for all the driving, they weren't far from the airport.

Antonio and Cirocco got out of the cab. As Antonio looked around, he felt very conspicuous. He had worn his best clothes, his gold cross and silver belt buckle, wanting to please Angelica when she picked them up at the airport. He'd even dressed Cirocco in a collared shirt and slacks and a brand-new cowboy boot. It suddenly occurred to him that it might be hard to get a taxi when they were ready to leave. He turned to the driver to pay him. "Could you come back in an hour?"

The man looked at his watch and nodded. "Possibly."

"I'll pay you twice the fare to take us into town if you do."

A smile broke out on the man's face. "I'll be here." He drove away.

Antonio looked at Cirocco and shrugged. "If he doesn't get a better offer, he'll be back."

The two men went into the restaurant.

They sat on a bench at one of the crooked wooden tables, and soon a young woman came to take their order.

"What would you like?"

Antonio answered. "We're pretty hungry. What do you have?"

"We will make what you like."

After some discussion the men decided on tortillas, beans, rice, and *carne asada*. Antonio warned Cirocco to fill up on the good food as Angelica seldom cooked Mexican style.

As the men talked, Antonio noticed Cirocco's eyes kept

266

looking over Antonio's shoulder. Finally, Antonio turned around to see what his nephew was looking at.

There was an old man sitting in a wheelchair by the entry to the toilets. The man was dirty and unshaven, and his hands were curled on his chest. A small gourd, a *bule*, was in his lap. The sight of the *bule* stirred long forgotten memories in Antonio, of being a child, working in the fields, and carrying the gourd filled with water.

Antonio turned back to Cirocco, whose eyes were still on the old man. "He looks hungry, should we ask him to join us?"

Antonio waited, wondering if Cirocco had heard him. But then Cirocco gave a very slight nod of his head.

Antonio rose. As he approached the man, he smelled a strong, unpleasant odor. Ignoring it, he said, "Excuse me. Could I ask you a question?"

The man looked at him.

Antonio found himself in the gaze of the most peaceful eyes he'd ever seen.

"I am eating with my nephew, would you like to join us?"

Instead of expressing surprise, the man looked toward the table where Cirocco was sitting and nodded as though responding to an invitation he'd already had time to consider. "I saw you come in."

Antonio stepped behind the wheelchair and rolled it to the head of their small table.

Antonio took his seat to the man's right. "I am Antonio and this is Cirocco. What is your name, *señor*?"

"Rico." He nodded first to Antonio, and then to Cirocco.

"What would you like to eat?"

267

"I'm not hungry or thirsty." He looked at Cirocco. His wise eyes seemed to study the boy's face.

Cirocco looked at the man with puzzled curiosity. "Won't you have something?"

"Perhaps a glass of water."

Hiding his surprise, Antonio signaled the waitress and asked her to bring the man water. She soon arrived with both the water and the food.

Antonio picked up his fork. "Do you live nearby?"

"Yes, across the street." Rico smiled, revealing a few scattered teeth. "I'm lucky to live so close to my work. God has been good to me." He took the glass of water and carefully poured some of it in the *bule*.

Cirocco glanced in the direction of the toilets. "What do you do?"

Rico's dark, placid eyes followed Cirocco's gaze. "Oh, you mean, what is my job?"

Cirocco nodded.

"I clean the toilets. I have had my job for many years." The man's voice was gentle. "For that I am grateful."

"What happened to you?"

Antonio kicked Cirocco under the table.

Rico settled back in his chair. "I was trampled by a horse many years ago." He dropped his gnarled hand to his leg. "Since then I can't walk."

Cirocco's gaze was on the man's twisted fingers.

"Later I got a disease in my joints."

There was something about Rico's manner that seemed familiar to Antonio. He closed his eyes for a moment, listening to the man's voice. There was something about him.

Cirocco winced. "Are you in pain?"

"I have been." Rico looked into the boy's eyes. "But the

268

real pain was when my wife left me and took my sons with her. She said she could not live with half a man."

Antonio glanced at Cirocco. There were tears in the boy's eyes.

Rico continued. "But I met a man and he healed my pain."

Cirocco's gaze retuned to the man's hands. "He must have been a good doctor."

Rico's gentle eyes did not leave Cirocco's face. "Yes, he was a great physician."

Moments passed. Rico seemed to be waiting for Cirocco to respond. But Cirocco said nothing. Instead he frowned and took a bite of his food.

As the men ate, the talk turned to the trip and the wonderful news about Manuel.

"So God has been good to you too." Rico placed his gnarled hands on the wheels of his chair. "Now I should get back to my job."

Antonio started to rise and help him.

"Sit. Sit. Finish your food."

Antonio and Cirocco watched the old man wheel himself to the toilets. Then they turned to their meal.

Cirocco used the last tortilla to wipe his plate clean. "He was kind of strange."

Antonio shrugged, then signaled the waitress.

The waitress brought their check and Antonio put the money on the table.

"Look, *tío*, he never did drink the water. He just put some in that *bule*."

It was true. Antonio glanced over his shoulder, looking toward the toilets. At exactly that moment Antonio realized what he had just witnessed and knew immediately that the lesson was for both of them. He looked at Cirocco. "I think the water was for you."

Cirocco frowned and tossed his head. "Now you sound as strange as he did."

"Cirocco, God comes to you where you are. He loves you." Antonio lowered his eyes. *He comes to you where you are because His followers fail Him* . . . why hadn't he talked to Cirocco about Jesus? Antonio's heart began to pound. He jumped from his chair, whirled around . . . but the man was gone.

He turned back to Cirocco.

"What's wrong, *tío*?"

Antonio slowly shook his head. "Nothing. You ready?"

Suddenly, Antonio felt time was short. He needed to talk to Cirocco about having a personal relationship with Jesus Christ. He would do it as soon as they got home. He felt a check in his spirit. Maybe he would do it on the plane.

The two men walked out of the restaurant. Antonio looked across the street, hoping that perhaps the man had gone home and was sitting by his front door. But the only building across from the restaurant was a church. He scanned the area. Seeing no one, he turned to Cirocco. "Let's look for our cab."

The two men walked up and down the street. First waiting on one corner, and then the other. But the cab didn't come. Finally, Antonio asked for directions to town and they began to walk.

Cirocco gave Antonio a lopsided grin. "Wish I had my board right now."

Antonio put his hand on Cirocco's shoulder. "I wish you did too."

Perhaps fifteen minutes had passed when an old car pulled

up next to them. There were two men in it. The passenger rolled down the window. "Where you two going?"

Antonio stopped. "Downtown."

The man smiled. "Want a ride?"

Antonio looked at the two men. Ordinarily this was something he wouldn't do. But this was Mexico, these were his people. He glanced at Cirocco. "Sure, why not."

Antonio and Cirocco climbed into the backseat, and the car took off.

Antonio looked out the car window, thinking about Angelica and the anniversary ring he would give her the day after tomorrow. *Thank You, Dios. You blessed me with extra work. If it were not for You, she would not have the ring.*

Cirocco jabbed him in the side. Antonio turned toward him.

The boy's eyes were filled with terror. A gun was resting on the back of the front seat, pointing directly at Cirocco's heart.

Angelica scanned the passengers gathering around the luggage conveyor. She tapped her foot. Antonio and Cirocco would probably be the last ones off the plane since Cirocco was disabled. She stood on her tiptoes, looking at each person walking toward the baggage claim. She couldn't wait to surprise Antonio with the news that Manuel was doing so well he'd been released from the hospital and everyone was waiting at Regalo Grande to welcome the two men home. The belt started moving and luggage began to appear.

As the stream of arriving passengers began to thin, she walked in the direction the people were coming from, looking at each face. But the familiar face of her tall, handsome husband was not among them.

She rechecked the flight number posted at the baggage claim, then dug in her purse for her cell phone. She flipped it open. No missed calls, no voice mail.

Maybe they would come to the baggage claim a different way since Cirocco couldn't come down the stairs. She positioned herself so she could watch the circling luggage and keep an eye on the concourse. People retrieved their bags and left. Eventually she was the only person remaining.

She checked her cell phone for the tenth time. Nothing. Why wouldn't he have called her if he wasn't going to be on the plane? Fighting a rising sense of panic, she walked to a row of chairs and took a seat. Knotting her hands under her chin, she began to go over in her mind everything he had said when he called her from San Jose del Cabo. As she thought, she continued to scan the area. Suddenly, in the distance she saw someone pushing a wheelchair. They were coming toward her. Right toward her.

She leapt to her feet. It was them. *Thank You, God, thank You.* She began to run toward the figures. As she approached she slowed. The person in the wheelchair was large and the man pushing the chair was very thin. She stopped.

It wasn't Antonio.

With that momentary hope snatched from her, the reality of the situation seemed magnified. They had not arrived on the plane. And they had not called. That was the thing that confused her the most. She walked back to where she'd been sitting.

There had to be a reasonable explanation. She sat down and took her phone out of her purse again. As she fingered it, she remembered once when she and Antonio had been traveling out of state, her mother had called her and left a message but the voice mail symbol hadn't come up on her screen. It wasn't until her mother finally reached them and told them, that Angelica was able to retrieve the message by calling into her voice mail.

Of course. That had to be it. Antonio had left a message on her phone but it hadn't registered on her screen. She dialed her own number and punched in the codes to retrieve messages.

There were none.

She stood. She needed to find out if he'd checked in for the flight she was waiting for. She had no idea how one would do that. After briefly hesitating, she took off for the ticket counter. They used the airport many times and she knew exactly where the counter was.

When she arrived, there was a line of people checking in. She looked for someone dressed in the airline's uniform, and spotted a woman helping someone fill out a form. She moved toward the woman and waited.

Finally, seeing an opportunity, Angelica spoke. "Excuse me."

The woman turned to her.

"My husband was supposed to be on a flight from Los Angeles that landed at nine thirty-five this morning. But he wasn't. I need to know if he checked in in Los Angeles."

The woman listened intently. "Perhaps he rescheduled his flight."

"He wouldn't do that without calling me. He has a cell phone." Angelica could tell by the woman's tone of voice that she had soothed a wife looking for an errant husband before. "I need to know if he checked in for that flight."

"I'm sorry. FAA regulations don't allow us to give out passenger list information."

Angelica stared at her, quickly becoming as angry as she was concerned. "So what am I supposed to do?"

The woman patted her arm. "I'm sure he'll contact you as

273

soon as he has his arrival information." The woman turned to a lady holding a child.

Angelica heard her cell phone ringing in her purse. It had to be Antonio. She opened her purse, grabbed the phone, and flipped it open. "Hello."

"Angelica, it's Mom. Instead of coming here, can you guys meet us at the hospital? Manuel has a fever."

Angelica felt her stomach churn. "Mother, they weren't on the flight. I don't know where they are."

"Is the plane late?"

"No, you don't understand, the plane arrived. They weren't on it."

The line was silent.

"Mother?"

"Here, talk to your father."

"What's happened, Angelica?"

The sound of her father's voice felt like a lifeline. "I don't know. They weren't on the plane."

"Angelica, there could be a hundred reasons for that. If you're sure they're not at the airport, come home and wait for his call."

"But why hasn't he called? Antonio has never done anything like this in our married life."

"You're talking about someone in a foreign country. There could be satellite problems, his battery could be dead and he isn't where he can charge it. There are a lot of perfectly logical reasons for him not to call."

Her father's strong voice calmed her. What he was saying made sense. Something had delayed them and Antonio would be calling soon. He could even already be on another flight. Maybe they had to board before he could call.

"Angelica, I've called Dr. Dorak. Manuel has a temp and I want him seen."

"I'll meet you at the hospital, Dad. I'll leave now."

She closed her phone and put it in her purse.

Angelica walked back to the baggage claim for one last look. People were gathered around the moving belt. She looked at the flight information board, a flight from New York. Passengers were grabbing their suitcases, others embraced. There was laughter and the general excitement of people who had returned home safely.

A vestige of the fear that had gripped Angelica earlier bubbled in her stomach.

Benito sat in a chair next to Manuel's hospital bed. By the time they had arrived at the hospital, Manuel's temperature had shot up from 99.5 to 104.2. Dr. Dorak had ordered several tests and started antibiotics, but the fever continued to rage. Manuel was admitted to the Pediatric Intensive Care Unit and a pediatric intensivist, Dr. Pfeil, was assigned to comanage the case. Benito looked at his watch. It was almost midnight.

He tried to slip the paper crown from his grandson's hand. But even in his sleep, the little boy's grasp on the tattered, soiled paper was firm. Manuel was always asking for his crown lately. At odd times reaching out, "Crown. Manuel crown." Especially tonight, clearly in pain, yet wanting to hold his paper crown.

Benito took his finger and stroked the child's flushed cheek. Manuel was burning up. The chest x-ray had been cloudy, pneumonia was mentioned. "Fight. You're an Amante. Fight," he whispered. He blinked rapidly. How long was it fair to ask Manuel to fight? How much did a little boy have to endure? How much did his mother have to endure?

Angelica had left the hospital in tears, sure something had

happened to Antonio and his nephew. Benito had offered more excuses, but she hadn't believed them . . . and neither had he. They both knew something was terribly wrong.

Benito put his elbows on his knees and his face in his hands. Everything was slipping away . . . even the ranch. If only there were some way to save it.

He'd thought about it many times before he put Regalo Grande up for sale. The only way would be to sell off almost all his other assets to generate enough cash to pay off the mortgages against the ranch. The same assets that provided his and Gen's annual earnings. It was a catch-22. To generate enough cash to keep the ranch he would have to wipe out their income.

He sighed. There was no point in dwelling on it. The ranch would have to be sold. Right now the only thing that mattered was finding Antonio.

Benito stood and began to pace. He had to do something. His entire life he'd relied on himself. He put himself through medical school, he excelled as a heart surgeon, he built Regalo Grande, he traveled the world, he was admired and respected by all who knew him.

Sitting on the couch, he folded his arms across his chest. He had stood in an operating room, held the human heart in his hands, and he repaired it. Hundreds of lives had been saved because of him.

His eyes drifted to the Bible Angelica had left on the side table. That was foolishness. He never accepted adversity, he never ran to God like the women did, expecting He would fix things. And he wasn't going to start now.

Benito chewed his lower lip, considering again something he'd thought of when Angelica first called saying Antonio was missing. Contacting the police here wouldn't help. Antonio wasn't in the Bay Area. He really didn't know if Antonio had made it to Los Angeles. It was possible that Antonio and Cirocco were not even in the country. The only thing they knew for sure was that the two men had been sitting at the San Jose del Cabo airport at about noon yesterday. Since that was the only thing they knew for certain, that was where he would have to start.

It was time to take control. Tomorrow he would fly to San Jose del Cabo. He would find out what had happened to Antonio and Cirocco. And he would deal with it.

He began to formulate a plan. He'd take the first flight out of Sacramento tomorrow. When he arrived in Mexico he would ask questions. He thought a moment. He didn't speak the language. . . . He'd take a picture of Antonio—he had a good wedding picture, and show it to . . . who? And say . . . what? He rose.

He would hire an interpreter. That's what he would do. They would go around the airport, and . . . The futility of the situation began to show itself. The police would have to get involved, looking for two men who didn't live there or know anyone there, one of them resembling a dated picture, and the other man Benito couldn't even describe.

He walked to Manuel's bedside and looked at the child's precious face. And how long would it take? The thought was sobering. How long did Manuel have? What if Benito was in Mexico and Manuel . . . He couldn't leave Manuel alone.

Benito felt his life unraveling. There was nowhere to turn . . . His grandson, his son-in-law, the ranch . . . He was losing everything he . . . he . . . he loved.

His heart began to pound, he felt sick to his stomach. He stiffened his neck, bracing himself against the truth.

There was no way out.

Manuel's face blurred as Benito blinked back tears. He set his jaw. The men had to be found.

Benito put his hand on the back of the chair and in a stiff, awkward motion he got down on his knees by his grandson's bed.

He bowed his head. Terse, angry words tore from his lips. "If You're who You say You are, then bring those men home."

Cirocco raised his head.

He didn't know how much time had passed. There had been brief moments of sunlight, but now there was only the moon. He twisted his head to the left. He could barely make out part of his uncle's leg and hand through the brush. Still, even through the eerie shadows he could see that the body hadn't moved. It had been a long time since they'd been dumped by the two men in the car. He fought to hold on to consciousness. But he couldn't. His last lucid thought was of his uncle.

Antonio was dead.

18

ANTONIO HAD STILL not called.

Angelica had finally gone to bed at 2:00 a.m. But even then, she lay with her arm extended, fingers touching the phone. Waiting, hoping, praying that she would hear something from him . . . from someone.

She picked up her purse from the kitchen table, where she'd thrown it the night before. She caught her breath. Stacked on the end of the table were the anniversary cards she bought for Antonio.

Today was their anniversary.

She stared at the cards. Flashes of the day she bought them flickered through her mind. She'd been smiling and giggling. He was coming home. She planned how she would meet him, staying out of sight until he got close to the baggage carousel. He would be looking for her. She imagined her tall, handsome husband, clean shaven, dressed professionally; he would have done that for her, casually looking across the concourse, trying not to appear anxious to see her. She would run to him . . .

She pushed the thoughts away. Instead of walking into

her husband's arms, she'd walked into the pit of hell. Every story she'd ever read about missing people haunted her. A mother's appeal on television for her missing daughter in Aruba; a husband pleading for the public's help to find his missing wife, abducted in a carjacking; a wife searching for her husband. Endless stories, whether here or abroad, all were dark and foreboding.

Angelica whirled around. Setting her jaw, she strode decisively through the garage to the van. Sometime during the sleepless night she'd made up her mind that she was not going to be a victim. She was not going to dwell on the "what-ifs." She would find every resource available and bring it to bear on the situation. She put the key in the ignition and turned it. Nothing.

She tried again. Not a sound. Dropping her hands in her lap, she tried to think what could be wrong. Why would the battery be dead? She looked around the interior of the car. Her purse was on the passenger seat . . . her purse . . . the overhead light. The overhead light must have been on all night.

When she'd pulled into the garage the night before, her cell phone had started ringing. It wasn't on the seat next to her, where she laid it. She turned on the dome light and found the phone had slid to the floor on the passenger side. The call was from her father, telling her Manuel's temperature had dropped slightly. She had jumped out of the van and ran in the house to tell Tex. She must have left the light on.

She tried the ignition again. The battery was dead.

Why did this have to happen? Why another thing? "Why, Jesus?" she called out. "You promised to never leave me or forsake me." She pounded her fist on the steering wheel. "But You have."

The gnawing sense of uneasiness that was always present

when she was away from Manuel surged within her. She needed to get to the hospital. Antonio would want—Antonio . . . Unexpectedly, the thought of being a single parent flashed through her mind. Fear, pure and icy, vibrated through her. No.

She grabbed her purse and computer case and got out of the van. She had to keep moving. She couldn't allow herself to feel or think. She had to get to the hospital. Now.

She walked around the van and got into Antonio's truck. The keys were in the ignition, as they always were. She started it.

The truck smelled like him. It held the unmistakable scent that was uniquely his . . . *"Angel, I love you"* . . . *"This my boy, he the one God give me"* . . . *guitar music.*

Pieces of the past were suddenly present with her.

Closing her eyes, she breathed deeply. She held her breath, the sweet scent filling her. In that single, transcendent moment, he was with her again. Tears rolled down her cheeks. She clenched her hands into fists, trying to hang on, trying to stop time, trying to stay with him.

"I need you, Antonio."

He was good and kind. His love had borne all things, believed all things, hoped all things, endured all things. His love had never failed her. "Please come home. I'm so scared."

Tears poured down her face. She wiped her eyes with the sleeve of her blouse.

She opened her purse, looking for a tissue. Finding none, she opened the glove compartment. Feeling around, she fingered something hard and square. She pulled it out. A small, black velvet box.

Her lips parted.

She raised the lid.

An exquisite band of diamonds sparkled before her. She

281

lifted the ring from the box, tilting it back and forth. It became a circle of light, dancing between her fingers. She took a ragged breath. It was beautiful. Each time she tilted it, arcs of diamond points evoked memories of the past . . . a time just after Manuel was born . . . sitting with her baby under the oaks . . . surrounded by a circle of light. And the strong, strong sense of God's loving presence, assuring her then that He was in control, that all things had worked together for good.

She pressed the ring to her lips, feeling the cool surface. A calm settled over her. For the first time since she'd left the airport, she felt the tightness in her chest ease.

A clear, singular thought presented itself. She had a choice.

She could choose to trust God, lean on Him, believe Him. Even in these most desperate circumstances. Or she could fall apart.

She eased the band onto her right ring finger. The beautiful, exquisite circle of light had somehow become a symbol of hope, of choosing, of believing. Of God's and Antonio's love for her . . . united as one.

Taking a few minutes, Angelica pulled herself together. She had to be strong for her children, for Antonio, for herself. She backed out of the driveway, and started to the hospital.

As she drove, Angelica thought about how word of the missing men had spread like wildfire through the school.

Tex had told her that the phone rang all night before Angelica had arrived home. Students, parents, and teachers wanted to gather and pray for the missing men. Tex took down all the names and messages of support. Many of the parents whose children belonged to the Mighty Warriors Club suggested a special meeting of the Warriors after school. By the time Angelica went to bed, she and Tex decided Tex would put out the word that the Mighty Warriors would be meeting in her classroom after school. Anyone who wanted to could meet and pray. The thought of corporate prayer for Antonio and Cirocco strengthened Angelica. She hoped she'd be able to attend for at least a short time.

She parked in the lot of the Sierra Medical Center and hurried into the hospital. From her father's call it sounded like the antibiotics were finally working.

As she neared Manuel's room, she saw his doctors in front of her. "Dr. Dorak. Dr. Pfeil."

They turned.

Dr. Dorak's face was filled with concern. "Good morning. I spoke to your father earlier." His gaze was intent. "How are you doing?"

She sensed the reference was to Antonio. "No news yet."

The doctor's kind eyes held her gaze. "I've been praying for him."

As they entered the room, Benito rose from the couch. His face was drawn, the circles under his eyes had deepened.

Angelica stepped quickly to the bedside. Manuel's eyes were closed.

Her father stood next to her. "His temperature spiked again this morning."

"What?" Angelica felt a wave of nausea. She reached out for her father's arm. She looked at Dr. Dorak. "Why is this happening?"

Dr. Pfeil answered. "We're not sure. It looks like pneumonia, but if that's what it is, Manuel should start responding. We've tested for numerous viruses and bacterial infections, but all the results have been negative. This morning I called Dr. Kleinlerer, an infectious disease specialist."

Angelica stood next to Manuel's bed. She couldn't believe

how much his appearance had deteriorated since the day before. She sought Dr. Dorak's eyes. "This is bad, isn't it?"

His expression was veiled. "We're going to do everything
humanly possible."

After her father left, Angelica spent the morning making
calls to Senator Evans's office, searching the Internet trying
to find people who had been in her situation, and calling the
airport to see if any luggage had shown up. It seemed that
no matter what she did, it led nowhere.

By the time her mother arrived in the early afternoon,
Angelica's Internet searches had generated leads to all kinds
of companies that searched for missing people. But every one
of them was for searches within the United States. The only
thing she found relating to foreign countries was horrific
stories of people who had gone missing on vacations. None
of the people had ever been found.

"Mother, I don't know what to do."

Her mother came and sat beside her. "I don't either, Angelica. Your father and I have talked about nothing else since
this happened."

"I'm praying that Senator Evans's office will be able to
give me some direction." She fingered the diamond band
on her right hand.

Her mother reached for Angelica's finger. "What's that?"

"I think it's my anniversary present from Antonio." Angelica told her mother how she'd found it in the truck's glove
compartment.

Her mother faced her and took Angelica's hands. "We've
got to keep the faith. God knows where they are."

"There's going to be a prayer meeting at the school in an
hour or so. Well, really it's the Mighty Warriors Club. I'd

really like to go." She glanced at Manuel. "But I'm so torn. What if he needs me and I'm not here?"

"Angelica, Anica needs you too. And—" her mother patted Angelica's hand—"I can't think of anyplace you could do more for Manuel than at a prayer meeting."

Angelica reached out to her mother and the women hugged.

"You go, honey. I'll be here. You can call me if you get concerned."

Angelica closed her eyes a moment. It felt right. "Thanks, Mom."

She rose, and after kissing Manuel good-bye, rushed out to the truck.

When she arrived at the school she hurried to Tex's classroom. Walking briskly, she breathed deeply of the cool, crisp fall air. It was a beautiful day. Any other time, she would have slowed her steps and enjoyed the peaceful, quiet afternoon.

But instead, she hurried on to Tex's homeroom.

It was empty. Her heart sank.

Had Jack O'Hare stopped the gathering? Had he called Tex into the office? She looked at her watch. It was 3:45. The meetings usually started at 3:30. She took a deep breath as anger rose within her. Enough was enough. Her son was desperately ill, her husband was missing, and her community wanted to pray for her. There was nothing about that that should cause a constitutional crisis. She turned on her heel and marched out the door and down the hall toward the administration building. She exited through a side door, to cut across the playground.

The minute she stepped out of the building, a wind whipped her hair into her face. She brushed the hair away from her eyes. As she did, she saw that there were groups of people pouring into the school's gymnasium. She stopped. Something was going on.

She angled across the grass, bypassing the administration building and heading directly to the gymnasium. As she approached, she saw Tex and Anica standing just inside the door.

"Mommy. Mommy." Anica jumped up and down, waving.

Angelica hurried up the gymnasium steps. "What's going on here?"

Tex shrugged. "It's the craziest thing. I returned the calls from last night and waited in my classroom after school. Well, people started streaming in. By three thirty, the room was overflowing. A lot of parents who came to pick up their kids just parked and stayed. I told everyone to come here to the gymnasium and I posted a note on the front of the office door since that's the way most of the people were arriving."

"And Jack O'Hare let you do that?"

Tex quirked her mouth. "He's not here today. So I had to make an executive decision."

"Isn't this wind something?" Angelica stepped farther into the gymnasium. Anica took her hand.

People who recognized Angelica stopped and spoke to her. Some giving her words of encouragement, some giving a quick hug and a sympathetic smile. Finally, the stream of people began to dwindle.

"Mommy." Anica squeezed her hand. "Look, it's Hugh Bris's mom."

Angelica braced herself as Norna Bris approached her.

Just as the small woman stepped through the door, a strong gust of wind slammed it shut behind her. She looked at the door and raised her eyebrows. Then, turning to Angelica, she straightened. Raising her chin, she primly clutched her handbag in her hands. "I'm so sorry to hear that your husband is missing." The words sounded rehearsed and crisp.

Angelica nodded. "Thank you."

Mrs. Bris turned back to the door and pushed on the bar to open it. It wouldn't move. She pushed it again. It opened a crack, but the strong wind outside kept it from moving any farther.

Angelica let go of Anica's hand. "Sweetie, I think it's time for you kids to start."

Angelica glanced at Norna Bris who was straining to open the door. Finally, the woman walked toward the back of the gymnasium, trying each exit door she passed. But none would open.

Angelica took a seat next to Tex along the side of the gym.

Jimmy Shultz, Anica, and their classmates Pete and Katie stood in front of the bleachers. Mr. Shultz stood behind them, holding a microphone. "Good afternoon." The huge room began to quiet. "Thank you all for coming. I'm Ed Shultz." He paused, reaching for Anica's hand. "As most of you know, Manuel Perez, a student here, has been fighting leukemia for the past two months." Ed Shultz gave a quick summary of Manuel's struggle, and then introduced Anica and Angelica.

He handed the microphone to Jimmy. Jimmy looked at the other three leaders of the Mighty Warriors Club. "Ready?" The children began to clap their hands in rhythm. Everyone stood, joining them. They led the crowd in a simple praise song.

When they finished, someone from the bleachers shouted, "God bless you."

From another quarter, "Amen to that."

287

Angelica felt a breeze as light as the hem of a robe brush over her feet.

She looked across the bleachers. There were dozens of familiar faces from Faith Community Church. She saw older siblings of Manuel's and Anica's friends. She was struck by how many young people were in the gym.

Everyone took their seats.

Tex whispered, "Yes, praise You, Jesus, for who You are. You are our refuge in time of trouble."

Though she had spoken in a whisper, a man on the farthest side of the gym spoke out. "Yes, Jesus, You are our refuge."

Angelica's eyes widened and she turned to Tex.

The room began to quiet.

Tex was sitting with her eyes closed and her hands raised, unaware that her voice could be heard throughout the gym. "I ask You, Holy Spirit, come to this place."

A voice from the back of the bleachers sounded in the room without effort, "Yes, come, Holy Spirit, come."

A gentle breeze moved through the gymnasium. At first discernable only as movement, but then becoming sound. And the sound became a voice, the most exquisite high voice, singing.

Many turned their faces upward. Others looked from side to side, searching for the source of the stirring song. But it was hidden from them.

As the moments passed, there was no sound except the singular, ethereal voice, surrounding all who were present, entering into sweet communion with the heart of man.

Lifting her hands wide and extending her fingers in welcome, Angelica closed her eyes and raised her face. She had heard the voice before, when she prayed with Maclovia in the nearby foothills . . . in the presence of God. Now, as

288

then, she couldn't understand the song as one understood the spoken word, but she felt it with every fiber of her being. She understood at a place beyond words, that Jesus was being magnified for who He is, the Son of God, the Savior, the hope of all mankind. Her hope this day, at this hour, at this moment. "Praise You, Jesus. I love You. I need You."

Somewhere across the room she heard, "Yes, praise You. Praise You."

Tex continued, "I will say of the Lord, 'He is my refuge and my fortress; my God, in Him I will trust.' Surely He shall deliver you from the snare of the fowler and from the perilous pestilence. He shall cover you with His feathers, and under His wings you shall take refuge . . ."

Angelica listened as Tex began to pray the ninety-first psalm for Antonio and Cirocco. Angelica found as she listened that she knew each word, "You shall not be afraid of the terror by night . . . He shall give His angels charge over you, to keep you . . ." She mouthed the words with Tex, yet, she had never memorized the psalm, she'd only read it at different times over the years.

A man's voice took over, continuing the recitation, word for word. When he finished, a young woman stood and began to pray a passage of the New Testament, and when she stopped someone else continued.

For the next hour, passages of the Bible that seemed tailored for the missing men were spoken against the backdrop of the beautiful high voice that magnified the name of Jesus Christ. And each verse came to Angelica, as she imagined the words came to all who were present, from someplace hidden in her heart, to be brought forth and used at this time.

People began to bow their heads, others knelt where they stood.

With the clarity found only in those moments one truly

longs for Jesus, Angelica knew that whatever the future held, Jesus would sustain her as He worked out His will in her life and in the lives of all those she loved.

Angelica heard someone begin to sob. She heard it with the same unusual clearness with which she'd heard all the voices. She whispered words of thanksgiving as she recognized the sound of brokenness from a deeply repentant heart.

Angelica opened her eyes. Directly in her line of sight was Norna Bris. Her hands lifted, reaching for her salvation.

Lightning cracked above Antonio's head as rain poured from the night skies. Once again, he gathered all his strength and tried to push himself up. This time he managed to get on his knees. Rocks and brush bit into his hands and legs.

He tilted his face, gathering water in his mouth. He had no idea where he was or how long he'd been here. He knew only that for a long, long time he'd been unable to move. His body seemed separated from his mind and ultimately, it was only the force of his will that stopped him from accepting death.

It wasn't because he was afraid to die, it was because he knew that he had not finished what God had for him to do. He had unfinished business with Cirocco, with Manuel, and with his wife. These were things he had come to understand in the hours he spent hovering between life and death, though he could not say how.

He breathed in deeply, and then, ignoring the pain that shot through his ribs, he stood.

Rocking back and forth, he scanned the area around him. Through the sporadic lightning flashes he saw Cirocco. With lurching, awkward steps he stumbled toward his nephew's body, finally falling on top of the young man. A moan escaped

Antonio's lips and darkness drifted over his eyes. He fought back. He could feel that Cirocco was alive.

Half lying on the boy, he put his face against Cirocco's face, his lips touching the boy's ear. "I love you. I'm here. Don't be afraid. Talk to me." He listened, but heard nothing.

He felt down Cirocco's arm to his hand. "If you hear me, squeeze my hand." He waited. But there was no response. The boy's eyes were closed.

What if Cirocco died? What if Antonio were speaking the last words his nephew would ever hear?

Antonio's chin dropped to his chest at the thought of losing the boy. If these were the last moments of Cirocco's life, he wanted to tell him the only thing that mattered. "God sent His Son to die for you. Whoever believes on Him will have everlasting life. It is as Mama Rose told you. If you call for Him, He'll come to you, Cirocco." There was no response.

If Cirocco died, Manuel would die also. Antonio looked at his nephew's bruised and swollen face.

Finally he whispered, "Go to the light."

Exhausted, he covered Cirocco's body with his own, and closed his eyes for what seemed like a moment. When he opened them, he was looking at the clear morning sky. He could hear the ocean in the distance.

He turned toward Cirocco and saw he was still breathing.

Antonio nudged him. "Wake up." He could see the boy's body had been badly beaten. Antonio looked at himself. He'd been stripped of everything but his shirt, pants, and shoes. Even his belt was gone. Suddenly, a thought occurred to him. He wiggled his toes. Their visas were still there.

Cirocco moaned. Antonio got on his knees. Bending over the boy, he slapped his face gently. "Wake up."

Cirocco opened his eyes, but they didn't register any recognition. His eyelids drifted shut.

Antonio stood and tried to pull his nephew up, but the boy slipped out of his hands.

Antonio made his way toward the sound of the ocean. He came to a rise and he could see a beach not too far in the distance. If he could get to the beach, he could find help.

Looking at the rough terrain, he hesitated. He didn't want to leave Cirocco behind, but there was no way he could carry the boy through the rocks that lay between them and the beach. He walked back to where his nephew lay. Squatting, Antonio shook Cirocco's shoulder. He moaned.

Antonio sat back on his heels trying to remember what had happened. The men had brought them here in a car and made them get out. They didn't walk for very long in the hilly area when one of the men hit him in the back of the head and started kicking him.

There had to be a road nearby.

He rose and walked in the opposite direction he'd planned to go, looking right and left for some indication of how they had come to this spot. He didn't walk far before he could see a natural pathway leading down the hill. He followed it. Ahead of him he saw a paved road. "Praise You, *Dios*."

He returned to Cirocco, got down on one knee and wedged his shoulder under Cirocco's chest. He grabbed the boy's hand and draped Cirocco's arm around his neck. With all his strength he hoisted the young man. Straining forward, Antonio managed to stand.

Half carrying, half dragging his nephew, he stumbled toward the road. He began to feel weak and nauseated, but he pressed on, thinking of Manuel. One more step. One more step. He couldn't go on. He had to go on. He squeezed his eyes shut, blocking out everything but the face of his son. One more step.

He felt blacktop under his feet. He released Cirocco's arm and sank to his knees.

"Señor! Señor!"

He didn't know if a minute or an hour had passed. Someone was giving him water. Cool, life-giving water. He opened his eyes and found himself looking into the eyes of a toothless old man, holding a *bule* in gnarled hands.

"Please, help my nephew."

19

GOOD MORNING, DAD." Angelica threw her coat and purse on the couch. "Has Dr. Dorak been by yet?"

"Not yet. And I'm staying here until he does. He and Dr. Pfeil were supposed to meet with Dr. Kleinlerer, the infectious disease doc, yesterday afternoon. They took some nose swabs and blood and did more tests."

Angelica pulled a chair next to her father. She looked at her son. "Mom told me that Senator Evans's office called about getting us some help in Cabo."

Her father nodded. "Yes, he's working through some personal contacts he has. We've got to get someone to start an investigation down there." He looked at Manuel. "If he'd just start improving, I'd go myself."

"You may have to, Dad." Angelica looked into her father's eyes. "I was thinking about it a lot last night. We can't just sit here waiting. I can take care of everything while you're gone. Between Mom and me, we can be sure someone is here with Manuel. Tex will help me at home. If something comes up on the sale of Regalo Grande, I can be a liaison for you."

"You've been thinking." He smiled at her. "I've been thinking too."

Angelica studied his face, waiting for him to continue.

"Sandi Greer called me last night." He held her gaze. "The people from Idaho who made an offer on the ranch aren't going to extend. They've changed their minds about moving away from their children and grandchildren." He looked at his hands. "I can't say I blame them." He shifted in his chair. "I've decided to take the ranch off the market for now."

Angelica sat up in her chair. "I thought you said there were financial considerations and you had to sell." After all her father had done for her and her family, she didn't want him to feel any pressure from her about not selling the ranch.

"Yes, it is about money. When I made the agreement with the buyers I thought there was a good chance I'd get a second offer right away. But I didn't." He paused. "Maybe that was providence."

Angelica sat stock still. *Providence*. She'd never heard her father use that word before.

"I can't maintain the hacienda and acreage *and* the lifestyle your mother wants. Monthlong trips with friends every spring and summer, new cars every year, and you know the kind of parties she likes to throw. But you know what?" He glanced at her. "Maybe that lifestyle really isn't necessary anymore." He released a deep sigh. "Your mother and I have been talking. We're going to the accountant as soon as we can and we'll see what can be worked out. I owe a lot of money on the ranch, but I can sell other holdings to pay off those debts. The problem is, that leaves us with dramatically reduced income." He shrugged. "I'm going to try and figure out something."

She understood exactly what her father was saying . . .

295

and she suspected why he was saying it. *God bless that man.* She reached for his hand.

"Thank you, Daddy."

Benito stood and turned his face away from her. He walked across the room and looked down the hall. He cleared his throat. "I thought I heard Dr. Dorak coming."

Angelica turned back to Manuel, allowing her father his privacy.

"Angelica, isn't that your phone?"

She jumped up and flew to the couch. She grabbed her cell phone from her purse. "Hello?"

"Angel?"

"Antonio?"

Benito rushed to her side.

"Antonio?" She was trembling so badly she could hardly hold the phone.

Her father took it from her. "Who is this?"

"This is Antonio. Can I talk to my wife?"

"Antonio!" Benito bellowed into the phone. He looked at Angelica. "It's Antonio." He dropped his hand to his side, the phone dangling from his fingers.

Angelica took the phone from him. "Where are you? Are you okay? What happened?" She sank to the couch, tears flowing down her cheeks.

"We're okay. How is Manuel?"

"He's not doing too well right now. He has a high fever, and they can't find out what's causing it. What happened to you? Where have you been?"

"Right after I talked to you, we went to San Jose del Cabo to eat. Instead of a taxi, we got picked up by some locals, and they robbed us and left us out in the countryside. But we finally found our way back to town. I'm so sorry. I know you have been worried sick."

Angelica closed her eyes. She felt like screaming at him. Why would he take a ride with strangers? "Do you have your papers?"

"We have our visas, but that's it. I borrowed money from a nurse to make this call."

"A nurse! Where are you?"

"Right now we're at a clinic. Just to get checked over. But I need you to wire me money and I'm not sure how to get the passports replaced here. I can't rent a car. They took my driver's license."

"How are you going to get out of there?"

"Angel, I'm a Mexican in Mexico. This is my country and I know how to get things done here. I think there's a Banco Internacional here. I'm sure the same people who arranged for the money to be sent to Guadalajara can have money sent here. I'll call you again later when I know more. I just wanted you to know we were okay."

The whole conversation seemed surreal. She didn't want to let him off the phone. She had a million questions. "Antonio, I need to talk to you. So much has happened."

"I've got to go now. I'll call you later. I love you so much."

He hung up.

Angelica sat for a moment, then she shot off the couch. "Dad. Dad. Antonio is coming home!"

She ran to her father and jumped up, wrapping her arms around his neck. As she hugged him, she felt his arms around her. But instead of the quick hug she always got, he held her.

As she quieted down, she noticed the uneven sound of his breathing.

He was weeping.

She laid her head on his chest. He tightened his arms

297

around her, as if she were the one being returned to him. The sweet poignancy of the moment deeply moved her.

"It's okay, Dad. I understand how you feel." She spoke into his chest. "Antonio and Cirocco are coming home."

Her father whispered into her hair. "He *is* who He says He is."

Mark Dorak's shoulders slumped. It was the worst possible scenario. And the outcome could be fatal.

He pushed his chair back from his desk. After reviewing Manuel's medical history, Dr. Kleinlerer had suspected an insidious fungal infection, aspergillus, could be the reason for Manuel's continued high fever.

Dr. Kleinlerer had immediately ordered a bronchial lavage. Microscopic examination of the fluid collected had confirmed the presence of the fungus.

Mark stood and walked to the window. The fungal infection probably started when Manuel had first gotten a fever weeks ago. His white blood cell count had been low then, and stayed low for an extended period of time. But when the course of antibiotics he'd been given had improved his condition, no suspicions of any underlying infection were raised. It wasn't until the white blood cell count rose and the fever persisted that the smoldering infection started to show itself.

The invasive fungus was daunting enough without the complications of AML and pneumonia. The three conditions being present concurrently was life threatening. If the pneumonia spread through Manuel's body, it was possible that septic shock could set in, and that could lead to disseminated intravascular coagulation.

Mark ran his fingers through his hair. He'd seen the horrific condition once before in a young cancer patient. It had begun a massive and uncontrolled coagulation in the patient's vessels and eventually his body ran out of coagulation proteins. Uncontrollable bleeding started. As the patient neared death, he began to sweat blood. Ultimately, he fell into a coma and died.

Mark strode to his desk and grabbed Manuel's files. He could not let that happen. He would find a way to arrest the disease.

As he walked to the Pediatric Intensive Care Unit, his thoughts turned to God. Manuel's illness could quickly become something beyond the reach of man or medicine. *Lord, I believe that You bring every patient who comes into my care. I want to be Your vessel, to be used by You. I pray You will give me wisdom in speaking to this family and in discerning what treatment will be best for Manuel.*

When Mark walked through Manuel's door, Benito had his arms around Angelica and they seemed to be crying.

Mark rushed to Manuel's bedside. The boy's condition seemed unchanged. He looked back at Angelica and her father.

Angelica stepped away from Benito and ran toward Mark, a smile lighting her face. She threw her arms around him, giving him a heartfelt hug.

"Dr. Dorak! Antonio and Cirocco are coming home. They should be here in a few days." Animated and energized, she told him about the phone call she received.

Mark looked at the father and daughter. "What an incredible story."

But the reality was, if Manuel didn't improve he would be too ill for the peripheral blood stem cell transplant. Mark searched for words to put the situation into perspective. "Right now we're going to focus on getting Manuel healthy.

The tests Dr. Kleinlerer ordered uncovered the presence of a fungal infection. Now that we know, we can start treating it."

The smile left Benito's face. "What kind of fungal infection?"

Mark explained exactly what the disease was, though he didn't go into all the possibilities of where it could lead.

Benito straightened, folded his arms across his chest, and listened without comment.

Mark knew that the retired heart surgeon understood the seriousness of what he was being told, and it was clear he didn't want to alarm his daughter.

Benito seemed to age in front of him.

Angelica's eyes narrowed. "Dr. Dorak, what does all this mean?"

"It means we will begin treating the infection aggressively. We'll start the tests that are part of the donor's preparations and we'll look forward to a successful outcome."

"The transplant will be done soon, won't it?" Angelica's face had filled with concern.

"That depends on how well Manuel responds to treatment."

He could see Angelica wanted more from him, but that was as far as he could go under the circumstances. The next forty-eight hours would be critical.

The room became silent.

Benito turned to Dr. Dorak. "I'm sure you're doing everything you can. Thank you." He held the doctor's gaze a moment, then faced Angelica. "I'm going to go home now. I want to wire money to Antonio as soon as possible and get those boys home."

He left the room.

As Mark began to examine Manuel, he could hear Angelica on the phone, sharing the fantastic news that the men had been found. But within moments he was completely focused on his patient. Manuel's breathing had become somewhat more labored, his fever was still 104. For the first time Mark considered having a tube inserted into the child's lungs and assisting Manuel's respiration with oxygen.

Mark glanced at Angelica.

He was glad Antonio would be home soon.

Antonio whispered a prayer of thanks. Over and over again, during the past twenty-four hours, from the bank manager who stayed after closing, to the taxi driver who lent Antonio an old truck, to the federal officials who helped him get his passport, as soon as he explained his situation, people had gone far beyond what was required of them to help him.

He pulled into the clinic's parking lot and got out of the truck. The doctor who had treated him and Cirocco the day before had insisted they come back before leaving. If it hadn't been for Cirocco, Antonio wouldn't have bothered. There was nothing that could be done about his bruised ribs, and his cuts and scrapes would heal on their own. Still, the doctor was concerned about Cirocco, thinking he might have a mild concussion. But Cirocco insisted he would be fine, and against the doctor's protests, they left.

A small hotel gave them a room and Cirocco rested there while Antonio arranged for their travel. Antonio received an unexpected blessing when he took off Cirocco's boot and found that the boy, after seeing Antonio put the visas in his shoe, had hidden his passport on the top of his foot.

Antonio helped Cirocco get out of the truck. The two

men went into the clinic, and after checking in, took a seat in the crowded waiting room.

Antonio stretched his legs in front of him. "As soon as we're finished here, we'll pick up my passport, take the truck back, and then we'll go try to get a flight to Los Angeles. I'm hoping the luggage is still there somewhere. We should be in Sacramento by this time tomorrow."

An older man on the other side of Cirocco leaned forward. "Excuse me. You from Sacramento?"

Antonio leaned forward. "No, we're from Sierra County."

"Oh." The man looked disappointed. "My son works in Sacramento. I thought you might know him. He was just here visiting me."

Antonio smiled. The little man obviously had no idea how big Sacramento was. "Where does he work?"

"He works at a horse ranch. I was in a bad accident." The man tapped his leg cast. "He came to see me. First time I've seen him in five years. The trip is dangerous, you know."

Antonio felt for the man. Antonio knew all about the dangerous trip across the border. The man would probably not see his son again for another five years, if not longer . . . if at all. "What happened to your leg?"

"I was running a tractor at my job, trying to plow uphill, and it fell on me." He clapped his hands together. "Just like that. Almost killed me. If it hadn't been for the hospital in La Paz, I would have died." He clucked his tongue. "That's some place. They gave me blood."

Cirocco sat straight up and whirled toward the man. "Blood?"

"Yeah. I nearly bled to death. But they gave me blood."

Cirocco looked at Antonio, his eyes wide. He turned back to the man. "How did they do that?"

302

The man shrugged. "I don't know exactly. It was in bags and it went down a tube into my arm."

Antonio realized that Cirocco's interest came from knowing he was going to be giving blood to Manuel. "This is my nephew. He's going to be giving blood to my son when we get back to the U.S."

The man nodded at Cirocco. "That boy will thank you. I never knew about such things. At the hospital they told me that there are people who give their blood each month so there is always a supply for people like me."

Cirocco smiled from ear to ear. "The people give their blood each month?"

The man smiled back at him. "That's what they said."

"Cirocco, in California I joined a club that helps people find blood that matches theirs. I couldn't help Manuel, but I might be able to help someone else."

Cirocco stared at Antonio for a moment. "I'm not going to die?"

"Die!" Antonio drew back. "No, you're not going to die."

Cirocco dropped his head and rubbed his eyes.

Antonio caught his breath. Had Cirocco thought he was going to die all this time? When Antonio had told Angelica that Cirocco seemed troubled, he never dreamed that this was at the root of it. It made sense now.

Antonio carefully raised his arm and put it around Cirocco's shoulder, pulling his nephew to him. Cirocco had planned to die so Manuel could live! Antonio reflected on the ordeal they'd just been through and the past that was Cirocco's life. His heart ached for all he had not done for the boy, and for the wasted years Cirocco had spent on the streets. He had failed the young man and that needed to be made right. He kissed the boy's forehead. "You are precious to me. I love you, man."

Cirocco was not going to die. Cirocco was going to live. With him. He tightened his arm around the boy. "I will never let any harm come to you. You are my blood."

After seeing the doctor, they finished everything they needed to do before going to the airport. Antonio found two flights that looked promising.

As they sat waiting, Antonio's thoughts turned to the conversation in the clinic. Cirocco had thought he was going to die when he gave his blood. The boy's courage humbled Antonio. And again he felt ashamed that he had not taken more of an interest in Cirocco before all of this had happened.

"*Tío?*" Cirocco's voice interrupted his thoughts. "I want to tell you something that happened to me that night." That night. When both had hovered between life and death. It was how they spoke of it now. "That night I had a dream."

Antonio waited patiently, letting the boy speak at his own pace. "I was cold, so cold. And I was surrounded by darkness." He hesitated. "At first I couldn't see anything but then I saw my mother. She was holding a baby in her arms. It was me. And I could see her eyes." His face softened. "How they loved me." He stopped, taking a steadying breath, then he continued. "But as I gazed at her I realized they were not her eyes . . . and then she became Mama Rose, sitting by my hospital bed in Guadalajara. Still, the eyes did not belong to Mama Rose. And then the face changed again . . . and it became your face."

Antonio hardly breathed as he listened to his nephew.

"But they were not your eyes, either." Cirocco blinked rapidly and looked away for a moment. "Then I heard a voice say, 'God sent His Son to die for you. Whoever believes on

Him will have everlasting life.' . . . And I knew they were the eyes of Jesus. He had been looking at me all my life."

Antonio wiped a tear from his cheek.

"Then I felt a blanket cover me. And I was not so cold anymore." He looked at his hands. "It was then I asked Jesus to save my life . . . and He did."

Antonio rubbed Cirocco's shoulder.

"But I had promised to give my blood to Manuel and I thought my life would end there. Then this morning in the clinic, I saw that it was worked out. It was as if Jesus had worked it out for me. Do you know what I mean, *tío*?"

Antonio looked in his nephew's eyes. "Yes, I know what you mean."

All things work together for good to those who love God, to those who are the called according to His purpose . . .

20

Angelica had talked to Antonio in Los Angeles and had fallen asleep expecting a call from him when he knew his arrival time in Sacramento. Instead it was her father's voice that awakened her. Dr. Dorak had ordered a tube to be inserted into Manuel's lungs. Antonio's call came later, and Tex went to pick up the men at the airport. When Angelica arrived at the hospital, her father told her they were having trouble keeping Manuel's oxygen levels up, even with the help of the ventilator.

"Dad, what time is it?"

"Two minutes later than the last time you asked me."

"Then it's two minutes closer to the time Antonio walks through that door." Angelica released a deep sigh. "I hope Dr. Dorak or Dr. Pfeil comes back soon. I feel like Manuel hasn't improved, even with the ventilator."

Sitting next to the hospital bed, with her hand on Manuel's arm, she could feel his fever through the sheets. A flicker of apprehension coursed through her.

Her eyes drifted to his flushed face as memories filtered through her mind . . . other days, other places. Rocking him in his nursery. *Mommy loves you.* Sitting by the stream at the ranch. *Mommy loves you.* Cradling him, sheltering him from the wounding words of other children. She tightened her grip on his arm. *Mommy loves you.*

Manuel had blessed her a thousand times over. Maclovia had known that would happen. When the doctors had told them that Manuel might have Down syndrome, Maclovia began to pray. Not for the healing of the unborn child, but for the healing of the heart of man. A tear slipped down Angelica's cheek. Manuel's presence in their lives had changed them. Especially her father. He had loved more deeply and lived more fully because of Manuel.

Antonio's voice!

She carefully eased her hand from the bed and rose, then hurried out the door to the hallway. "Antonio, Antonio."

She was in his arms, her face in his chest, feeling him, touching him. His strong arms holding her.

A moan escaped his lips. "I love you so much." He whispered to her, stroking her hair. "I'm here now. Shhh. Shhh."

And as was his way, though anxious to see his son, he stood in the hall and let her take from him all she needed. Whispering to her, reassuring her, calming her . . . bringing light into the darkness.

Finally, she stepped back, wiping her eyes.

Behind his shoulder she saw Tex and a young man. The boy's face was bruised and his lip was swollen. Even though she knew what had happened, she was shocked by his appearance. "You must be Cirocco."

He smiled at her, but didn't speak.

"Honey, he doesn't understand you."

"Oh, sorry." She nodded at Cirocco. *"Mucho gusto."*

His smile broadened.

307

Antonio looked past her. "Where is my boy?"

Angelica took Antonio's hand and led him into the room.

Benito met him at the door and the men shook hands. "It's good to have you back, son."

"It's good to be back." Antonio turned toward Manuel, then stopped.

Angelica looked at him. His face had gone pale. He slowly moved toward the bed.

Suddenly, Angelica realized Antonio hadn't seen Manuel for almost two months. Antonio hadn't gone through the chemo and its hellish aftermath, the mouth ulcers, the wrenching vomiting, the rashes, the fevers, the sleepless nights and endless days.

Sorrow and sadness etched Antonio's face. "He has suffered too much."

Manuel's appearance had deteriorated dramatically since Antonio had left. Caring for him day to day, Angelica hadn't thought about it. She hadn't allowed herself to think about anything but getting him well, taking him home, having her son with her. But Antonio's words jarred her. Manuel's frail body was lost in the sheets, tubes, and machines surrounding him, his breathing labored. She felt like she was seeing him for the first time.

Stepping next to him, she kissed Manuel's head. "Sweetie, Daddy's here. Can you wake up?"

Manuel was unresponsive. Her heart started to pound.

"Dad, what's wrong?"

Benito stepped in front of Antonio. "I'm sure he's fine. While you were in the hall, he opened his eyes and looked right at me."

Benito lifted Manuel's eyelids.

Suddenly, her father put his hands on her son's shoulders. "Manuel. Manuel."

"Daddy, what are you doing? What's wrong?"

"He's beyond sedation. I'm going to get a doctor." Her father ran from the room.

Angelica gripped Manuel's shoulders. "Wake up, Manuel. Please, wake up." She felt like she couldn't breathe. "Manuel. Manuel." She could hear her voice rising. "Do you hear Mommy?"

She sought Antonio's eyes. But they were focused on his son.

Dr. Dorak burst into the room, with Benito at his heels. An alarm sounded.

Angelica whirled around, eyes scanning the machines. Manuel's oxygen level had plummeted, and his heart rate had dropped to sixty beats a minute. Through all of Manuel's hospital stays, she'd never seen these numbers that low. Her eyes cut back to her son. A faint blue tinge was visible on his face. Fear seized Angelica in a death grip, as Dr. Dorak checked the leads on the heart monitor.

Benito grabbed her arm, pulling her away from the bed. "Get out of the way."

Antonio jumped backward, knocking over the chair by the bed as Dr. Dorak pushed in front of him.

The doctor placed his fingers on the child's neck.

Angelica felt a wave of nausea go through her stomach. Why was he taking so long to get Manuel's pulse?

The doctor shook Manuel, calling his name.

Angelica looked at the number on the heart monitor. Thirty. "What's happening to him? Do something!" She searched Dr. Dorak's face.

Her eyes returned to the monitor. Two zeroes flashed on

the screen—the tracing went flat as a squealing triple beep pealed through the room.

Dr. Dorak leaned over Manuel and began chest compressions, shouting over his shoulder, "I need help here!"

Antonio wrapped his arms around Angelica, pulling her back as people rushed into the room.

Benito knotted his hands into fists. "No."

Dr. Pfeil stepped next to the bed. "What happened?"

Dr. Dorak continued the chest compressions. "His grandfather caught me in the hallway and said Manuel was unresponsive. When I came into the room, his oxygen level and heart rate were dropping. Then he became asystolic."

A respiratory therapist stepped to the head of the bed, disconnected Manuel from the ventilator, and placed a blue plastic bag at the end of the tube, giving him breaths every few seconds.

A nurse took Dr. Dorak's place, continuing chest compressions.

Dr. Pfeil addressed a nurse who stood beside the code cart that had been wheeled into the room. "Give him zero point one mls of one to ten thousand strength epinephrine IV push."

Dr. Dorak nodded. "And get a set of labs."

Angelica watched in stunned horror as people pulled medications and equipment from the cart. A nurse placed a syringe in Manuel's IV and blood tubes were handed off to a nearby care assistant.

Two or three minutes passed.

She turned to her father. "What's happening?"

"They're giving the epinephrine a chance to circulate. It should help his heart to start beating again."

Angelica closed her eyes. *Oh God, send Your angels to save Manuel. You are God, You can stop this. I beg You, save my little boy. He has suffered so much. Stop his suffering now.*

Dr. Pfeil's voice cut into her thoughts. "Let's stop CPR and see what we have."

Suddenly, everyone paused, and all eyes turned to the heart monitor. The tracing remained flat.

"He's still asystolic." Dr. Pfeil's words hung in the air.

Angelica cried out, "Don't let him die." Antonio's arms tightened around her.

Dr. Pfeil motioned to the nurse at the code cart. "Let's give another round of epi."

"Angelica. Antonio." Dr. Dorak had stepped behind them.

They turned toward him.

Dr. Dorak took Angelica's hand. "Manuel is a fighter. But his heart and lungs have become extremely weak." He looked into Antonio's eyes. "There is nothing we can do now to change that."

Suddenly, the room became quiet.

Angelica looked toward the hospital bed. Everyone was facing the heart monitor.

The flatline marched across the screen. Defying the doctors, the nurses, the drugs.

"Keep trying!" Angelica screamed. "Don't stop. You can't stop now."

She heard Antonio's quiet voice behind her. "No, Doctor." He stepped next to her. "Please stop." He turned toward her, his eyes searching hers. "Let him go to God."

She pushed in front of Dr. Pfeil, throwing herself onto the bed, taking Manuel in her arms.

Antonio gently pulled her back.

Dr. Dorak touched Angelica's shoulder. "Manuel is leaving us."

The moment Dr. Dorak's fingers touched her, a flame appeared in her line of vision. She pressed into Antonio.

The flame grew larger, seemingly burning away everything around her until there was nothing but the golden light. And within its midst a door. And through the door, she saw a glassy sea sparkling like crystal. She felt Antonio's cheek next to hers.

She didn't move, yet the water came closer to her. The sea shimmered, and as she watched, one by one, the diamond points of light grew larger, revealing that each point of light was in fact a prayer.

Trumpets blew, heralding the day and the hour. The time of God's choosing to act on the prayers of His people.

The points of light began to burst. She heard Anica speaking: "Jesus, please heal Manuel. Don't let him hurt anymore."

Another point of light glowed, then broke open. Her father's husky voice: "If You can hear me, stop his suffering."

As a silvery wave crested, releasing sparks of light, the voices of schoolchildren whispered simple, sweet requests for their friend.

A swell on the surface, the voice of her husband: "You have given me a son and I love him with all that I am. He is life to me. But now, he is sick. *Dios*, You are my only hope. Only You can help us."

The sea began to roil, and in the midst of a multitude of prayers she could hear them all. Petitions for her son, offered up, but yet unanswered. Those of little faith became mist and fell back into the sea, those imbued with the Spirit of God rose again and again, higher and higher, louder and louder. Seeking God's mercy, pleading for His will.

His will.

There were other prayers sounding in the background. And though she couldn't say how, she knew that they were part of Manuel's journey. She heard a mother praying for her son: "Give my child a home. Keep Cirocco safe wherever he is."

A woman's prayers: "Work in the lives of those two people so Ines can be reunited with her son."

An old man's voice: "Teach Mr. Benito to pray, so he will know You. Do whatever You need do, Lord, so he turn to You."

A husband's voice: "Only You can change hearts, Lord. My wife is a good woman, but Norna's hardened her heart to You. I beg You to meet her somewhere, someday soon."

A man's plea: "This will be Shawn's last summer, where can we find hope?"

A wind began to blow, catching up the essences of the prayers and carrying them into the future where their fruit would be multiplied into the lives of people not yet born, weaving a tapestry, working all things together for good.

As the wind died down, the sea became a field of flowers, and in the air above them, Angelica heard her own voice. "Oh, God, send Your angels to save Manuel. You are God, You can stop this. I beg You, save my little boy. He has suffered so much. Stop his suffering now."

Manuel appeared in the center of the field. His body was now straight and strong, and his mind had full understanding. He reached forward, his eyes filled with wonder.

Angelica looked ahead of him. He was not alone. A man and a woman stood in front of him.

A diminutive figure . . . and . . . an old woman.

Angelica's heart began to race. She knew them.

Poppy and Maclovia each took one of Manuel's hands. And when they touched the boy, their bodies became spirit.

313

Everything beyond the field of flowers fell away and the heavens opened as a scroll. The presence of forgiving love flooded toward her.

In the distance was the throne of God. Proceeding out of the throne was a river containing the water of life, and upon the river was a light. Love made perfect.

The light became a man. And the man held a crown.

Jesus.

And the scent of roses.

The two with Manuel moved away and Manuel stood alone before his Savior.

Manuel reached out, as she had seen him do so many times in the past months.

"Jesus, my crown?"

Jesus knelt beside him. "You are blessed by my Father; take your inheritance, the kingdom prepared for you since the creation of the world."

Jesus placed the crown on Manuel's head, then lifted the child into His arms.

Angelica called out, "Manuel!"

But he couldn't hear her.

"Manuel, Manuel."

"Angelica, he's gone." It was her father beside her.

A voice called out, "Time of death 10:33."

She leaned her head back, looking into Antonio's face.

His eyes were focused straight ahead, on something in the distance.

"Thank You, *Dios*."

It was right that it was a beautiful fall day. Autumn leaves falling. Manuel had loved to play in the leaves that Antonio

314

swept into piles on the lawn. Diving in, wiggling back and forth until he was buried . . . until he was buried.

Angelica watched as the small, white casket inched its way into the earth. Standing straight, heels together, her shoulders square, gripping Antonio's hand, tears pouring down her cheeks. The debilitating grief she'd surrendered to the day of Manuel's death hovered all around her. But she would not give in. She had been charged with a purpose. She'd come to realize that. In the depths of her grief, in the darkness of the nights since his death, and on her knees before God.

Manuel had fully lived the life he'd been given. Always expecting the best, and always finding it. Never sorry for himself, never holding back, and never giving up. He had never understood he should give up . . . not even in the last days of his life.

Manuel had called her to a higher standard.

She took the crumpled tissue in her hand and wiped her eyes.

"Our Father who art in heaven, hallowed be Thy name. Thy kingdom come, Thy will be done, on earth as it is in heaven." Angelica lifted her eyes as Pastor Steve's words slipped into her thoughts.

His will be done . . . and God had called her to a higher standard. That was the meaning of her life now.

She closed her eyes, trying to recapture the moment that the will of God had been revealed to her. The omniscience of His plan. The unremitting purity and rightness of it. His thoughts were higher than her thoughts, His ways higher than her ways.

A crown. A crystal sea.

And with that revelation had come an understanding. She was to share the Truth she'd been given. And God, who prospers what He ordains, had shown her how He would bring that to pass.

Death was not an ending, but a beginning. The certainty of that had been gifted to her in the darkest moment of her life.

A gift to be shared. *Un regalo.*

"Don't worry, Dad. It's going to work out." Angelica snapped her cell phone shut as she walked across the parking lot of Sierra Medical Center. Her father had called to tell her that the offer they received on the ranch the day before had fallen apart. After the accountant confirmed there was no way to pay off the ranch with other assets and still have a monthly income, her parents had lowered the price.

The prospect of selling the ranch had become more wrenching for her father since Manuel's death. She didn't understand why, but instead of turning on God, her father had begun to turn to Him. He even confided in her that he prayed God would help them keep the ranch. The way he said it reminded Angelica of the term "mustard seed of faith."

The heels of her shoes clicked in sharp staccato as she strode down the hall toward Dr. Dorak's office. It had been only two weeks since the funeral, and the smells and sounds of the hospital assailed her. She was still raw. She lifted her chin and set her jaw. Remembering Manuel's courage, she willed her tears away.

Angelica waited for the receptionist to finish her phone call. "Good morning. Would you tell Dr. Dorak I'm here for our appointment?"

Angelica took a seat in the waiting area next to a woman holding a little boy. Bald and thin, he sat listlessly in her lap. Angelica's heart filled with compassion for them. She set her lips in a firm line. *I bet Pasha's velvety nose would bring a smile to that little face.*

"Angelica, come on back." Beth stepped toward her and gave her a warm hug. "How are you doing?"

"I'm doing okay." Angelica drew a deep breath. "At the moment." The women's eyes met and they hugged again. "Really, I'm okay." Angelica straightened. "You go ahead with the next person. I know the way."

Dr. Dorak rose from behind his desk as Angelica came into his office. She hadn't seen him since the funeral, yet there was a sense of continuity in the room. As if the time that had elapsed was but a pause in an ongoing conversation.

They embraced, and Angelica took a seat across from him.

She looked Dr. Dorak in the eye. "You knew, didn't you?"

Dr. Dorak nodded. "There is no holier ground than at the side of the bed of one of His little ones on their way Home. That's when God brings His healing, and death is defeated." He paused. "God showed me what awaits these children when I was still a kid myself. My job is to make things as easy as possible for them and their families while they're still with us."

"Is that what gave you the idea of a camp for kids with cancer?"

Dr. Dorak smiled. "You bet. A place where they can go and be kids again. And I want to have it set up so moms and dads can stay too. A place to make wonderful memories, for families to be families again, away from the sterile atmosphere of a hospital. I want to have staff onsite, and other services too. Ideally, it would be a place that meets not just physical but emotional and spiritual needs. A very special place."

"Poppy's Place."

317

"Excuse me?" Dr. Dorak tilted his head.

"I wondered if we could call it that."

The doctor continued to gaze at her.

Angelica leaned forward and folded her arms on the desk. "I have a proposal for you."

He looked at her, waiting.

"My father doesn't want to sell the ranch. We've discussed a number of ideas, trying to find a way for him to keep it. But it always comes down to him needing monthly income. If he leased the facilities to you for a camp, it would give him monthly income."

Dr. Dorak straightened in his chair. "Tell me more."

"My parents would retain the residence and two acres. The balance of the property would be leased to you. You make all your own improvements. If the camp is ever closed, we would have your improvements appraised and buy them back from you." She caught her breath and continued. "I'll work there full-time. For free, until the camp gets going, then I'll become a paid employee." She looked into Dr. Dorak's eyes. "I've been where those parents are, and I know something they've yet to learn. I think I can help lighten their load and ease their pain. That's my heart's desire."

"What does your dad think of all this?"

"I haven't gone over it with him yet."

Dr. Dorak raised his eyebrows.

"I've been involved with my family's finances many times over the years. There isn't a doubt in my mind that he'll agree it's a sound business decision. But even more important, it's a way to honor Manuel's memory."

Angelica sat back in her chair. "And there's another thing."

Dr. Dorak looked amused. "I'm waiting."

"We had to move heaven and earth to find a peripheral

blood stem cell match for Manuel because ethnic minorities are so underrepresented in the National Marrow Donor Program. I want to raise public awareness about that. There's a huge Hispanic population in this area and all are potential donors. We can work out something with the local blood centers. Maybe do some events."

Dr. Dorak pushed his phone in her direction. "Why don't you call your dad and tell him you've got a deal."

Angelica picked up the phone and dialed.

Benito answered.

"Hi, Dad. I think you should call Sandi Greer."

"What are you talking about, Angelica?"

"Regalo Grande isn't for sale."

The line was silent for a moment.

"Why would you say that?"

"I'm on my way up there, Dad. I'll explain everything when I get there."

She hung up.

Rising, she extended her hand. "Let's shake on it, Mark."

Angelica turned and left.

As she walked down the hall her steps quickened. She was going to the ranch. Not to arrange for its sale, but to arrange for its future. She began to run.

Out the door, across the parking lot, and into the van, never looking back.

She pulled onto the street. As she drove toward the Sonoma Mountains, her thoughts returned to the day her father had told her he'd built the ranch for her and her mother. A gift to his family. Now the ranch would become a gift of hope and love to many families, not just here, but throughout the world.

Un regalo. Un regalo grande.

EPILOGUE

Poppy's Place, Eighteen Months Later

"Antonio, let's take a walk." Angelica took the hammer out of Antonio's hand and set it on a sawhorse. "Cirocco, we'll be back later."

Cirocco climbed down off the ladder with ease, as though he'd had his new leg for years, not months. He poured more paint into his paint tray. "You no need hurry back. I keep working."

"Cirocco, you're speaking English like a native."

He smiled broadly. "I study hard so I will go to college." He wiped the excess paint off the brush and climbed back up the ladder.

Angelica took Antonio's hand and they stepped out of the barn into the flower-scented air of an early summer afternoon. They walked past the new bunkhouses and the little chapel that was her father's contribution to the camp.

"What's up?" Antonio's dark eyes searched her face. He knew her so well.

Angelica looked away for fear he would read her thoughts. "It's a beautiful day and we've hardly seen each other this week. First, it was the big party and dance to thank everyone who's helped make Poppy's Place a reality. And now it's all the last-minute things that have to be done for opening day. I just thought it would be nice to take a walk." She guided him toward the drive.

Antonio smiled at her. "It's all been worth it. I know your parents are happy with the way it's worked out. Your mom loved having the party at her house."

Angelica nodded. "The highlight for her was dancing with Senator Evans."

"The highlight for me was watching Cirocco dance with his mother." Antonio slipped his arm around her waist. "Cirocco told me that when we take Ines back to Guadalajara, he wants to visit Santa Sophia. He wants to take his mother there on a Sunday afternoon when the mariachis are playing in the plaza." He pulled her closer to him. "While Cirocco dances with his mother, I'll be dancing with you."

"Oh, I forgot to tell you." Angelica pulled away and stepped off the drive. "Tex told me she and Mark have set a date. They're getting married this Christmas." Antonio followed behind her. "I know they'd like to get married here at Regalo Grande since it was Manuel who brought them together."

They ducked under the oaks.

Angelica turned and took Antonio's hand in hers. "How long has it been since we've sat beside the stream?"

Antonio pulled her to him and kissed her. "Too long." He looked into her eyes. "What are you up to, *señora*?"

"I have a gift for you." Angelica held his gaze. "You know I had an appointment this morning in town."

Antonio nodded.

"Well, while I was out I picked up something I had made for you."

Antonio waited for her to continue.

Angelica glanced past him, to the base of the big oak they were standing beneath.

Antonio turned around.

Leaning against the trunk was a guitar.

Antonio took two long strides and picked it up. Turning it back and forth, he examined it. He gave a long, low whistle as he ran his fingers over the inlaid rosewood that formed a single rose on the top of the guitar. He turned to her.

Their eyes met and neither spoke. It had been almost two years since Antonio had owned a guitar. Angelica had saved for months. There was little extra money with all of Manuel's hospital bills.

"Play for me," she whispered.

Antonio pulled the guitar to his chest and closed his eyes a moment. Then his fingers touched the strings.

At the first strains of music, Angelica pressed her fingers to her tummy.

Antonio opened his eyes and looked into hers. He began to play. Slowly at first, tilting his head, but his eyes, intense and focused, did not leave her face.

The tone of the music intensified as his fingers stroked the strings.

A summer breeze rustled through the trees around them.

Antonio began to play with abandon. His eyes filled with love.

Without speaking a word, he stood before her, little by little letting the raw emotion that he reserved for their most intimate moments flow through his fingers and into the music.

The wind seemed to catch the notes and the trilling vibrato danced through the air.

Holding his gaze, she received the music. Its beauty touched her, caressed her, tears slipped down her cheeks.

His eyes never left hers as he bore witness to what she meant to him and how deeply he loved her.

Slowly, he allowed the music to become a sweet melody, then he quieted the guitar with his hand. Setting it down, he stepped toward her. "Thank you." He lifted her fingers to his lips and kissed them.

It took her breath away.

She waited a moment. "Antonio, I have another gift for you."

His dark eyes searched hers.

He waited for her to continue. "Yes?"

"We're going to have a baby."

Antonio's lips parted.

Her voice trembled. "A little boy."

He scooped her into his arms and swung her in a circle. "This is more than any man deserves."

He set her down and took her hand, leading her to a boulder by the stream. He sat and pulled her onto his lap. Then wrapped his arms around her.

Something stirred within her heart.

Suddenly she realized, for the first time since the day of Manuel's death, she felt joy.

She closed her eyes and rested her head on Antonio's chest. The beat of his heart, strong and steady, sounded in her ear. She was in the arms of a man who adored her, carrying a child whom a love tested by fire had brought into being. Tomorrow fifty desperately ill children and their parents would arrive at the ranch and be touched by the natural beauty and gifts of Regalo Grande. And because Manuel had lived . . . and died . . . she would be able to minister to them.

And we know that all things work together for good to those who love God, to those who are the called according to His purpose.

Romans 8:28

ACKNOWLEDGMENTS

When I first felt God calling me to write this story, I knew it would take His divine hand to accomplish it. I needed expert resources in three areas: HLA antigens and their role in peripheral blood stem cell transplantation, the lab testing and ethics surrounding bone marrow donation, and information about the culture of doctors and the workings of a pediatric hospital. Three doctors, respected and esteemed in their fields, graciously agreed to helped me.

Dr. Mehmet Tevfik Dorak, expert on Molecular Immunogenetics and the HLA System, Genetic Susceptibility to Childhood Leukemia. The book could not have been written without you. The months you spent helping me plot this book and the additional months you reviewed dialogue and storyline allowed me to craft a tale that incorporated the scientific details of the subject in a way I never could have accomplished on my own. But what I am most grateful for is the time you spent teaching me what I needed to know and your constant encouragement during my moments of doubt and uncertainty.

Dr. David Senitzer, DABMLI, DABHI, director of the HLA Laboratory, City of Hope National Medical Center. Thank you so much for taking the time to meet with me and for your patient, kind, and consistent guidance through the course of writing this book regarding not just the practical but the ethical considerations of blood donation for this life-saving procedure. Your commitment to maintaining the highest ethical standards in these matters of life and death is only part of the reason you are esteemed and admired by your colleagues. Again, thank you for the months and months of your dedicated support.

Dr. Harvey Cohen, Chief of Staff, Lucile Packard Children's Hospital, and Chair, Department of Pediatrics, Stanford University School of Medicine. I am deeply grateful for all your help. Your prompt and thorough responses to my many questions about the culture and inner workings of a hospital were critical in the writing of this book. I will always feel indebted to you.

I am convinced I would never have connected to any of these men were it not for the continuing work of my prayer partners. Thank you, Tex Gaynos, Glenn and Donna Wimer, Renae Moore, and Betty Willems.

Thank you to my editors: Jennifer Leep, without you this book could not have been published; Carol Craig, your knowledge, and most of all your caring concern keep me striving for excellence; Susan Lohrer, your uncanny ability to get to the core of what I'm trying to say continues to amaze me. Thank you for all you do.

I also want to acknowledge my family. Antonio, my sons, and my parents, Col. and Mrs. Nicolaus Gaynos, who share in my joy and rejoice in my success. It was Dad who came up with the idea for Angelica's final gift to Antonio. Also, those dear friends and acquaintances who have encouraged and helped me along the way—Sue Callen, Barbara Rostad, Joan Hust, Susan Pearson, Deb Greer, Beth DeHoff, Pedro Rivarola, Lu Ann Kolenda, and Carolyn Kellie. Those of you who shared deeply personal and painful experiences with me, I hope this story somehow comforts you.

And a special thanks to my agent, Natasha Kern, who has been on my writing journey from the beginning. At times walking in front, to lead me. At times walking behind, to let me shine. But who has always come alongside me when I needed her most. Your support has been unfailing, and your judgments unerring. I cannot view my successes without seeing you.

And to the Creator of the universe . . . I write because of that empty grave. I write because of Your saving grace. I write for the Truth at Calvary.

AUTHOR'S NOTE

One of the reasons I wrote this book was to raise public awareness about the shortage of minority donors to the various marrow donor programs in the United States and elsewhere. This dramatically reduces the chances of Hispanics, African Americans, Asians, and other minorities to find unrelated donors when a life-saving transplant is needed.

Prior to writing the book, I thought that donating bone marrow was a horribly painful procedure. I learned that new advances in the field mean that now it is often possible to donate peripheral blood stem cells through a process of apheresis, similar to donating platelets at a blood bank.

There are also ongoing efforts to increase the banking of umbilical cord blood stem cells (this is not the same as embryonic) for non-Caucasians. MaxCord is an organization on the leading edge of that endeavor is.

Manuel would not have died had a match been found quickly. Please consider saving a life by donating to the National Marrow Donor Program, www.marrow.org; the Icla da Silva Foundation, www.icla.org; or Kids Beating Cancer, Inc., www.kidsbeatingcancer.com.

As Christians, we know in a deep and profound way that the life is in the blood. Our Savior shed His blood for us. I would love to rejoice with you should you decide to become a donor. Please write to me at: Box 3781, Coeur d'Alene, ID 83816.

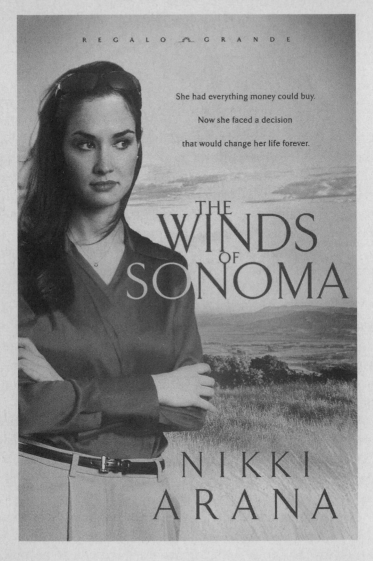

Can love overcome the crisis
that threatens her family?

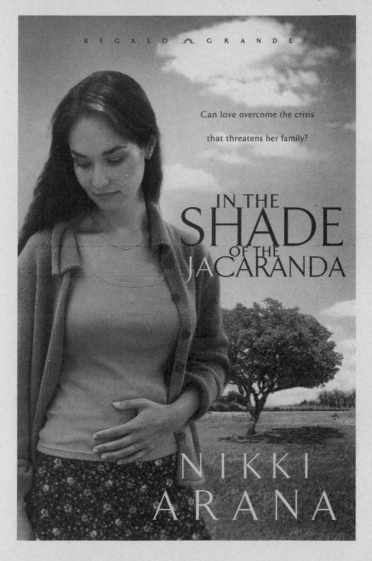

Book 2 in the R E G A L O ☀ G R A N D E series